~ chapter
one

"Err-a-er-er-errrr!" The high-pitched crow of the rooster had Andi Cooper moaning a half-awake protest. Rolling over on the soft mattress, she caught a whiff of frying bacon, which indicated that her mother was preparing breakfast. Andi's eyelids fluttered, and she glanced at her lace curtains billowing in the morning breeze.

"Don't wanna go to school," Andi grumbled, and pulled the pillow over her head, but then smiled sleepily when she remembered that she didn't have to get up. She was twenty-eight years old and was only home for a visit. Snuggling beneath the patchwork quilt, Andi sighed, begging her brain to slip back into the delicious dream she had been having involving Brad Pitt, a big brass bed, a red feather, *oh yeah,* and handcuffs. With a long sigh that segued into delicate snoring, Andi slipped back into her interlude with Brad . . .

"This won't hurt a bit," Andi assured him with a saucy smile as she cuffed his wrists to the bedposts.

"*I would be shaking in my boots,*" Brad responded with a grin, "*but you've removed them along with my clothing.*" (Her dream Brad is the long-haired cowboy version from Legends of the Fall.) "*Not that I'm complaining,*" he added.

"*Oh, I don't think I'll hear any complaints from you,*" Andi told him with a throaty laugh. Leaning closer, she swirled the red feather over his chest and then down his abdomen, making his muscles clench, which highlighted his amazing six-pack. Andi teased and tickled with the very tip of the feather, going farther and farther south until Brad was moaning and arching up off the mattress.

"*Andi, please,*" he begged, his voice a low growl, as he strained against the handcuffs.

"*Please . . . what? Is this perhaps what you want?*" With a wicked chuckle, Andi leaned down and placed her mouth . . .

"Er-a-er-er-errr!" The damned rooster jarred Andi from her destination and her dream, making her almost levitate off the bed. Eyes wide open this time, she blinked at the fingers of sunlight curling through the window. With a little squeal of pure frustration, Andi squeezed her eyes shut, trying to conjure up bodacious Brad once again.

"Annndeee! Breakfaaast!" her mother called from the bottom of the stairs.

"I don't want breakfast, I want Brad!" Andi grumbled loudly, pounding her fist into the pillow.

"You want bread? But, sweetie, I made biscuits. Would you rather have toast?"

"No, Mom, biscuits will be fine," Andi called to her. "I'll be down in a few minutes." With a weak laugh, Andi put her cool hands to her warm cheeks as she recalled the

contents

Wild Ride

LuAnn McLane

A SIGNET ECLIPSE BOOK

SIGNET ECLIPSE
Published by New American Library, a division of
Penguin Group (USA) Inc., 375 Hudson Street,
New York, New York 10014, USA
Penguin Group (Canada), 90 Eglinton Avenue East, Suite 700, Toronto,
Ontario, Canada M4P 2Y3 (a division of Pearson Penguin Canada Inc.)
Penguin Books Ltd., 80 Strand, London WC2R 0RL, England
Penguin Ireland, 25 St. Stephen's Green, Dublin 2,
Ireland (a division of Penguin Books Ltd.)
Penguin Group (Australia), 250 Camberwell Road, Camberwell, Victoria 3124,
Australia (a division of Pearson Australia Group Pty. Ltd.)
Penguin Books India Pvt. Ltd., 11 Community Centre, Panchsheel Park,
New Delhi - 110 017, India
Penguin Group (NZ), cnr Airborne and Rosedale Roads, Albany,
Auckland 1310, New Zealand (a division of Pearson New Zealand Ltd.)
Penguin Books (South Africa) (Pty.) Ltd., 24 Sturdee Avenue,
Rosebank, Johannesburg 2196, South Africa

Penguin Books Ltd., Registered Offices: 80 Strand, London WC2R 0RL, England

First published by Signet Eclipse, an imprint of New American Library,
a division of Penguin Group (USA) Inc.

First Printing, March 2006
10 9 8 7 6 5 4 3 2 1

SIGNET ECLIPSE and logo are trademarks of Penguin Group (USA) Inc.

LIBRARY OF CONGRESS CATALOGING-IN PUBLICATION DATA

McLane, LuAnn.
    Wild ride / Luann McLane.
       p. cm.
    ISBN 0-451-21762-4
    1. Resorts—Fiction. 2. Amusement parks—Fiction. 3. Love stories, American.
I. Title.

PS3613. C5685W55 2006
813'.6—dc22   2005027258

Printed in the United States of America

Wild Ride

Whiplash

details of her naughty dream. "A red feather?" she whispered, shaking her head. "What was up with that?"

With a sigh and a long stretch, Andi tossed the quilt back and swung her long legs over the side of the bed. "Pretty pathetic when the best sex I've had in a long time is a figment of my imagination," she grumbled, rubbing the sleep from her eyes. Looking around her old bedroom, though, Andi had to smile. Her mother hadn't changed a thing since she had moved out to study journalism at Indiana University. Her trophies and medals for swimming were displayed on a shelf, which was the only sport as a gangly teenager she could master. Of course, her real talent had been as captain of the debate team. She may have been a geek, but she could argue with the best of them.

Andi pushed up from the bed and picked up a plump pink teddy bear, won for her at the county fair, junior year, by Keith Gavin, fellow geek and all-around nice guy whom all the girls, with the exception of her, had ignored. With a grin, Andi picked up a picture of Keith and her, both with big hair and braces, at the junior prom. "Oh Keith, why couldn't I fall for a nice guy like you or one of Mom's farm boys that she still hopes I'll marry?"

Putting the gold-framed photo down, Andi shook her head, thinking she had no intention of getting married anyway. She enjoyed her career as a freelance travel writer. It had been her ticket off the farm, not that she didn't love it here, but just to visit. She used to daydream about exotic places as she mucked out the barn. Now that she was living the life she had only dreamed about, she wasn't about to give it up for a guy . . . not even Brad Pitt.

Nope, she would, well, *bet the farm* that there wasn't a guy on the planet who could make her give up traveling the world.

"Andi?" her mom called from downstairs, a little impatiently this time. "Are you coming down soon?"

Andi took two long-legged strides to the doorway and shouted, "In a few minutes. I'm just going to wash up."

"Time's a-wastin'. Hurry yourself up."

Andi glanced at the digital alarm clock and shook her head. "Good lord, it's only seven o'clock." Farmers were early-to-bed, early-to-rise kind of creatures. She, however, was not.

After a quick trip to the bathroom, Andi reached into her closet and pulled a Midway High School T-shirt and an old pair of gray sweats from a hanger. Tugging on the clothes, she left off her underwire bra for comfort's sake since after breakfast she planned to veg on the front porch with a pitcher of sweet tea and a good book. Andi had to grin when she looked into the mirror. "Now if I had filled out this T-shirt like this in high school, maybe I could have gotten a date."

A "late bloomer," her mother had called her. While Andi knew she wasn't a beauty by conventional standards, she was finally comfortable in her just-under-six-foot frame, and managed to get her fair share of male attention. Her curly red hair had softened to more of a strawberry blond thanks to so much time spent outdoors, and although she had to be careful, Andi was one of those rare redheads who could achieve a light, sun-kissed tan. Hazel eyes, which changed from green to brown with her mood, tilted slightly at the corners, giving her otherwise girl-next-door appearance a bit of allure.

While taming her curls into a sloppy ponytail, Andi glanced over at the poster of the New Kids on the Block pinned to the wall. Maybe sleeping in her old bedroom surrounded by teen-idol pinup posters was her reason for dreaming about celebrities. She started to head out the door when she paused to pick up a picture of her younger brother, Jack. One of the reasons Andi had come home for a visit was that her mother had been distraught when Jack had announced that he was staying in Nashville to pursue a career in country music instead of coming home to work on the farm.

Andi had seen Jack's announcement coming, knowing full well that his ever-changing major at Vanderbilt was a thinly-veiled ploy to live in Nashville for the past five years and play his music at Tootsies. While Andi was happy to pass the black-sheep torch to her brother, she felt sorry for her mom, who was having a major case of empty-nest syndrome.

"Andrea Jane, your breakfast is getting cold!" Her mother shouted, more than a little agitated this time. Andi grinned. Some things never change. All through school, it had taken her mother three warnings before Andi finally stomped down the stairs. What was it about coming home that turned you from a responsible adult back into a kid?

Andi knew that the fourth shout was going to be "Andrea Jane *Cooper*" and the very real threat of feeding her breakfast to the dog. The aroma of her mom's strong coffee and crisp bacon wafted up the hallway, making Andi bound down the stairs as she used to do in high school, except now she had breasts that jiggled like Jell-O with each descending step.

At the bottom of the stairway, Andi was about to greet her mother, but after looking into the kitchen she came to a startled halt, causing some residual jiggles. This drew the undivided attention of Walter Weaver, who was leasing some acreage from her father. More importantly, he was number one on her mother's list of most-eligible farmers.

"Hey there, Andi," Walter said to her breasts. Scooting back from the breakfast table, he stood up, dwarfing her petite mother who stood there giving Andi a my-God-you-are-*braless* glare. As tiny as she was, Daisy Cooper could be intimidating, but Andi stood her ground, defiantly *not* crossing her arms over her braless boobs even though she really wanted to. How was she to know that her mom would be pushing Walter on her at breakfast, for goodness sake? Geez, couldn't a girl get a cup of coffee first?

"Hi, Walter," Andi said, feeling her cheeks grow warm. She wished she had the nerve to bounce her breasts a bit, just to watch him come undone. Turning to her mother, Andi said with forced sweetness, "Mom, I didn't know Walter was coming for breakfast."

"I wasn't going to, but your mama insisted when she found out that all I had to eat this mornin' was a bowl of Froot Loops."

"A boy needs more than Froot Loops, for goodness' sake," Daisy said defensively. "Don't you agree, Andi?"

Walter was shifting his stance from one booted foot to the other, looking a bit uncomfortable. "I think I had better get on out to the fields," he said in his quiet way, drawing a protest from Daisy.

Andi suddenly felt a little rotten. Walter was a nice guy

and it wouldn't kill her to have breakfast with him. Besides, the scrambled eggs, strips of bacon, and golden biscuits were calling her name. "Oh, stay for a another cup of coffee," Andi offered, motioning toward the table with a swing of her arm, forgetting that this would cause a major breast bobble.

Walter blinked rapidly and Daisy made a strangled coughing sound. *Oh no.* At this point Andi really wanted to salvage the situation, and said the first thing that entered her mind, a really bad habit of hers. "Oh, stay, Walter. I don't know about you, but I could eat a horse."

If possible, Walter blinked even more rapidly. Now, the comment was a common enough one, but with her tight T-shirt and freewheeling breasts, it somehow sounded, well, sex-related. The statement sort of hung in the air, and no one seemed sure how to answer.

Recovering from a faux pas wasn't exactly one of Andi's strong points, either. She usually managed to dig herself in deeper and did so now, in rapid fashion. "Uh, not a *horse,* horses are too big. Maybe a cow. Ew, no, maybe I could eat a . . ." She was saved from further farm-animal examples when her cell phone, hooked on her pants, started playing a tinny version of "When the Saints Go Marching In." Raising her index finger in the air, Andi said, "Uh, excuse me."

Andi took the call out on the front porch, willing to talk to just about anyone in order to get away from Walter, her mother, and the whole "eating a horse" thing. "Hello?"

"Hi, Andi, this is Janelle Portwood, of *Living Large* magazine."

Andi's heart picked up speed as she sat down on the

front porch steps. Janelle was editor-in-chief and Andi had wanted to do a piece for *Living Large* for a long time. "Hi, Janelle. What can I do for you?"

"I've got an incredible assignment for you. A cover story."

Andi's heart pumped harder.

"We're going to do a huge spread on Wild Ride Resort and we want *you* to write the article."

Her heart sank.

"Andi? I know, I know, you must be speechless. Now, get a load of this. The resort, of course, is booked solid, so Oliver Maxwell is going to put you up in his very own penthouse apartment overlooking the island. I've heard it is spectacular."

Andi closed her eyes and shook her head sadly.

"Andi? Recover, girl. Hey, I don't care if you scream for joy."

Andi wanted to scream, all right, but in frustration. She forced the next words past her lips. "I can't do the story, Janelle."

"What? You're kidding, right?"

After taking a deep breath, Andi explained, "I hate the place."

"You've been there?"

"Yes, when it was called Crystal Island and owned by Graystone Cruise Lines. Janelle, the island was a pristine treasure that Oliver Maxwell, in my opinion, *ruined*. The thought of one of his roller coasters marring the beauty of the island makes me sick. I'm sorry, but you'll have to find someone else. The Club Med–meets–Coney Island concept just turns me off."

"Oliver Maxwell wants *you* and made it abundantly

clear that he wouldn't settle for anyone else. He thinks you're the best travel writer going." Janelle's compliment had a bit of an edge to it.

Andi really hated to burn this bridge, but felt compelled to be up-front. "Janelle, you know I tell it like it is in the articles I write. I refuse to pull any punches. I'm very enthusiastic about places that I love, but bluntly to the point about places that I don't. With the travel industry still recovering, I'd hate to pan a place that is attracting so many tourists."

Janelle was silent for a moment and then said, "I totally get what you're saying, but you might be surprised by Wild Ride Resort. Everyone I know who has gone there has loved it. It's really tastefully done."

Andi wasn't convinced. "I don't see that happening."

"Well," Janelle said slowly, "I never promised a glowing article. Controversy sells magazines, too."

Andi felt a little surge of hope, but said, "I don't feel quite right having Oliver Maxwell put me up in his penthouse and then bashing his resort."

"Would you be okay with it if he knows this is a possibility?"

"A probability."

"Whatever. I'll call him and explain the situation. If he agrees, are you in?"

Andi thought about Walter and her mother waiting inside the farmhouse for her and said, "I'm in." But when a twinge of guilt hit her in her empty gut, she added, "Just give me until the end of the week. I'm visiting my mother after almost a year of traveling and I want to spend a few more days with her."

"No problem," Janelle said, with the perkiness back in

her voice. I'll give Oliver Maxwell a call and get back to you. Now, go enjoy your mother."

Andi walked slowly back into the farmhouse, wanting to cause as little jiggle as possible, all the while wondering what she had just gotten herself into.

Dangling horizontally from the safety harness, Max examined a section of the roller-coaster track that had been causing just enough shimmy to give his passengers a rough ride the night before. His crew had fixed the problem but he wanted to check things out for himself. With his forearm he swiped at beads of sweat rolling into his eyes while checking out the first curve of a spiral turn.

Everything seemed to be running smoothly, but roller coasters could be temperamental creatures and even the smallest malfunction could shut the ride down, which would not exactly be popular with the tourists. This one was a smaller but no less exciting version of his signature amusement-park roller coasters. Max had named this ride the Dolphin because it ran parallel with the beach, mimicking the twisting and diving, yet graceful and playful swim of a dolphin until coming to a smooth stop inside the lobby of Wild Ride Resort.

With a grunt, Max hefted himself onto the small plat-form, pausing to admire the panoramic view of the At-lantic Ocean. "Man, I could use a swim," Max muttered as he tugged his damp white T-shirt over his head and used it to mop the sweat from his face. The cloudless blue sky, although beautiful, meant the day would be a scorcher.

After swiftly descending the narrow series of steps leading to the ground, Max was deciding whether to take a dip in the hotel pool or to swim in the ocean when Krista Ross, his entertainment and marketing director, came rushing his way. A cool, sophisticated blond, Krista somehow managed to look fresh in the sweltering heat. Did the woman ever break a sweat?

Dressed in a lime green halter sundress that exposed tanned, toned shoulders, Krista had an all-business frown on her beautiful face. "Max, we need to talk."

"If you continue to scowl like that, you'll get wrin-kles," he said, knowing she wouldn't even crack a smile. "You know you look good enough to eat in that dress," he said, giving her a once-over.

"Max, you *can't* make comments like that to an em-ployee. It's sexual harassment."

"It was a compliment."

Krista put her hand on one slim hip. "You're just try-ing to get a rise out of me, aren't you?"

"And you make it so easy." He was rewarded with her lips twitching to form a grin before the frown returned. "Okay, what did I screw up now?" He started walking toward the pool and she fell in step beside him. Even in high-heeled sandals she only came to his shoulder, so he slowed his pace for her sake.

"I just took a call from Janelle Portwood of *Living*

Large magazine and she said that you requested Andrea Cooper to do the cover story they promised us."

Max nodded. "Yes. I think she's a great writer. Her articles make you feel like you're *there,* you know. I wanted someone who could capture the feel of Wild Ride Resort. I think she can."

Krista put a hand on his arm, scrunching up her nose when she encountered sweat. "Have you ever read one of her pieces when she hates the place?"

"No."

"She can be really snarky."

"Your point?"

"Max!" She stopped in her high-heeled tracks. "Bad publicity is *not* a good thing."

"How could Andrea Cooper not love this place?" With a grin, Max made a sweeping gesture toward a twenty-thousand-square-foot circular beach-entry swimming pool glistening in the morning sunlight. Two smaller pools fed into the main one via cascading waterfalls. Snow-white, with a deep red tiled roof reminiscent of old Florida, the main hotel curved around the pool, in sharp contrast to the deep blue sky.

"Max, you've got to take this seriously. Andrea is highly qualified, but strongly opinionated. We might be the hottest destination in the industry, but that can change, especially in our present economy. We need a five-star rating from her."

"We'll get it," Max said firmly. He toed off his shoes, wanting to dive into the cool water before the pool opened to the resort guests. "An hour from now the pool will be filled with people having fun in the sun while being catered to by our staff."

Nodding, Krista tucked a lock of blond hair behind her ear. "Yes, I realize that. And when the sun sets, we'll transform this place into a sultry, sexy no-holds-barred carnival for adults. There's no other place quite like Wild Ride, Max."

"That's part of the appeal."

Krista sighed. "The people who love Wild Ride keep coming back for more, but you know as well as I do that this place isn't for the faint of heart."

Max trailed his big toe in the water. "Do you seriously think a world traveler like Andrea Cooper will fall into the faint-of-heart category? She's probably seen and done it all." Knowing he'd get another rise out of Krista, he added, "If she's lucky she'll get to do me."

Krista wagged her index finger at him. The twang she kept carefully hidden reared its Southern head. "Don't you dare go having sex with her! Good God almighty, that could lead to disaster!"

Max made it a personal quest to make her lose control at least once a day, just to keep things interesting. He had met Krista at a frat party while completing graduate school at Georgia Tech. Krista had been fending off the unwelcome drunken advances of her date. Max had been about to deck the jerk when Krista had taken the matter into her own hands and kneed the guy in the balls. "Sex with me never leads to disaster, I'll have you know." He chuckled, sending Krista into orbit.

"Max, for once in your life, will you be serious?"

"Sugar, you're serious enough for the both of us."

"Don't call me or any other woman, especially Andrea Cooper, *sugar.*"

"Lighten up, Krista," he said in a teasing tone, but

meant it. They had remained friends since college and he loved her like a kid sister. Rough around the edges when he met her, she had transformed herself into a savvy businesswoman, but Max wished she would relax and let some of her real personality shine through the polished surface. Once in a while Max could still get Krista to let her hair down, but those times were becoming few and far between.

"Max," Krista began in that clipped, no-nonsense tone that grated on his nerves.

"Yes?" He innocently raised his eyebrows just before he dipped his big toe beneath the water and gave her a good splash.

With a little squeal, Krista gave him a hard shove, sending him into the pool. Max laughed as he hit the surface. Twisting his body, he sliced through the water with long strokes, enjoying the silky feel of the water against his heated skin.

As he swam laps, Max's thoughts drifted to Andrea Cooper. Judging from her writing style, he imagined her to be the model of cool sophistication, a champagne-and-caviar, Prada-wearing, high-maintenance chick. Max knew the type well, and he knew how to handle them. By the end of her stay, he planned on having Andrea Cooper eating out of his hand.

⌦ chapter three

"Well, damn!" Andi muttered when a dollop of mustard dripped from her corn dog and landed on her white V-necked shirt. With a small napkin, she dabbed at the yellow blob, making it worse. Since she had checked her luggage through to Wild Ride Resort, there wasn't any way to change into a clean shirt. With a shrug and a sigh she finished the corn dog, washing it down with a cherry slushy.

Shading her eyes against the glare of the sun, Andi spotted the ferry approaching the dock. Since it was a Friday afternoon, not many people waited with her to board the boat. Tourists for the resort arrived and departed on Saturdays for the weeklong stay or arrived on Thursday for an extended weekend. Andi wasn't supposed to arrive until Saturday, but she liked to slip into a destination unannounced to see how the management would handle her early arrival. Admittedly, this was not a very nice thing to do, but it had proven in the past to be a real indicator of how many stars the resort deserved right off the bat.

Hefting her purse onto one shoulder and her leather laptop case onto the other, Andi boarded the ferry, selecting a seat up front. During the forty-minute ride, she read the information she had already gathered about the resort and also about Oliver Maxwell.

Pursing her lips as she read his bio, Andi had to admit to herself that the man had an interesting past. As a child, Maxwell had traveled the country with his parents, who owned and operated a traveling carnival. Homeschooled by his mother, he learned at an early age how to assemble and repair the carnival rides by working with his father. Over the years, improving the design of the faster rides became a passion that carried over into adulthood. After earning a master's degree in mechanical engineering, Maxwell had formed his own company and become one of the most sought-after roller-coaster designers in the world. Both his wooden and steel designs consistently won the coveted Golden Ticket Award year after year.

"Humble beginnings," Andi mumbled, feeling a twinge of admiration. Flipping to the next page, she blinked at the glossy picture of Oliver Maxwell. "Wowsa." Wavy black hair, light blue eyes, and a killer smile had her pausing on the page for way too long. Dressed in a pale blue polo shirt open at the throat and khaki shorts, he casually leaned one broad shoulder against a palm tree, looking sexy as hell.

The man was positively drool-worthy if you went for tall, ruggedly handsome kinda guys, which she did. No, he wasn't a pretty boy, but rather looked like he would be at home on a football field or with a tool belt slung low on those lean hips or doing something outdoorsy and physical like chopping down trees. Angling her head at the photo, Andi thought *or perhaps something indoorsy and physical, like making love all night long.*

Slapping her hand against her forehead, Andi realized she had sex on the brain way too much, lately . . . or then again maybe not nearly enough, depending on how you looked at the situation. Regardless, she was going to have to keep her distance from Oliver Maxwell and not let him influence how she felt about Wild Ride Resort.

After closing the media kit and tucking it in her leather case, Andi stood up and leaned against the front railing. Ocean spray misted her face and hair, leaving a salty taste on her lips. Taking a deep breath, Andi inhaled the briny tang of the sea while trying to clear the sexy image of Oliver Maxwell from her head without much success. The ferry cut through the white-capped water as they came closer and closer to the island that had been a day-excursion destination for a small cruise line.

Andi felt a surge of anger at the commercialization of the pristine paradise that had once been little more than a bird sanctuary. In her travels, she had seen more and more development of beachfront property and wetlands, which in her opinion should have been protected for the wildlife that depended upon it.

"Wow," Andi breathed as Wild Ride Resort came into view. She couldn't help but be impressed by the beautiful hotel overlooking the crescent-shaped beach dotted with sunbathers lounging beneath large red umbrellas. Just past lumpy sand dunes and sea oats waving a welcome in the ocean breeze, Andi could see thatch-roofed tiki huts and rows of lounge chairs surrounding a huge swimming pool buzzing with afternoon activity.

"Where is the doggone roller coaster?" she wondered out loud. "Oh!" Just then, over to the right of the hotel, she spotted a flash of blue winding through the palm trees and tall cypress. Somehow, Oliver Maxwell had managed to all but hide the roller coaster until it came shooting above the trees and then disappeared. "Oh!" Andi covered her mouth in surprise once again when the roller coaster popped above the treetops, and then popped up once more before slipping, as smooth as you please, into the second story of the hotel.

Except for the roller coaster, though, Wild Ride Resort looked like a typical upscale tropical playground, making Andi curious as to what it was about the place that had created a waiting list to get in. While she knew that the resort was transformed at night into a carnival of sorts, photographs weren't allowed after dark and she had learned from the brochures that it was a rule that was strictly enforced, giving real meaning to the phrase, "what goes down on the island stays on the island."

The ferry cruised past the beach and headed over to an inlet that was a small marina for the island. A colorful row of jet skis bobbed in the water. Several boat slips were empty but Andi had read about deep-sea fishing and scuba-diving excursions, two of the few activities not covered in the all-inclusive itinerary.

Andi sighed as the captain skillfully eased the boat up next to the dock, wondering once again if she was making the right decision by coming here to do the article. While she had been around the world and had seen some pretty crazy things, when push came to shove, she was still an Indiana farm girl. The whole air of mystery had her just a teensy bit nervous and she wondered if she would be clicking her ruby slippers before her stay at Wild Ride Resort was over.

Oh, come on, Andi, she mused, giving herself an internal pep talk, something she had done since she was a child to get through scary situations. *You've ridden a camel in Egypt. Well okay, that was a mistake . . . who knew they spit? Think of another example. How about the elephant ride in Africa? Ew, bad memory there, too.* In truth, though, there weren't too many things she was afraid to try unless they involved heights, the sight of blood, (shiver), or spiders. Other than that, she was good to go.

Stepping off the ferry with the aid of the very cute captain, Andi lifted her chin and said to herself, *Wild Ride Resort, here I come. Show me what you got.*

"Will you be riding the Dolphin roller coaster into the lobby?" the cute captain asked with a dimpled smile.

"Oh, my God, no."

Squeezing her shoulder, he said, "I understand. Afraid of heights?"

Andi nodded. "That and the whole twisting, turning, flipping-you-upside-down part. Other than that, I'd be down with it."

He chuckled and then said, "You can enter the lobby by taking the stairs over by the pool. It's about a five-minute walk from here to the hotel. Would you like for me to call a shuttle?"

"No, that's okay. I could use the exercise."

He nodded. "Just follow the pathway and have a nice stay. Your luggage will be sent up to your room."

"Thanks," she said and began walking, suddenly re-thinking the whole arriving-a-day-early thing. Maybe it wasn't such a good idea, after all. Or very nice. After all, Oliver Maxwell was putting her up in his very own apartment and here she was booting him out a day early. Why is it that impulsive moves seem so smart at the time, but then end up in disaster?

She paused at a fork in the pathway. A dolphin-shaped sign pointed the way to the roller coaster. Andi remem-bered reading in the brochure that it was, "an exhilarat-ing way to begin your stay at Wild Ride Resort." Hearing a low rumble, she looked up just in time to see the blue dolphin-shaped front car dipping toward the ground in a spiral motion while passengers whooped and screamed.

No, thank you.

In pure fascination, though, she had to watch as it twisted and turned in and out of the trees before whizzing into the hotel. Andi grudgingly had to admit that it was rather sleek and sexy and for a moment wondered if she should give it a whirl.

But luckily, the insane moment passed and she headed over to the steps where she could enter the lobby without losing her corn dog. Pausing at the entrance to the hotel, Andi gazed out over the pool. "Magnificent," she said with a low whistle. The sweet smell of coconut-scented sunscreen and the heavy beat of calypso music drifted her way, making her want to shimmy into her swimsuit and grab a frozen strawberry daiquiri. But first things first, she thought and entered the lobby.

"Nice," she breathed, turning in a complete circle to take it all in. After seeing as many hotels as she had, es-pecially over the last year, she was darned difficult to impress. The lobby was open and airy with a tropical theme that used bold, bright colors instead of the pastels that Andi was used to seeing. The feel of the place had an instant energy but was oddly soothing at the same time, Andi thought. She was itching to get to her laptop to take notes.

The building was ten stories tall, and the rooms opened to a hallway overlooking the lobby. Andi smiled when the Dolphin entered the second story almost soundlessly on a track that exited at the other end of the lobby, much like the monorails at the Contemporary Hotel in Disney World. Tacky, crass, vulgar, and the whole list of words she thought she would be using to describe Wild Ride Resort simply did not apply.

At least not yet.

Still feeling a bit guilty about arriving early, Andi was about to approach the front desk when she heard a petite blond woman just to her right mention her name to the concierge. "Andrea Cooper arrives tomorrow and Max said to cater to her every whim, no matter how big of a bitch she turns out to be."

Pretending to check for messages on her cell, Andi strained her ears to hear more of the conversation. *Bitch? Well!*

The blond shook her head. "Max insisted on having *her* write the article."

"Why?" the concierge asked.

The blond shrugged her slim shoulders. "She's good, but, unfortunately, nasty if she doesn't like the place."

Uh, that would be called being honest, Andi wanted to tell her. People work hard all year to go on vacation. Nasty would be giving five stars to a resort that didn't deserve it.

The blond shook her head and said, "You know Max. He thinks he'll get his five stars one way or another. I told him to keep his hands to himself. A travel writer scorned is nothing to mess around with. Especially her." She shrugged again. "Anyway, whatever the snob wants, make sure she gets it, okay?"

"So she's a snob?" the concierge asked.

The blond shrugged. "They usually are. Globe-hopping Prada-wearing nose in the air."

He nodded. "I get the picture."

Snob? *Snob!* Andi looked down at her mustard-stained blouse and almost laughed. She flicked her cell phone shut, wondering if smoke was curling out of her ears. The thing about redheads and tempers was not an old wives' tale. She was seething. Oh, so "Max" thought he could squeeze five stars from her, did he? "Ha!" *Oops,* she had said that out loud and people were looking. Plastering a smile on her face, she marched over to the front desk and announced her arrival.

chapter four

Max turned his back to the pelting spray of the shower, hoping to soothe his tense neck muscles. He was sure going to miss this spacious two-headed shower stall while bunking in his office suite. It was a small price to pay, though, if Andrea Cooper came through with a five-star rating. Krista had gotten all over him again about requesting Andrea Cooper and although he had pretended to be confident about wanting her, Max was nervous. He totally respected Krista's point of view but he had ignored her last incoming call to his cell phone. Enough was enough.

Max angled his head forward while rolling his shoulders, letting the pulsating water work its magic. Some people got headaches. His body always reacted to stress with pain that started in his neck and shot through his shoulders and down his back. At times like these, Max wondered why in the hell he hadn't retired as he had planned to instead of turning this island into a resort.

When the pain subsided, Max lathered up his body, thinking that the next thing on his agenda was an ice-cold beer, followed by a steak dinner, and then maybe getting laid. God knew it had been a while. Damn, he was getting half hard just thinking about it. With a groan, he palmed his penis, but refused to get relief with that method.

He wanted a woman. He needed an endless kiss, smooth skin, firm breasts filling his hands, his mouth. He needed to sink into silky heat, slow and easy, all night long. Damn, when was the last time he had done an all-nighter? Found a woman he couldn't get enough of?

He couldn't remember.

There wasn't a day that went by that Max didn't get a key card slipped in his pocket with an explicit invitation, and while his reputation for being a player made for great tabloid reading, Max hadn't done much over the past ten years but work his ever-loving ass off. It had been difficult to find a steady girlfriend who would put up with traveling the globe and living on the road for months at a time while building a roller coaster, only to arrive home, take a breather, and start the process all over again.

Max turned off the water and fingered his wet hair back from his face. Yeah, he had made a fortune; earned a reputation as an international playboy. Bought his own damned island. But in reality?

Max was lonely.

The women who approached him on a daily basis were mostly after a vacation fling, offering an empty invitation that Max found himself accepting less and less. With a sigh, Max stepped from the tiled stall and toweled dry. That cold beer was calling his name, so he tucked the edges of the towel around his waist and made a beeline for the fridge.

Imagine his surprise when standing in his kitchen was a tall redhead with a longneck in one hand and her blouse and bra dangling from the other.

"I guess it must be happy hour," Max said drily not knowing if he was angry or grateful at the intrusion.

Her mouth moved but no sound came out.

After a lingering glance at her perfect breasts and endless legs, Max decided to be grateful. "Who sent you up? Danny?" It wouldn't be the first time.

"No, I . . . uh . . ." The blouse and bra slipped from her fingers and she shook her head mumbling something that sounded like "mustard and shirt."

"Mind sharing?" he asked and eased the cold bottle from her fingers.

"Wait, I need—"

"Thanks," he tipped the bottle back, and then guzzled a long, satisfying swallow.

"Um, D-Danny didn't send me." She backed up while covering her breasts with her hands.

So she wanted to play coy . . . how cute. "Oh, well, remind me to thank whoever did. Now don't go hiding those bodacious breasts from me." Max lowered his head and nuzzled her neck.

"You don't under . . . mmmm . . . stand." She pushed at his shoulders, thus freeing her breasts, allowing Max to cup them in his hands . . . *ahh*, warm, soft, and yet so firm.

"Oh, I think I do." He dipped his head and lightly licked one nipple while thumbing the other one in light circles.

"No, I . . . need to . . . tell . . . this is . . . *God* . . ."

When she groaned Max tugged on the nipple with his teeth and then raised his head to capture her half-open mouth with a kiss. She mumbled against his lips, as if she wanted to say something, but Max didn't have talking on his mind. He deepened the kiss, loving the taste of her warm, sweet mouth. Whatever she was trying to say dissolved into a groan and he felt her relax.

She suddenly came alive in his arms. Threading her fingers through his wet hair, she kissed him back, moving sensuously against him, making her pebbled nipples graze back and forth across his bare chest. And she was tall . . . where Max had to stoop to kiss most women, he merely had to tilt his head down to kiss her. God, it felt good to have a woman fit perfectly against him, molding against his body in all the right places.

Without breaking the kiss, Max pulled back just far enough to cup one breast, kneading the fullness against the palm of his hand. Then, with his thumb and index finger, he teased the nipple, rolling and tugging until he was rewarded with hearing her whimper low in her throat.

And still, he kissed her . . . the never-ending kiss he had been denied for so long. "I want to taste you everywhere," he whispered hotly in her ear.

"Oh, *yes,* that would be . . . *what?* No, you . . . I . . . we *can't* . . ." Andi's body hummed with sexual need until she couldn't think straight.

"Sure we can," he murmured low and softly into her ear. "It's been so long and you feel so right." He tugged on her earlobe with his teeth, sending a jolt of heat all the way to Andi's toes.

"Oh, I *know*," Andi said with a long sigh and a hot shiver. "So very long."

"Let's just slide those shorts off," he whispered as he nuzzled her neck with warm, wet kisses.

"Okay . . . mmmmm, that feels so . . . oh God, *no!*" She gave his shoulders a little shove knowing that she had to put some distance between herself and his incredible mouth.

"What's wrong?"

Andi put her hands up to cover her breasts. "I'm," she swallowed and said softly, "Andi." She winced. "Sorry about the, uh, confusion." She tried to put a businesslike edge to her breathless voice but it was difficult to be businesslike while standing there half naked and weak-kneed. "I um, came early."

"Well, not to worry, Andi. I can make you come again."

Oh God. She shook her head. "No, I . . ." Okay, this was really awkward. She felt heat creep into her cheeks and said in a rush, "I'm Andrea Cooper."

For a long moment he just blinked at her, finally saying, "The . . . the travel writer?" It was more of a horrified statement than a question. "Oh, I uh . . ." He took a swift step backwards and somehow got his feet tangled up in her discarded shirt and bra. "Why didn't you . . . ? Whoa!" He stumbled backwards and her shirt slid on the smooth tile causing him to flail his arms but go down with a solid thump on his ass. His hands slapped against the floor and he just caught himself before his head hit the tile. The bath towel fell open, sliding from his hips in sort of slow motion, and his penis sprang forward like a jack-in-the-box.

"Ohmigod," Andi shouted, rushing forward. "Are you okay?" She tried not to look . . . *there,* but he was aroused and *wow,* magnificent. "Oh!" Andi instinctively put one hand over her eyes but then one breast was exposed. "Oh," she said again, slapping her hand back over her breast but the other hand over her mouth, flashing him the other breast. Realizing she must look like she was dancing a kinky version of the Macarena, Andi put both hands over her breasts, but he wasn't paying any attention anyway.

Max was frantically trying to cover himself but the towel was bunched up beneath his hips and when he tried to stand to remedy the situation Andi noticed that his bare feet were somehow hopelessly hooked in her twisted bra straps.

"Let me help."

"I'm fine." He tried to kick his feet free of his bra bondage, succeeding in making his situation a tangled mess.

Unsure of what to do, Andi did manage to grab her shirt. Turning her back to him she tugged it over her head.

"Damn!"

Andi pivoted in time to see that Oliver Maxwell had folded his big body into a sitting position but was still having trouble untangling his big feet. She shook her head and had to swallow a smile. This was the roller coaster-tycoon/international playboy? "Allow me," she said, knelt down, and unhooked the metal clasp where it was snagged in a bit of white lace. She unwrapped the bra from his feet and then stood back up.

"Thanks." He yanked the towel back in place. Looking up at her he said, "On a humiliation scale of one to ten, um, this is way off the charts."

"It wasn't all your fault. If I hadn't spilled mustard on my blouse I wouldn't have been standing half dressed in your kitchen. I was about to throw my shirt in the wash when I decided I needed a cold beer. I'm sorry."

"I think that should be my line." He pushed up to his feet holding the towel in place. "Can we start over?"

Andi grinned. She was finding it hard not to like him. "Sure."

"Great. Andi Cooper, I'm Oliver Maxwell but everybody calls me Max."

"Nice to meet you, Max," Andi replied and held out her hand to him.

Max engulfed her hand in his warm grasp. "Welcome to Wild Ride Resort."

"Thanks, but uh, Max?"

"Yes?"

"You just lost your towel."

chapter five

"Oh shit." Bending over, he quickly retrieved the towel.

Andi had to bite her tongue in order not to laugh.

"Sorry for the language."

"No problem."

"And for losing my towel again."

"I thought it was just another warm welcome."

"It was totally an accident, I swear." He raised his hands in mock surrender . . . and the towel dipped dangerously low.

"You're about to flash me again." With a chuckle Andi took a step closer to Max. She reached over and tightened the loose knot at his waist but she wasn't prepared for the jolt of pure heat caused by the mere brush of her fingers against his warm, smooth skin. Andi saw his ab muscles tighten and quiver. The realization that she had the power to arouse this incredibly sexy man caught her by surprise. Growing up tall and gangly with flaming red hair, Andi had never felt physically attractive, but a glance up at Max told her that he found her downright hot.

Her heart pounded with excitement but Andi stepped back even though she wanted to reach over and splay her hands over his magnificent chest . . . oh, and then tip her head up for another scorching kiss. She had a feeling keeping her relationship with Max on a professional level was going to be impossible and Andi prided herself on being professional. She felt her heart sink to her toes but with a determined lift of her chin said, "Max, I need to go."

"You mean as in leave the island and not write the article?"

"My editor won't be happy about it, but she can get someone else."

"But I want you."

Her heart all but stopped at his vehement statement and she wished that it meant something else entirely. Trying to keep her voice steady, she said, "Well, I've learned that you can't always get what you want. I just don't think we can keep this on a professional level given our . . . uh, introduction."

Taking a step backward, Max said, "Look, I'll keep my hands to myself. We'll keep this on a purely business level."

She gave him an I-don't-think-this-will-work look.

"Really, I will."

"Okay," Andi said slowly, trying not to feel disappointed that he thought he could actually do this. She was already thinking of throwing herself at him again.

Clearing his throat, Max said, "Well, then, I'd better pack some clothes."

"I hate to put you out." God did she ever. Maybe she should offer to let him stay. After all, the place was huge. No, that would be too dangerous. "I could just stay in a regular room to get the feel of the hotel, anyway."

He shook his head. "It's booked."

"You don't hold rooms back?"

Max grinned. "We don't do much holding back here at Wild Ride." His grin faded a bit when he said, "I should pack and get going."

Andi nodded, trying to think of a reason for him to stay, but knowing she should let him go for both personal and professional reasons. "I'll go shower while you pack."

"If there's anything you need . . ." His voice trailed off and he took a step toward her. "Listen, if you'd like, I could show you around, take you to dinner?"

Andi felt herself being drawn to him like a magnet to a refrigerator. She forced the next words past her lips. "That probably wouldn't be a good idea."

He nodded. "Right." He stood there looking disappointed and a bit uncertain. "Well, then . . ." His eyes met hers and he said softly, "You know you're nothing like what I expected." He shifted from one bare foot to the other. "I mean that in a good way. You're more down to earth . . . warm . . ."

"Max, you're not anything like what I expected, either."

He gave her a crooked grin. "Sorry about your luck."

She smiled back. "I didn't mean it as an insult."

"Andi?"

"Yes?" Her heart thudded.

"I know I promised to keep my hands to myself and I

will, but I'm asking for one last kiss before we start the new program."

He mistook her not-being-able-to-find-her-voice thing as a no, and looked so damned disappointed that Andi wanted to fly into his arms. Knowing full well that she was playing with fire, she whispered, "Okay."

With a smile that flat-out melted her heart, Max slowly walked toward her. Threading his fingers through her hair, he kissed her softly, so sweetly. The briefest touch of his tongue sent a jolt of longing all the way to her toes. Just when her eyes fluttered shut and she was about to wrap her arms round him, he pulled his mouth from hers.

With an unsteady intake of breath, Max leaned his forehead against hers. With a weak chuckle, he murmured, "That was a mistake." His instant reaction to the brief kiss was evident beneath the bath towel.

Andi *so* wanted to be bold enough to put her hand over his arousal, rub her palm over his hard length, and then yank the towel to the ground. For once in her life it would be awesome to dominate, to rule, to just throw her inhibitions out the window. She wanted to caress his hot, velvet skin as she closed her fingers around him . . .

But she didn't. She might be a world traveler but deep down she would always be an Indiana farm girl. "I'll go take that shower now," she said, embarrassed that her voice was a bit shaky. She turned to go, but Max stopped her with a hand on her shoulder, his dark eyebrows drawn together in a frown.

"Andi, I want to give you a word of caution. When the sun goes down, Wild Ride Resort takes on a life of its own. Some nights can get a little crazy. I try to keep it under control with undercover security, but they can't be everywhere."

Andi gave him a reassuring smile. "I've been all over the globe, Max. I can take care of myself."

His frown remained. "I'm sure you can, but still, I'm going to leave my card on the kitchen counter. Call me if you need me . . . for any reason, *okay?*"

"Okay," Andi said firmly, since he looked so worried.

Max smiled then, and Andi wanted so badly to kiss him again that she turned away in a hurry before she did something crazy like throw herself into his arms. After entering the bathroom, she leaned against the closed door and slid on shaky legs to the cool tile floor. Putting her face in her hands, she didn't know whether to laugh or to cry.

Not being much of a crier, Andi shoved that notion aside, but laughter didn't fit her mood, either. In a word, she was . . . confused. If anyone had suggested that mere hours after arriving at the resort she would have contemplated sleeping with Oliver Maxwell, Andi would have said that they were out of their ever-loving minds. While Andi had been around the world, she hadn't exactly been around the block. Casual sex just wasn't her thing.

"My God, what am I thinking?" And then she realized she hadn't been thinking. She had been feeling. And somehow she knew that sex with Oliver Maxwell would be anything but casual; it would be unbelievable.

And it wasn't going to happen.

chapter
six

Max took the duffle bag that he had hastily packed and tossed it onto the leather couch in his office while uttering a curse. He wanted to see Andi Cooper again, dammit.

And *not* on a professional level.

Hell no, he wanted to be up close and very personal with her. But he had given his word that he would keep his hands to himself, and so he would. Ah, damn, but it had been so long since a woman had moved him the way she had . . . and he wanted more of it. A lot more of it.

Not that it was just about sex. Max could walk out to the pool and have a bikini-clad beauty in his bed in nothing flat. For whatever reason, he had felt a connection with Andi that went beyond the physical. There was just *something* about her that brought out every damned primal male instinct that he possessed, including the need to protect her. There was an air of innocence about her and he wanted to keep her safe. In his mind, Andi Cooper needed someone at her side after dark at Wild Ride, that someone being *him*.

The nights, he knew, could fluctuate from wild and crazy to dark and sensual, depending on the crowd, the music, the tides, the moon? Who knew? Max had yet to figure it out, because every night was different. And it was one of the reasons he didn't allow pictures to be taken. Photographs could never capture Wild Ride Resort after dark. You had to experience the feel, the smell, the rhythm . . . the heat.

After reading Andi's work, Max believed that she could capture the essence of what it was like after the sun went down on the island, replaced by glittering lights, pulsating music, spicy food, and potent drinks, but with unexpected twists and turns not unlike those of one of his roller coasters. Safe . . . but with the illusion of danger.

But he had expected Andrea Cooper, the world-wise travel writer, to be altogether different from the fresh-faced beauty that had blown him away. Sure, he could have his security keep a close eye on her, but that could only go so far. No, *he* wanted to be at her side with his arm protectively around her waist, hugging her close . . . letting every guy on the island know . . .

"Fuck!" Max scrubbed a hand over his face. What in the hell was wrong with him? He barely knew Andi Cooper and yet she had him turned inside out; had him acting like a jealous lover!

"Max?" Krista blew into the room like a miniature hurricane. "Oh, thank God you're here. I've been scouring the island for you. Where have you been?"

Max opened his mouth to reply but Krista rushed on.

"Listen, don't you dare go up to the penthouse. Andrea

Cooper has arrived a day early." Krista narrowed her eyes as she continued, "You know she did it on purpose to get us all frazzled and everything, but we fooled her and whisked her, pretty as you please, right up to your place. Ha, she thought she could catch us with our pants down." Krista wagged a finger at him. "But don't you go up there! Make me a list and I'll go up and get whatever you need. Okay?"

"Uh, that won't be necessary." Under other circumstances, Max would have found this whole situation rather amusing. Not only was Krista good at her job, but she managed to provide comic relief without even trying. She was smart as a whip and sexy as hell, but a damned drama queen. Max pitied the poor bastard who tried to tame her.

Krista's gaze flicked over to the couch. Her blue eyes widened when she spotted the duffle bag. "You've been up there? Was she there?"

Max opened his mouth and almost managed to get in a word, "Uh . . ."

Krista gasped. "She was! Max, you *have* to answer your cell and your pages. I tried to warn you not to go up there. Dammit, I thought you were working in the Dolphin all morning or I would never have sent Andrea Cooper up there." Krista took a step forward with her fists on her hips and demanded, "So, what happened?"

There wasn't much that could embarrass Max, but he felt the telltale heat of a blush creep up his neck.

"Oh. My. God. Tell me you didn't have sex with her."

"Not exactly."

"What do you mean, not exactly? It's a yes-or-no question."

Max took a deep breath and blew it out. He knew from painful experience that Krista would hound him until she got the details. "Well, I was in the shower."

"Oh God, I don't like where this is going."

"Do you want to know what happened or not?"

"Go on."

"Okay. After I got out of the shower, I wrapped a towel around me and headed to the kitchen for a cold beer. Standing in my kitchen was this beautiful redhead with a longneck in one hand and her shirt and bra dangling from her other hand. You can imagine how I got the wrong impression."

"Oh God."

"Yeah, I thought Danny had sent her up—"

"Oh God, oh God!"

"Do you want to hear this or not?"

Wincing, she shook her head.

"Anyway, I sort of . . . look, she had amazing breasts so I—"

"Felt her up? You felt up Andrea Cooper's breasts?"

Max felt the need to defend his . . . his something. "I didn't know who she was."

Krista blinked at him. In other circumstances Max would have been proud to render her speechless. "I was fresh out of the shower. She was standing there in my kitchen . . . half naked," he said lamely.

"So you felt the need to feel her up? Is that all you did? No, don't tell me. I can't take it."

"Well . . . no. But it didn't go that far . . ."

"What were you thinking?" she asked through gritted teeth.

"I told you I thought Danny had sent her up. I didn't know—and then my towel—"

She gasped. "You . . . you *exposed* your . . . your *package* to her?"

"It was an accident. I slipped and got all tangled up in her bra and—"

"No!" Krista raised her hands in surrender. "I don't want to hear any more."

Max leaned against the edge of his desk. "Listen, don't you tell a soul, you hear me? I don't want people gossiping about Andi. This was my fault, not hers."

Krista's expression softened and she gave Max a curious look. "So, you like her."

"Yeah."

"Good!" She snapped to attention. "We can use this to our advantage, after all. Are you seeing her tonight?"

"No," he said firmly. "I promised her I'd keep our relationship on a professional level. And I'm not about to use her."

Krista puckered her lips. "Don't think of it as *using* her. More like schmoozing. Okay?"

"No."

"But—"

"No, Krista. But I do want security to keep an eye on her tonight."

"You seriously think Andrea Cooper, world-class traveler, needs to be shadowed?"

"She's . . . she's . . . I don't know, vulnerable. I want her protected, in case some asshole decides to come on too strong."

Krista clicked her tongue against the roof of her mouth and smiled. "Well, well, *well*. The mighty Oliver Maxwell is smitten."

"I'm not smitten." Damn, there was that frigging blush

again. "I don't get smitten. What the hell is smitten, anyway?"

"Look in the mirror and you'll know. My God, I didn't think there was a woman who could bring you down."

"I barely know her."

"You almost made love to the woman."

Made love. Max had always thought of it as having sex. It hit him hard that there was a difference.

"Earth to Max?"

Max blinked at Krista. "Sorry, what?"

"I asked what you were going to do about her?"

"I gave her my word that I would keep my hands to myself. I won't use her, Krista, so give it up."

"Okay, big boy, I hear you loud and clear." Leaning closer, though, Krista said with a little wag of her finger, "However, let me give you some advice."

Max crossed his arms over his chest. "Go on."

Krista put her fingertip to his chest and gave him a little nudge. "You promised to keep your hands to yourself."

"Yeah, in a moment of insanity."

"Let *her* take the lead."

Max frowned. "What?"

"It's simple, really. Just be your charming self, Max. Let Andrea Cooper come after you."

Max wasn't convinced. "She's not going to come after me, Krista. She wants to keep our relationship professional. And how the hell can I make her want me when I can't even touch her?"

Flipping her hair over her shoulder, she said, "Charm her with your great sense of humor. Your intelligence."

Max grinned. "Now, there's a novel idea."

Krista shoved him in the chest with her finger again. "I'm serious. Ditch the *player* crap and be with her the way you are with me."

Max frowned. "How am I with you?"

"You're the real Oliver Maxwell. Not the roller-coaster designer, or the successful businessman, or the sexy play-boy. You're just Max."

Max grinned. "Yeah, but I want the touching part, too."

Krista shrugged and then squeezed his biceps. "Give her a little flex of muscle. Flash your killer grin if you must. Just be subtle." She gave him a little punch in the arm. "But most of all, just be yourself."

"Who could resist the real me, right?" He grinned, but didn't feel as cocky as he wanted Krista to believe. Sometimes he wondered who he really was anymore.

"Andrea Cooper won't be able to resist you, or Wild Ride, Max. I've got a good feeling about this and you know my hunches are always spot-on."

Max knew that Krista was putting a new spin on the situation. She was an expert at using the cards dealt to her and somehow coming up with a winning hand even when she had to bluff her way through.

With a glance at her watch, Krista said, "Got to run. I've got a conference call with Travis Mackey's agent in twenty minutes."

Max raised his eyebrows. "The rodeo star turned country singer?"

Krista nodded. "He wants Mackey to finish up his summer tour here with a concert and maybe a music video."

"You said yes, I hope?"

Krista wrinkled her nose. "Country music? I'm not so sure."

Pushing away from the edge of the desk, Max said, "Are you kidding? Travis Mackey's one of the hottest acts going. Women love him."

"I was thinking more along the lines of Jimmy Buffet or the Beach Boys. You know, beach music."

Max chuckled. "You've never listened to Travis Mackey, have you?"

She did the little hair-flip thing. "It's not my taste, Max. You know that."

"It used to be."

"Don't go there."

Max raised his hands in surrender. "Okay, but Mackey's music isn't what you think. He's country, but does some very beach-friendly island-type stuff. He'd be perfect."

Krista leaned over and gave Max a quick peck on the cheek. "I just don't know if country music fits in here. Maybe I'll do an online survey. I do want to have a Labor Day blowout." She shrugged. "We'll see."

"Wait a minute." Max walked over to the entertainment center that held his television and CD player. Looking through his music collection, he said, "Aha, here's Travis Mackey's CD." He handed the case to Krista.

She looked at the cover, snickered, and held it up to Max. "He's walking on the beach shirtless, wearing a cowboy hat. Now, how goofy is that?"

Max shrugged. "He's had three hit singles off the album, so it's obviously working for him."

She handed the case back to him, but Max shook his head. "No, go ahead and give it a spin. You might just enjoy him, Krista."

She wrinkled her nose at him. "Right, a pretend cowboy." Tapping the plastic case, she said, "Sex is selling this thing, not his music."

"I like his music."

"You would."

"By the way, he isn't pretending. Mackey was a world-champion bull rider."

She shrugged. "Whatever. I'll see you tonight."

Max scrubbed a hand down his face and then flicked a glance at his wristwatch. In a few short hours it would be dark, but Max knew that when the sun set on the island, things only got hotter.

⤜◠ chapter
seven

A ndi stood on the balcony of the penthouse wearing one of the sexiest outfits she had ever worn in her life. No, make that *the* sexiest. And it was the most conservative outfit in the pile of clothing strewn across Max's bed. Not that she had a choice. Somehow, between the mainland and Wild Ride Resort, her luggage had been lost.

Andi took a swallow of her second beer and sighed. Having her luggage lost was not uncommon in her travels, but having only a boutique chock-full of barely-there clothing to choose from was. So now, instead of the khaki shorts and basic blouses, a sensible black evening dress, a one-piece bathing suit and basic Hanes for Her underwear, Andi had a variety of clothing that looked as if she had purchased them from a Victoria's Secret catalog. Not that the clothes weren't sexy, frothy, and beautiful.

They were just *so* not her.

And yet Andi's gaze kept traveling over to the big bed.

She had shopped with a kid-in-a-toy-store attitude . . . except that these items were definitely for adults. Giggling and blushing, she had been egged on by the store clerk and had purchased some items that she knew she would never wear . . . or would she?

She walked over and let her fingers sift through the colorful pile of bras and panties. Goodbye sensible cotton; hello lace and silk. She picked up a pair of hip-hugging short shorts that the clerk had gushed over, telling her that they made her legs look a mile long. Andi had always hated being so tall but the clerk had insisted that she had an amazing body and had picked out clothing that highlighted all of the body parts Andi had always tried to downplay . . . her legs, her breasts, and her red hair. Everything on the bed was short, tight, and boldly colored . . . but there was *one* outfit that stood out.

Andi sighed as she picked up the leather corset that laced in a crisscross pattern up the front. "I'll never wear this. What was I thinking?" But just touching the cool smooth leather gave her a little thrill. A leather thong, a garter belt, and thigh-high stockings rounded out the uber-sexy outfit that looked like something Catwoman might wear. "God," Andi said, shaking her head. If that wasn't enough, a small tasseled whip and black stilettos came with the ensemble.

Andi never would have even had the nerve to pick up the outfit to look at it but the boutique, although upscale and classy, had an entire room full of similar leather and lace outfits, lotions, oils, and some interesting toys . . . and had been packed full of eager customers. The clerk had explained that Wild Ride was all about fantasy and that if the leather corset was totally out of her comfort zone then that was all the more reason to buy it.

"I'll never wear it," Andi said again but for a moment she imagined Max handcuffed to the bed totally at her mercy. Closing her eyes, she swallowed, and wondered how it would feel to dominate, to control, to bring a man to his knees with need. Feeling foolish, she turned away from the bed.

If the sexy clothing wasn't enough, Andi also had to replace her lost cosmetics and another sales clerk at the fancy hotel boutique had insisted on giving her a makeover while raving over her cheekbones, or whatever. Now, instead of her "easy, breezy" Cover Girl foundation, mascara, and blush, Andi had a boatload of expensive makeup in smoky, sultry, shimmering shades. She had seven separate items for her eyes alone, for Pete's sake: eyebrow liner, three shades of eyeshadow, one light shade for the brow bone to give her eyes a "lift," one for the crease for "drama," and a medium shade for the lid. Eyeliner, she was told, was an absolute must, along with an eyelash curler that scared the bejesus out of her. Even the mascara was an ordeal . . . one coat of white extender before two coats of black mascara. Sheesh. Then there was custom-blended foundation, concealer, blush, lip liner, and lip gloss . . .

High maintenance was a royal pain.

But Andi had to admit that the results were kind of, well, amazing. She wore a sea foam–colored off-the-shoulder peasant blouse tucked into a flirty multicolored skirt with little beads dangling from the hem. Matching beaded earrings swung from Andi's earlobes and gold bracelets jangled at her wrist. Strappy sandals rounded off her bohemian look.

For the first time in her life, Andi thought she might actually look *hot*. Maybe it was the residual effects from the mind-blowing encounter with Max, or the fact that she was, for the first time ever, wearing a thong, but Andi felt sexy. Wearing a thong, she decided, just made you feel a little bit naughty. She wondered what Max would think of her new look and then wanted to kick herself for thinking of him. Again. For the millionth time that afternoon.

"How could I not?" Andi grumbled. After all, she was staying in his penthouse, surrounded by his things, drinking his beer! And by *God* the lingering smell of his aftershave had her in a constant state of arousal. With a delicious little shiver, she remembered the feel of his hands on her bare skin and the heat of his mouth locked with hers.

With a little squeal of pure frustration that sent a seagull squawking away, Andi tipped her bottle back and drained the last of the beer. She put the bottle down with an angry thump. *Damn you, Oliver Maxwell,* she thought, *for rocking my world and then walking right back out of it.*

Andi decided right then and there that tonight she wasn't going to stand on the sidelines and take notes like the good little travel writer she was . . . oh, no, she was going to jump into the thick of Wild Ride Resort. And if she just happened to run into Max? Well, she would be professionally polite. Distant. Maybe she could even pull off . . . *haughty*. Yeah, she'd show him.

Goodbye, farm girl. Hello, thong-wearing sex kitten.

Besides, this place was teeming with good-looking guys. Who needed Oliver Maxwell, anyway?

She did.

Which was why she was going to steer clear of him.

With a deep intake of sea air, Andi looked out over the Atlantic Ocean. The sun, glowing reddish-orange, was sinking low over the water, sending streaks of orange across the deep blue sky. As the horizon darkened, there was a kaleidoscope of vivid purple, red, and orange. Andi noticed that the lights of the hotel and the courtyard surrounding the pool were dimming as if in sync with the sun. Shadowy twilight cloaked the resort and for a heartbeat everything seemed all at once to go dark, still, and quiet.

"Oh . . . oh, *my*," Andi breathed. Her hand involuntarily came up to her mouth as a multitude of sparkling lights burst forth in the distance. She could see the top of a Ferris wheel above the tall cypress trees. Music and laughter traveled on the night breeze and Andi could faintly smell buttered popcorn, sweet funnel cakes, and cotton candy.

"Max's Moonlight Madness," Andi whispered, repeating what the brochure had called the glitzy carnival that came to life every night at twilight. She had read that the hotel all but shut down and the Dolphin stopped running and now she realized that it was true. With her hands gripping the railing, Andi watched for a few more minutes, feeling herself drawn to the hint of energy and excitement in the air. Andi felt a shiver of anticipation as she shut the sliding door of the balcony. Pausing only to pick up her tiny beaded purse, she let herself out the door of Max's penthouse. With her heart pounding, she pressed the down button for the elevator.

After the buzz of activity all day long, the hotel was almost eerily quiet as Andi made her way through the lobby. Everyone, it seemed, was at the carnival. Andi suddenly felt alone and more than a little nervous, glad to have Max's card and her tiny cell phone tucked away in her purse. Not that she planned on calling him. It was just comforting to know that she could. Odd, really, since she was used to traveling on her own in foreign counties, exotic locations. But a feeling almost palpable in the air hinted of something wild and wicked beyond the tall gates where Max's Moonlight Madness awaited.

chapter eight

"Have you seen her?" Max asked Krista yet again, trying to keep the impatience from his voice. With narrowed eyes, he scanned the crowd, hoping to spot Andi's strawberry-blond head.

"Max, I'm not certain what she looks like."

"A tall redhead. She stands out."

Krista shook her head. "I don't know what you're wigging out about. This is an island. She has to be here someplace. I think you're more worried about who she's with than where she's located."

Max shot Krista a look, but she had hit a little too close to home. The thought of Andi with someone else set his teeth on edge. He was, though, a bit worried. The crowd tonight was loud, rowdy, and damn, it was still early.

Shrouded by tall trees, Max's Moonlight Madness was fenced in to keep out wildlife for the protection of both the animals and the people. Beyond the fencing was a wildlife sanctuary off limits to visitors. The carnival itself was set up much like a village with brick-paved streets and storefront shops set up café style, which created an Old World atmosphere. Off to the left of the main street was an area with traditional carnival rides including a Ferris wheel, a merry-go-round, the classic whip, and the tunnel of love. One street over had a variety of games of chance, palm readers, and roving musicians.

"Where the hell is she?" Crossing the street, Max wound his way through the sea of people with Krista trying to keep up. Normally he would have slowed down for her short stride, but tonight he was a man on a mission.

The evening air felt thick and warm, smelling of the earth, the ocean, and food. With the rum punch flowing, Max made sure that food was readily available and consumption was encouraged. Usually, Max would indulge in a paper cone of hot, sugar-roasted almonds, a guilty pleasure since childhood, but tonight the scent of cinnamon failed to tempt him.

Max had other things on his mind.

A bead of sweat rolled down his chest, causing the thin fabric of his tropical-print shirt to stick to his damp skin. Max absently unbuttoned the top three buttons, allowing the night breeze to give him some relief from the heat. When Krista pressed a cold plastic cup of punch into his hand, Max paused to take a big swig.

"Hey," Krista said, putting a hand on his arm, "there's a tall redhead."

Max looked in the direction where Krista pointed. His heartbeat kicked it up a notch when he spotted Andi standing in a semicircle of people watching Maury the Magnificent perform magic tricks. As a child, Max had been dazzled by Maury's lightning-quick slight of hand when he had performed his magic for Max's father's carnival. Maury had then moved on to Vegas but, like many of the old carnival workers, was happy to accept Max's offer to retire to a beach bungalow on the island working at the carnival in the evenings. With his tufts of white hair, barrel-chested body, and impish grin, Maury the Magnificent charmed the crowd gathered around his small stand.

"Max, *is* that Andi?" Krista took a sip of her own punch and then raised her blond eyebrows in question at Max, but he had his eyes on Andi. Shaking her head, Krista muttered, "I'm guessing she is."

Max nodded absently, grinning when Maury plucked a big daisy from behind Andi's ear, and, after bowing deeply, presented it to her with flair. Andi tilted her head back and laughed, making Max feel cheated when the sound of her laughter was lost in the noise of the crowd. In his mind, Max reproduced the throaty sound, becoming a bit agitated when the guy standing next to Andi leaned in and said something in her ear that had her laughing again.

"She doesn't exactly look like she needs your protection, Max."

With a frown, Max realized that this was true. Andi appeared to be holding her own, having fun. His eyes narrowed when it appeared that she was flirting. And what the hell was she wearing? A sexy little off-the-shoulder number, and a short skirt that showed off her forever-legs to perfection. Max felt his body quicken in reaction to those slender legs, wondering what her legs would feel like wrapped around him.

Bullshit. He didn't need this; didn't need *her*.

"Hey, where are you going?" Krista demanded when Max turned away, having seen enough.

"You're right. She doesn't need me." Max polished off the punch and crushed the cup in his fist.

Krista reached up and yanked on his sleeve. "You mean after all of this, you're going to turn and walk away?"

"You betcha."

"Max—"

"Krista, there are reasons why I should keep my distance from her anyway."

"And maybe one big reason why you shouldn't."

Looking down at Krista, he shook his head. "Give it up. She seems to like the place. I feel confident that we'll get our five stars."

Krista shook her head back at him. "That's not what I meant. You seem so into her, Max. I've never seen you have such an immediate reaction to a woman and I've known you for a long time."

"Krista, I just met her."

She shrugged. "I realize that."

"So, what are you telling me, here?"

"Don't give up so soon." Krista swallowed and then said, "She could be, you know," she swallowed again and then said, *"the one."*

Max thought Krista was kidding and was about to make one of his jackass comments, but something clenched in his gut at Krista's expression. She was serious, but then Krista was always serious. What surprised him was that she seemed to believe in the romantic notion that there was "the one" out there somewhere. For a moment, Krista's carefully crafted don't-mess-with-me-attitude slipped, revealing a softer side that few people knew existed.

But then, with an uncharacteristic chuckle, Krista glanced down at her plastic cup and said, "What in the world have they spiked this punch with?"

"Krista," he began, but she stopped him by putting her hand in the air.

"You handle this the way you want to, Max. I'm over-stepping my bounds."

"That's never stopped you before."

She gave him a ghost of a smile. "True. So, let me say one more thing."

"Go on."

"Don't be a weenie."

Max had to chuckle. "A . . . a *weenie*? I haven't heard that word since I was about nine."

Her lips thinned and there was a hint of a blush on her cheeks. With a little flip of her hair over her shoulder she said tartly, "Hey, if the shoe fits."

Max puffed out his chest in mock horror. "I've never been a weenie. I have, however, been a hot dog."

Krista poked him in the chest but she actually smiled. "Then don't start now. Forget about business. If you want Andi Cooper, go after her." Handing him her half-empty cup, she said, "I've got to run."

"Krista, wait . . ."

She put a hand in the air again. "You're on your own, bud. I know I'm your right-hand man, but I can only do so much. Getting the girl is your job." With a wiggle of her fingers in the air, she said, "See ya."

Max drew in a deep breath and blew it out. Normally

by this time of night he would be munching on his roasted almonds and mingling with the crowd, keeping a discreet eye on things. "Ah, to hell with it," he grumbled, thinking he should do just that. Maybe find another woman to take his mind off of Andi. Sipping the rest of Krista's punch, he surveyed the crowd, looking for a woman to approach. His gaze, though, kept sliding back to Andi and the guy next to her. His eyes narrowed when it suddenly became apparent to him that Andi was no longer enjoying the guy's attention.

With an angry toss of the cup in the trash, Max weaved his way over to Andi, who was slapping at the guy's roving hands. Max slid his arm about her waist and with a pointed look at the jerk said to Andi, "Hey, baby, I've been looking all over for you."

"Oh?" Andi questioned, but looked relieved to see him.

Max whispered in her ear, "Play along." And then he bent his head and kissed her.

Andi's eyes widened in surprise, but at the touch of Max's mouth to hers, she melted quicker than the cotton candy she had consumed earlier that night. The palms of her hands came up to rest on his chest. She could feel the solid warmth of his skin beneath his thin shirt and it sent her own heart racing. He tasted faintly of rum punch, pineapple, and raw heat, and by God she wanted to devour him right then and there.

But Max suddenly broke the delicious contact and took a step away. Andi blinked at him, a bit dazed.

With a slight grin, he said, "I think we convinced your admirer to take a hike."

"Oh . . . y-yes. I think we did." She sounded throaty,

breathless. Embarrassed, she swallowed, cleared her throat and said, "Thank you for coming to my rescue."

"My pleasure," he said with a crooked grin.

My pleasure, too. "Not that I didn't have the situation under control, but still, thanks." Had a guy ever come to her rescue before? She didn't think so. Unless you counted when her brother had punched Pete Thomas in the nose for pinching her butt.

"Sorry about the whole kissing thing." Max shrugged and said, "It was either that or punch the guy's lights out and I thought it would be pretty embarrassing to be thrown out of my own resort. It was a spur-of-the-moment decision."

"It got the job done." Andi felt a stab of disappointment. Right, the kiss had just been for show. "No problem." But there was a problem: she wanted him to kiss her again. Right now.

"So, you're not angry?"

She waved her hand in dismissal. "Of course not. Quick thinking on your part. No biggie. Really. Forget about it. I know I have." She waved her hand again, but then let it fall limply back to her side, realizing she was protesting way too much.

"Good, it's forgotten, then."

"Totally. Poof . . . gone." She waved her hand over her head.

Something flickered in his blue eyes. Disappointment?

Max paused, but then said, "So, then, if I promise to be totally professional, will you walk with me? I'd love to show you around the carnival."

Andi hesitated, knowing it would be rather hard to concentrate with him so close. She needed to be taking notes for her article and Max would most definitely be a major distraction of the sexy kind.

"Remember, I have inside connections," he said with that damned killer smile. "I can give you some really juicy material."

Oh, I bet you could, she thought, resenting that he could stand there looking so at ease when she had the almost uncontrollable urge to yank him close and kiss him. It didn't help that the first three buttons of his blue shirt, dotted with tiny palm trees, were open showing a generous slice of tanned chest, lightly furred with dark, silky hair that had just hours ago had tickled her breasts. She barely suppressed a moan. Moaning right about now would definitely be embarrassing.

"Andi?"

She had that whole tongue-tied thing happening while he looked at her expectantly, maybe even hopefully, making it so damned difficult for the next sentence to pass her lips. "I . . ."

His eyebrows rose.

She swallowed and then said in a rush, "I don't think that would be a good idea." Something about Max made her come completely undone. Steering clear of him was the plan. It was the right thing to do and for the most part she was a doing-the-right-thing kinda girl.

His smile faded a bit. "I'll keep my promise." He held up the three-fingered Boy Scout salute. "Scout's honor."

"Were you ever a Boy Scout?" Hard to picture.

With a shake of his head, he admitted, "No, there weren't any Boy Scout troops in a traveling carnival."

Or a Little League team, Andi thought. No high-school football or prom night. Normal stuff that he had missed.

"Hey, don't look at me like that," he said gently, but close to her ear in an effort to be heard over a crowd that was swelling, getting louder. "My childhood was not normal by any standards, but I wouldn't trade it for a thing."

The slight defensiveness in Max's voice suggested otherwise, but Andi gave him a smile and nodded. She realized that she would love to hear more about his childhood. She wanted to get to know Max; learn everything about him.

But she shouldn't.

Andi opened her mouth to tell Max that she was going to be on her way, solo, but just then someone nudged her from behind, propelling her forward. Her hands landed on Max's shoulders and his hands went around her waist to steady her. She expected him to immediately remove his grip, but he didn't.

"Andi, the crowd tonight is a bit on the wild side. I really want you with me." His hands remained firmly on her waist and he gazed down at her.

Oh, there he went again, making her feel ultra-feminine. Making her want to kiss him. If he picked her up right now and slung her over his shoulder, she wouldn't utter a peep. With that thought in mind, she giggled. She tended to laugh when she was nervous, an annoying habit that often gave people the wrong impression.

"Andi, I'm serious."

She gave him a slow smile, surprising them both. "Well don't be. This is a party."

A muscle ticked in his jaw. "Yeah, and it sometimes gets out of hand no matter how hard I try to keep things under control."

Andi sighed. "Okay, you can show me around."

"Good," he said with the killer grin back in place. "Uh, I hate to break the no-touching rule right off the bat, but you need to hold my hand just to keep you with me in the crowd, okay?"

Andi nodded, and had to bite her bottom lip to keep from smiling. "Okay." She took his offer, loving the feel of her smaller hand engulfed in his warm grip. She hated to admit it, but he did make her feel safe.

"Would you like anything to drink or eat?" he asked close to her ear.

"I've already had a soft pretzel and cotton candy, so I'm good. I could use something to drink, though."

"Rum punch okay?"

Andi was about to request a bottle of water, but then thought *what the hell,* and said, "Sure."

Max snagged two cups of punch from a stand on the corner and handed her one. "We keep it simple at night. We only have the drink of the night, which tonight is the punch, but we also offer bottled water, soft drinks, and beer."

Cold and sweet with a bit of lime for tang, the punch was the kind of tropical concoction that would hit you all of a sudden and Andi made a mental note to take it easy. One cup, she told herself, and then switch to water.

"So everything over here is still all-inclusive?" Andi had to lean in close to him to be heard over the laughter, music, and general buzz of the crowd. Max had angled his head to hear her and Andi accidentally brushed her mouth against his the curve of his ear. Quickly averting her face, she took a gulp of punch to hide her embarrassment . . .

And her reaction.

❧ chapter
nine

Max frowned. Andi had just asked him something, but he had gotten distracted when her warm breath tickled his ear. He was about to ask her to repeat the question when a clown on stilts walked by, drawing her attention. Andi tilted her head back and laughed and Max was once again distracted. The delicate curve of her throat, the soft swell of her breasts peeking just above her peasant blouse, had him longing to put his mouth there where he could lick her smooth skin and inhale the slight floral scent of her perfume. Averting his gaze, Max tried to think of other things.

Max spotted Krista in the crowd. She smiled and gave him a thumbs-up. Other workers, friends, waved and greeted him, but he didn't stop to chat. He wanted this time with Andi all to himself.

Max liked the feel of her hand tucked in his as they strolled through the streets. He enjoyed watching her reaction to the surroundings that were getting more wild and wacky by the minute. They stopped on the corner to watch some spontaneous break dancing by some middle-aged men who had obviously never attempted to spin around on the ground before. This prompted others, equally bad, to challenge them.

"Ohmigod," Andi managed to sputter in between her laughter. "What is up with that?"

Max shrugged and said in her ear, "I see this kind of thing all the time. My theory is that the stress levels of your average Joe are so high that when they vacation here, they just let it all hang out." He grinned. "It's one of the reasons that I don't allow photographs on the premises."

Andi watched a heavyset guy attempt a handstand without much luck. She giggled and said, "Not a Kodak moment."

"Exactly. I want to give these guys the freedom to cut loose. Next week they'll be back at the office."

Andi nodded and then smiled up at him. "Kinda like spring break for adults?"

Max chuckled. "Yeah, I guess you could put it that way." He led her through the streets, pausing here and there to take in the antics of the crowd. Pointing to the Ferris wheel, he asked, "Want to go for a ride?"

Andi wrinkled her nose. "Sorry. I have this thing about heights. I'm okay when I have solid ground beneath my feet, like up on your balcony, but dangling in one of those little cars? No thanks."

"So you don't like roller coasters either?"

He sounded so disappointed that Andi had to smile. "I *like* them. The Dolphin is sleek and beautiful. And I was fascinated by some of the research I did on roller coasters."

"Like what?" he asked pulling her back from the crowded street to a more secluded spot next to a building.

She grinned. "You're going to think I'm a complete moron, but I didn't realize that there aren't any motors or power source involved . . . pretty amazing when you think about it."

Max nodded. "Even with the most complex roller coaster the fundamental principles are the same. Newton's first law of motion."

"I know this one!" Andi said with a lift of her chin. "An object in motion tends to stay in motion."

"Very good. Roller coasters are driven almost entirely by basic inertial, gravitational, and centripetal forces all manipulated to give you an awesome ride."

Andi angled her head at him. "Yeah, but after that first big hill how does it keep going?"

Max smiled, obviously loving this subject. Raising his hand, he mimicked the motion of a roller coaster ascending a hill. "Well, the first hill is called the *lift hill* and is used to build up a reservoir of potential energy." He let his hand swoop downward as he explained, "As gravity takes hold the potential energy changes to kinetic energy and propels the train up the next hill. The coaster tracks serve to channel this force and control the way the cars fall."

Andi frowned. "Yeah, but what about all of those loops and twists and turns?"

"It's a constant change between potential and kinetic energy. This continual fluctuation in acceleration is what makes roller coasters so exciting."

"Or so scary."

Max shrugged. "I guess scary and exciting go hand in

hand. But you're actually putting yourself much more at risk driving to the amusement park than riding the rides. And even then most of the injuries are from the people riding not following the rules and not the ride itself." With a chuckle Max asked, "So, have I changed your mind? Will you ride the Dolphin with me?"

Pursing her lips, she gave him a shake of her head. "I *so* want to. It looks like so much fun, but I'm afraid not." She put a hand on his arm. "It's not like I'm a big weenie or anything, but . . . hey, what are you laughing at?"

"Nothing, it's just that someone accused me of being a weenie earlier."

Grinning, she raised her eyebrows at him. "Really?" she asked over the noise of the crowd. "What are you supposedly afraid of doing, Max?"

Max paused and then answered, "Going after something I want."

With a little shiver Andi wondered if he was talking about her. *Nah.* With a sideways tilt of her head, Andi said, "Oh, come on, Max. You seem pretty confident. What could *you* possibly be afraid of going after? You seem to have everything a guy could want."

Pulling her close, he said in her ear, "You might be surprised."

She gave him a serious look and said, "Well, whatever it is, go for it. Life is too short for regrets."

Tilting her chin up with his finger, Max gave her a smile. "I'll take that advice, Andi. Thank you."

She smiled and said, a bit breathlessly, "There's the spirit."

God, Max wanted to kiss her. But he didn't because he had made a promise not to, leaving Max waiting for Andi to make the first move. He remembered Krista's advice to woo her with his sense of humor, his intelligence. Well, right about now he felt pretty damned stupid. How in the hell had he ever gotten himself in this situation? He also remembered Krista saying to flex a muscle, give her his best smile . . . but Max didn't want to win Andi over with male charm, which left the ball, as the saying went, in her court. With a deep breath, he passed the ball to her, saying, "Well, Andi, what would you like to do? I'm yours for the rest of the night."

Andi blinked at Max and swallowed. She wasn't stupid. She knew what he was up to. He was throwing this whole not-touching, professional nonsense right back at her. Ohmigod. *Was* she the thing he wanted, but was afraid to go after? No. Couldn't be. God, maybe this was just jet lag catching up with her.

"Andi?"

"I think I had better head back. It's been a long day."

"Okay, I'll walk you back."

"That won't be necessary. You must have things you need to do. I'll be fine."

"Please, indulge me. I'll feel better knowing you're safe."

"Okay."

He smiled with such obvious relief that Andi had to smile back. She wasn't sure if it was because he really was concerned for her safety or thought he had another chance at . . . what? Sleeping with her? Was this what this was all about? Or was it still all about the damned five stars? Andi put a hand to her head, suddenly feeling a bit woozy.

"Hey, are you all right?"

"Just tired."

With a small frown, Max slipped his arm about her waist. "Let's get you back to the apartment."

Andi didn't argue. With a weak smile, she said, "I think I'm about to crash and burn." It suddenly dawned on her that it was pushing midnight and she had been up since four-thirty that morning.

Max ushered her through the crowd using several shortcuts back to the hotel. In record time, he had her back up to his apartment and was unlocking the door.

"Can I get you anything?" he asked, once they were inside. "Water? A soda? Something to eat?"

"I'm okay," she answered softly, touched by his concern. "Just low blood sugar and a bad case of jet lag. I didn't realize how late it was."

He stood there in the hallway looking uncertain but then said firmly, "Let's get you over to the couch. I'll get you some orange juice and something to eat."

"No really, I'm . . ." she began, but a wave of dizziness washed over her.

"That's it." He scooped her up in his arms and gently deposited her on the leather couch. Turning an end-table lamp on low, he said, "Don't move."

"You're terribly bossy," she grumbled, but couldn't help but smile.

In nothing flat, he returned with a small plate of cheese and crackers and a glass of orange juice. "Thank you." Andi accepted the glass and sipped the cold juice, licking the pulp from her lips. "You don't have to babysit, Max. Really, I'll be fine."

His brow furrowed. "You look a little pale."

"I'm a redhead. We always look pale."

Her joke didn't faze him. "I'm staying."

"All night?"

He gave her a short nod. "To be on the safe side."

Andi swallowed a mouthful of cracker, washed it down with juice, and said, "No way."

Max raked his fingers through his hair, making it stand up on end. "I'll be worried that you might pass out or something."

"I won't. I'm fine. It's just been an extraordinarily eventful day." Oh, okay, that was embarrassing to say after what had occurred between them. "I mean, you know, a long day."

Max looked at her for a long moment and then said, "Okay, I just want to get you into bed and then . . . no, not *get* you into bed, I mean, get you *to* bed . . . you know, to sleep . . ." he trailed off and looked at the floor.

Andi had to smile. Could he get any cuter? Could she want to kiss him any more than she did at this very moment? "Max?"

Raising his head, Max looked over at her. "Yes?"

"You're so adorable, but you can leave now." Pushing up from the couch, she turned in the direction of his bedroom, but this time alone. Pity.

∽ chapter
ten

Adorable? *Yeah, right,* he thought, but was somehow pleased that Andi thought so. Adorable was good, right? Or was it a nice way of saying that she thought he was goofy? For God's sake, he suddenly felt like an insecure love-struck teenager.

Max watched Andi exit the room, thinking that there was no way he was leaving. She was still a bit unsteady on her feet. With a low groan he looked at the leather sofa, not nearly long enough for his six-foot-four-inch frame. But if he tried to go to one of the bedrooms, she might hear him and send him out the door. This way, he could check in on her during the night or come to her aid if she passed out or whatever. While Max didn't think her passing out was a probability, it remained a possibility, one he wasn't willing to risk.

As he sat down on the cool, slippery leather, Max realized that in just a few hours, Andi Cooper had gotten under his skin. He already cared about her; didn't want to leave her. No sex needed, he thought with a wry grin. Now, how about that? After a jaw-cracking yawn, Max stripped down to his boxers, turned off the lamp, and attempted to find a comfortable position on the couch. Reaching up, he pulled the afghan his mother had knitted for him from the back of the couch and in a few minutes of wondering what Andi was wearing to sleep, he was off to dreamland.

The annoying sound of a cell phone ringing filtered into Max's slumbering brain. Blinking, he fumbled for the phone, managing to roll off of the couch with a thud and a muffled curse while tangling his long legs in the stretchy afghan. It was still dark outside, and while frowning at his phone, he noted with a groan that it was only six o'clock. "Krista," he grumbled, to the only one on the island who would be awake at this ungodly hour.

"Where are you?" she hissed.

"In my penthouse," he whispered.

"You're with Andi Cooper?" She sounded pleased.

"No," he said, trying to untangle his legs from the afghan."

"I'm confused."

"So am I, but no, I'm on the couch, well on the floor . . ."

"So you didn't, *you know* . . ."

"No!" Max repeated, forgetting to lower his voice. "Krista, is there an important reason for this call?"

"I . . . well, no."

"Then I'm going back to sleep. I suggest you do the same," he said, remembering to whisper.

"I'm about to go for my morning run."

"Right." He had forgotten that Krista considered sleeping a waste of time.

"I'll call you later."

"No, I'll call *you*." He flipped the phone shut, grimacing at the small click that sounded like a loud *crack* in the quiet room.

Holding his breath, he hoped that Andi had remained asleep. He sat there on the floor for a long moment while considering whether to sneak out, check on her, or climb back up onto the couch and attempt sleeping when he knew he would only think about Andi in his bed without him. What would she look like, all sleep-rumpled and heavy-eyed, her red-gold curls tumbling around her shoulders? *Sexy as hell,* he thought as the picture formed in his mind. What would she do if he went back there right now and slipped under the covers with her, ran his hand over her warm skin, and kissed her awake?

Cursing the fact that he had promised to keep his hands to himself, Max decided he had better sneak out before she found him there when she had told him to leave. Of course, thinking back, she hadn't really *ordered* him to leave, or kicked him out. She had only said that he *could* leave.

Still undecided, Max froze when he heard the faint sound of movement . . . the rustle of covers, the slight creak of a door opening, and then the startling sound of his phone beginning to ring. Damn! He quickly answered it.

"Max!" Andi whispered fervently, surprised but grateful when Max immediately picked up. "I think there's someone in the penthouse." She clutched her small phone in one hand and Max's card in the other while trying to peek through the slightly opened bedroom door. She swallowed when she heard noise, thinking she should locate her can of mace. Was the intruder coming her way? Oh, why hadn't she let Max stay last night? "Max, I think he's coming towards me!" Dropping the phone, she squinted in the darkness for a weapon of sorts. She picked up a pillow. No! A pillow? Where the hell was her purse and the damned mace?

Oh God, she heard heavy footsteps heading her way! Her heart pounded and blood roared in her ears. I'm not going down without a fight, she thought, raising her fists. *I'm big and strong,* she told her scared self and then scooted over to cower in the corner of the dark room.

"It's okay!" the intruder said.

Yeah right. She wasn't born yesterday. Her heart about pounded out of her chest when the bedroom door opened and a really big male entered the room. With a blood-curdling yell Andi forced her shaking legs to run forward. She tackled the big guy from behind while praying that Max was on his way to rescue her. He went facedown on the bed with a whoomp and a big bounce. *Oh, no, now what?* She hadn't thought that far ahead.

"Wait, stop!" His words were muffled and he struggled but couldn't do much with her straddling on his back. For once Andi was grateful for being big. Ha, she had done it! Now if only Max . . . "Ahhhh!" Andi screamed when she was immediately turned over to her back. Squeezing her eyes shut she started flailing her fists while bucking her hips but her arms were immediately pinned above her head while the big bad guy's body flattened her into the mattress.

"Andi!"

"Max?" she croaked. She opened her eyes and

squinted in the darkness. Relief flooded her entire being. "You scared me to death! I told you last night to leave." She tried to sound angry but the fact that he still had her pinned to the bed made her voice come out husky.

Angling his head, Max said, "Uh, you said you *can* leave now. Not that I *had* to go." With a rather sheepish shrug, he continued, "See the difference?"

"That's mincing words, don't you think?"

"Guilty," he said, but then continued softly, "but only because I was worried about you."

"Oh. Well, as you can see, I'm fine."

He gave her a slow grin. "Oh, that I can see. In fact, I would say more than fine."

Andi's eyes widened when a few realizations bombarded her all at once. Max was wearing nothing but boxer briefs. His dark hair was sleep-tousled, flat on one side, sticking slightly up on the other, but he somehow managed to make bed-head look sexy. Andi's body went on instant sexual alert at the delicious feel of his body molded to hers. She swallowed, feeling her breasts swell, nipples tighten and . . . *Oh God,* she suddenly remembered she was wearing her new satin nightie instead of her usual extra-large T-shirt and said the first thing, *okay the second thing,* that came into her mind. "I . . . you . . . lost my clothes."

Max frowned. "What?"

"My luggage never arrived. I had to buy, or rather, Wild Ride bought me all new clothes. I . . . don't usually, uh . . . wear this kind of thing."

"You should."

Oh, God. Her heart started to thud. "I . . . I think it has a robe. I should go and—"

"Don't."

When Andi raised her eyes to meet his heated gaze, she knew she had a decision to make. There really was no in between. "Max—"

"I know. I'm heavy." He rolled to the side . . . and right off of the bed, landing on the floor with a muted thump and a curse.

"Oh, my God!" Andi put her hand to her mouth and looked down at him. "Are you okay?"

He chuckled and said, "Was that smooth or what?"

Andi tilted her head to the side and laughed. "You're adorable."

"Be honest, is that another word for goofy? I have to know."

"Sorta."

Max pursed his lips. "Thought so."

"But in an adorable way." She knelt down next to him and said, "You know I had this impression of you being such a player and now . . . well . . ."

He grinned while rubbing both knees. "You realize that I'm not so smooth."

What she realized was that she was falling for him hard and whiplash-fast.

"I know, I know, but *not so smooth* in an adorable way."

"Yeah, the adorable part makes all the difference." She itched to touch him. Trail a finger down his chest. She had to fist her hands in order to not do so.

He looked up at her. "Andi? I'll keep my promise."

"What promise?"

"Not to touch you. Keep my hands off, whatever the hell I so insanely promised not to do."

She frowned. "Oh, okay." *Not* okay.

"But there *is* a loophole."

Andi raised her eyebrows and immediately perked up. *Loopholes are good.* "Fill me in."

"*You* didn't make any such non-touching promise."

"Ah, so you're saying it's legal for me to touch you?"

"Perfectly. Encouraged, even. You do the touching and we can never say that I seduced you, mixing that whole five-star business with . . ."

"Pleasure?"

"Yeah. Pleasure."

Andi smiled, realizing that the five-star rating wasn't even an issue anymore. She had already fallen in love with the resort. Tastefully constructed, totally unique, with two-thirds of the island untouched and protected. So different from what she had expected. Andi, however, kept this knowledge to herself. This whole being-in-control thing was a total turn-on. "Well, okay," she said slowly, while gathering up the nerve to say the rest of her sentence.

Max shook his head. "I hear a 'but.' "

Andi felt heat creep into her cheeks. "I'll have to, well, make sure you keep good on the no-touching promise."

His blue eyes widened and his eyebrows shot up. "Go on."

"Well, I'll have to secure you to the bed, you know, tie you to the bedposts. Are you okay with that? I mean, it *would* totally put you at my mercy." When Max opened and closed his mouth a couple of times but failed to speak, Andi licked her lips and asked, "Are you game?"

Max blinked at her for a moment and Andi had to suppress a grin. In the past forty-eight hours she had morphed from sensible into a sex kitten and didn't quite know how or why. Maybe it was the sexy clothes, or the Wild Ride atmosphere . . .

Or maybe it had taken the right man to bring it out in her. *Oliver Maxwell,* she thought with a grin, *where in the hell have you been all my life?*

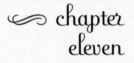
chapter
eleven

"Uh, yes, I'm . . . I'm game," he answered weakly. "Sure, yeah, have your way with me." Max thought his heart was going to pound right out of his chest. This was quite an unexpected turn of events. Not that he was complaining. Hell, no.

Andi crooked a finger at him and said, "Come along, then."

Max scrambled to his feet and then plopped down on the bed ready and willing.

"I'm going to freshen up," she said over her shoulder. "You go find two silk neckties for me, okay?"

"S-sure."

"And a condom or two."

He swallowed. " 'Kay."

"I won't be long," she said as she disappeared into the bathroom.

"Good." Since he was hard enough to pound nails. Ties, he needed ties. And, God, to brush his teeth. Rushing from the room, Max dashed into his walk-in closet and snagged two silk ties, rushed over to the spare bathroom, brushed his teeth, and found a box of condoms underneath the sink. Thank God for small favors.

Hurrying back to the bedroom, he hopped onto the bed and waited with a thudding heart and an anxious penis for Andi to return. He waited. And then waited some more until well, he was becoming a little worried and a bit less excited. Max was beginning to feel foolish perched in the middle of the bed clutching two neckties. Just as he was starting to give up hope, the door to the bathroom opened very slowly. His heart thudded in anticipation but Andi failed to appear.

"Andi?" he angled his head in an attempt to see around the half-open door. "Are you coming out?"

"Um . . ."

Max grinned. Oh, so she was a bit shy. "Come on out, sweetie." Maybe she was rethinking the necktie thing. "It's okay. We don't have to . . . *holy shit* . . ." he whispered. If he hadn't been in the middle of the bed he knew he would have fallen off. His almost-asleep dick came to immediate attention at the amazing sight of Andi Cooper decked out in a leather dominatrix outfit. "W-wow." Starting at the bottom he drank in the sight of her spiked heels and thigh-high black stockings held up by a black garter belt. She wore black leather panties and a black leather corset laced up the front. Her breasts were shoved high, spilling out of the corset, revealing just a hint of dusky nipples.

And she was holding a whip.

With his heart pounding wildly Max realized that the outfit was one from the Wild Ride boutique. He also knew how much courage it must have taken for Andi to put it on for him and he decided to play this to the hilt. One smile, one flippant remark, and the mood would be ruined. He widened his eyes in mock fear and raised his wrists in a tie-me-up gesture of submission.

Andi had been totally prepared to hightail it back into the bathroom but the sizzle in Max's blue eyes let her know that he was into this and willing to play along. Plus, the outfit gave her a sexy siren power that was hard to ignore. Taking a step into the bedroom, she planted her spiked heels in a wide stance and slapped the whip against her thigh. Pursing her glossy red lips (the clerk in the boutique had insisted that this was the only shade to wear with black leather) she cocked one eyebrow and let Max look his fill.

"Do you like what you see?" She forced a hard edge to her voice but when Max opened his mouth to answer she pointed the whip and said, "You're not permitted to speak, *slave*."

He nodded.

Andi fully expected a grin, but he only lifted his wrists higher. Walking slowly over to the bed (hoping she didn't stumble in the spiked heels, something she never wore). She snapped the whip and was rewarded with a soft but audible *crack*. When she reached the edge of the bed she leaned over to give him an enticing view of pushed-up cleavage, and with deliberate slowness let the tasseled end of the whip graze lightly over his chest, stopping when she came to the big bulge in his black boxers.

With a haughty lift of her chin, she took the silk neckties from his slack fingers. Leaning over, she secured one wrist in a slipknot to the headboard and then walked all the way around the bed to give him a view of her bottom bared by the leather thong. Max's swift intake of breath almost made her smile, but she ground her teeth together and continued to play the part. After tying his other wrist to the slats in the wooden headboard Andi stood back and let her gaze travel over him in what she hoped was a contemptous manner.

"Are you ready?" she asked in a short clipped tone.

He nodded mutely and Andi noticed a bead of sweat roll from his temple and down his cheek. Because the curtains were still drawn the room remained in darkness, but the overhead paddle fan made the curtains flutter so that bright sunlight flickered in and out, giving the whole thing a surreal feel. There was no sound in the room except for their breathing and the slight whir of the fan.

Andi cracked the whip just above the erection so very evident beneath the soft cotton of his boxers. "Raise your hips," Andi ordered. When Max obeyed she held the whip in her mouth and then used both hands to slowly peel his boxers down his hips to mid-thigh, wanting to restrict his movement so that she remained in control.

Her breath caught at the proud thrust of his penis and while she longed to touch him, she merely grazed the steely length with the tassel of the whip up and down . . . up and down until he was arching up off of the mattress while tugging at the ties.

"Andi . . ." His voice was hoarse, pleading.

She quelled him with a look and cracked the whip.

"I need—" he began but she stopped him this time by hitting him in the chest with the whip, knowing full well that the blow was nothing more than a caress against his skin.

"I know what you need," she purred. Snagging a condom from the nightstand, she climbed onto the bed and straddled his legs. Willing her fingers not to shake she first let her tongue swirl over the head of his penis and then rolled the condom on. Andi's heart pounded as she came to her knees and let him stare up at her while she popped open the metal snaps of the leather thong and tossed it to the floor.

Max willed himself to remain silent but the sight of her mound made him groan. Neatly shaved, the dark red hair was an enticing line that he wanted to run his finger down before sliding it inside of her. Straining against the ties, Max raised his head, needing to cup her ass and bury his face between her thighs. "Andi. Enough! Untie me," he growled.

She gave him a wicked smile and inched closer until he could almost taste her. She smelled of sweet perfume and woman. Sweat trickled down his face and rolled down his chest. He was more frustrated and excited than he thought possible. His heart pounded; his dick throbbed. "Andi!"

"Beg," she breathed.

"Please."

While staring into his eyes she placed her hands on his shoulders. With a little gasp she slowly let him sink into her wet heat. Her head lolled to the side. "God, you feel so good inside me."

"Untie me. I need my hands on your skin."

"No . . . mmmm, no way. *I'm* in control." To prove it Andi started a slow rhythm, getting used to the feel of him inside of her. He was so big, so hard. She felt his muscles bunched with effort and his skin hot and slick with sweat beneath her hands. This power felt intoxicating . . . exciting. She gripped his broad shoulders harder for support, hoping that her shaky legs wouldn't give out. Leaning in, she pressed her mouth to his and kissed him deeply while moving her hips in a slow sensuous rhythm.

Max groaned into her mouth and arched up from the bed going deeper, harder. Andi felt the beginning blossom of an orgasm but her legs were giving out without his hands around her waist for help. She moved faster. Her thighs quivered in protest and her hands slipped from his shoulders. She splayed them against his chest. The rapid beat of his heart pulsated against her palms.

"Free me!"

Her eyes locked with his. "No . . . I'm . . ."

With a growl he thrust upward, sending her flying over the edge. The orgasm ripped through her, making her arch her back and then fall against his chest. For a long moment they both lay there . . . stunned.

"I . . . I can't move," Andi finally said with a weak chuckle.

Max kissed her on top of the head. "I'd be willing to stay like this all day long, but my arms feel like they're going to pop from the sockets."

"Oh!" Pushing up for leverage, Andi tried to loosen the knot but her shaky fingers weren't of much value. "I think I'm going to have to cut you loose." With a little moan she slid her body from his.

"There are scissors in the top drawer in the bathroom."

Nodding, Andi swung her leg over his hips and scooted from the bed. Her legs felt as if they were made of rubber but she managed to make it to the bathroom and retrieve the scissors. She felt self-conscious in the now bottomless leather outfit. She wobbled on the heels, almost turning an ankle as she approached the bed. "I'm sorry," she said as she cut through the ties.

"I can buy new ones," Max said. "I hated the green one anyway."

Andi caught her bottom lip between her teeth. "No," she said softly, wincing when he rubbed his wrists. "Did I hurt you?"

Max grinned. "Yeah, it hurt so good."

Andi shook her head and looked at the carpet. She hated to think that he thought she was all about sex . . . kinky sex at that. "I don't know what got into me. This outfit was a whim. I never intended to wear it. You must think—"

"Stop it right there," he said softly. Putting his index finger beneath her chin, he forced her to look up at him.

"I think you are amazing."

She swallowed and looked at him. "But—"

"But *nothing*. Don't you think I realize that this is way out of your comfort zone, Andi? That only makes it more exciting. This wasn't just about sex. This was about you."

Andi gave him a trembling smile that hit him right in the gut. He was falling for her . . . hard. "Now," he said, undoing the laces of her corset, "while the whole S&M thing was so good, I really feel the need to touch you." He ran a fingertip over her exposed nipples, smiling when she shivered. She wobbled on the spiked heels and had to grab his shoulders while he continued to unlace her until she was standing before him in her garter belt, hose, and heels. "Get in this bed," he said. "Now we're going to do this my way."

Andi eased onto the bed and smiled. Holding her wrists up to him, she said, "I'm all yours."

Max grinned back. He knew she was being playful but he hoped her statement was all too true. "Mmmm, no need to tie you up. Feel free to touch me wherever you like." Dipping his head he took one rosy nipple into his mouth. "God it feels so good to taste you, to touch you. I was going crazy with wanting to feel your skin." He threaded his fingers through her hair. "I want to touch you everywhere," he said and then tilted her head back for a long kiss. "You know, I wanted to make love to you all night long, but all day long is quite all right by me. Afterwards I'll bring you breakfast in bed. Sound good?"

"Oh . . . *yeah.*"

chapter twelve

Andi wound her arms around Max's neck and gave him a shy smile. "I've never had breakfast in bed." Damn, now why did she just admit that to him?

"Well, I've never been tied to a bed, so I guess we're even." He tucked a lock of hair behind her ear and then tilted her chin up with his knuckle. "I think it's safe to say that neither of us is very much like what the other expected. I was expecting Andrea Cooper to be an uppity, snobby socialite and quite frankly, I've had my fill of those types, but I don't think I could ever get my fill of you."

Andi ran her fingertip across the fullness of his bottom lip. He had a great mouth. "Well, we have the rest of the week to find out," she said with a smile, but then thought that a week wasn't nearly long enough. And then what? Could she just walk out of his life? Her smile faltered. Maybe this was a huge mistake.

"Hey, Andi," Max said softly. "Tell me what you're thinking."

Tracing a fingertip over his collarbone, she said, "I . . . oh, nothing." She attempted another smile but her lips trembled.

"Come on, Andi," he gently prodded. "You usually don't have any problem saying what you're thinking. Now is *not* the time to clam up."

"You know me so well?"

Max shook his head. "Not nearly enough."

"You want honesty, then?"

"Please."

Andi was struck by the serious expression on Max's face. He looked almost fearful as he waited for her to reply and she fell a little bit harder for him, which of course was the main problem. She was falling in love with a man she barely knew . . . falling so hard and so fast that there was sure to be a crash landing.

"Andi?"

She swallowed and said, "I . . . I know we've just met." And she was sitting in his lap stark naked. She paused, not knowing quite how to phrase her next thought.

"Andi, go on. Baby, I'm all ears," he said gently.

His obvious erection said otherwise. Andi couldn't help but see the humor and glanced down.

"Okay, not *all* ears. Damn, I'm trying to be serious, here. Bear with me."

Her lips twitched.

"Poor choice of words," he said, but his lips twitched, too. The lighthearted moment passed, though, when Max threaded his fingers with hers. "Tell me what you're feeling."

Andi nibbled on her bottom lip for a moment and then said, "Excited, exhilarated . . . scared."

"Airtime."

She raised her eyebrows. "What?"

Max grinned. "Airtime is that butterflies-in-your-stomach sensation that you get when a roller coaster reverses course and climbs or descends at a high speed. It causes you to rise from your seat and sort of free-float. The more airtime, the better the ride."

"So, you're comparing being with me to a roller-coaster ride?"

"I get that airtime feeling in my gut every time I look at you, Andi."

Of course, she had to kiss him. It was a long delicious kiss that would have led to something much more, but Andi's stomach growled and Max insisted on bringing her the promised breakfast in bed.

Andi watched Max, gloriously naked as he padded on bare feet, searching for his boxers that she had tossed to the floor. She spotted them on the potted fern, but was enjoying the sight of him naked too much to point it out. When he tossed the green nightie to her, she shook her head. "I'd rather wear one of your T-shirts."

Max grinned. "No problem. I think that you'll look incredibly sexy in my shirt." Tugging open his dresser drawer, he located a blue T-shirt and tossed it at her.

"Thanks. By the way, your boxers are dangling from the fern."

"And you've known this how long?" He fisted his hands on his hips and stood there, ignoring the boxers.

Andi felt her cheeks grow warm. It was one thing to sneakily watch him, but now that he was looking right at her, she kept her eyes on his face. "Only a minute," she said in a small voice.

"I'll stay naked if you want me to," he said with a grin.

"God, no."

Chuckling, he tugged his boxers on. "I'll be back with a feast. You rest up. I hope you know you're not leaving this bed for the rest of the day."

Andi swallowed. "The whole day?"

He nodded. "You're in for some serious airtime."

Andi found out that Max wasn't kidding. The rest of the day was spent in his arms, only taking brief breaks for essential things like eating and sleeping. By the time the sun was sinking low in the sky they were both limp noodles, barely able to make it to the balcony, where they shared a delivered sub sandwich and a couple of ice-cold beers.

Andi sipped her beer from where she was wedged between Max's legs on a lounge chair. He kissed the back of her neck and she giggled. "Your lips are cold."

"Mmm, but your skin is warm." He reached around and absently cupped her breast, loving it when her nipple hardened beneath his thumb.

"Are you going over to the carnival tonight?" Andi asked.

"No, I told Krista to watch over things and to only contact me in an emergency."

"You can go if you want to. I'll be fine."

"I don't want to." Max leaned in and kissed her. "I want to make love to you out here under the stars."

Andi giggled. "I think we might have already had enough sex to qualify for the *Guinness Book of World Records.*"

"Are you complaining?" he teased.

"Not at all."

Max was amazed that he wanted her again. Right now. To hell with letting the stars come out. The problem was that his body was so sated that he could barely move. Still, he couldn't keep his hands from touching her. Placing her beer bottle on the ground, he was content just to hold her.

"Max . . ."

"Shhh."

"I'm . . ."

"I know. Me too. But just let me touch. Just lean back against me and watch the beautiful sunset with me."

She was naked beneath his shirt and the cotton fabric rubbing against her sensitive skin was softly sensual. Leaning back against Max's bare chest, Andi watched the orange ball dip lower in the sky, spreading fingers of deep color across the horizon. The lights of the hotel dimmed with the setting sun and Andi sighed with contentment. Twisting in the lounge chair, she wrapped her arms around Max's neck and kissed him. "Thank you for an amazing day," she said with a sleepy sigh. She put her cheek against his chest and smiled when he rumbled with a low sexy chuckle.

"My pleasure."

Snuggling in his arms, she smiled, kissed his chest, and, a heartbeat later, fell fast asleep.

ﾟ chapter
thirteen

The next few days took on something of a pattern. After breakfast, Max worked for a few
hours in his office while Andi wrote her article. After
lunch, they met by the pool, enjoyed a frozen cocktail or
two, and then headed back to the penthouse to make
love, nap, and then have dinner. They spent the evenings
at the carnival, where workers began to know Andi by
name and to expect her to be with him. Max couldn't remember a time in his life when he had been happier . . .
except for one thing.

The week was drawing to an end.

Max was pondering this problem while sitting at his
desk in his office when Krista walked in.

"Oh," she said with a grin. "So you're actually
working."

"Very funny."

"So may I have a moment of your time before you go
running back to your love shack?"

Max swiveled his chair away from the computer monitor to face Krista. "Sure. By the way, have I told you that I really appreciate you picking up the slack for me?"

Krista arched one blond eyebrow. "You can show your appreciation in my next paycheck. Two words: big bonus." She shrugged. "I kind of like being the boss, anyway."

"Wow, I would never have guessed."

"Now who is being funny?" Krista came closer to the desk and asked, "So, how is it going, lover boy? Do we have our five stars in the bag?"

Max narrowed his eyes at her. "Krista . . ."

She raised both palms in the air. "Just kidding. Boy, you're sensitive. You've got it bad."

"Krista, what the hell am I going to do?" Max asked, leaning back in his leather desk chair. "The thought of Andi leaving makes me crazy."

Krista leaned one slim hip against the desk. "Are you in love with her?"

After blowing out a breath, Max answered, "It hasn't been long enough to know for sure, but I'm heading in that direction, faster than the first hill of the damned Dolphin."

Krista shrugged. "Ask her to stay on for a while. Give you more time together."

"What if she says no?"

Krista rolled her eyes. "She looks as love-struck as you. You guys are gag-me in love."

"Gag-you?"

Krista grinned. "No, actually, I'm loving it. The mighty Oliver Maxwell has fallen."

"Oh, like it can't happen to you?"

With another shrug of her shoulders, Krista said, "I guess if the right guy came along."

Pursing his lips, Max muttered, "You mean a guy with the right qualifications?"

"I prefer to call it standards."

"Meaning money," Max said, but when something like hurt flashed in her blue eyes, Max was immediately sorry. "I'm an ass."

She grinned. "Sometimes. But you're not wrong. Max, you know I have money issues. I made my mind up a long time ago that when I marry . . . that is, if I marry, the guy will be loaded." She held up her index finger and added, "But sophisticated. Cultured."

"Boring jackasses."

Krista rolled her eyes again. "This isn't about me, Max. You're the one in love."

"Potentially."

"Oh pul-ease. You're a goner." Her cell phone rang and she glared at it. "Travis Mackey's manager."

"You've got him booked for a concert, right?"

"His manager is demanding the moon."

"Then give it to him."

"You're killing me. I could get the Beach Boys for half the price."

Max gave her a pointed look.

"Okay, okay. You'll have Travis Mackey. Now, when are you going to ask Andi to stay? Tonight? Boy, you've got to. She leaves tomorrow, right?"

Max nodded. "Yeah."

"Do you want a special romantic dinner set up in the penthouse?"

"Could you take care of that?"

"I might as well. I've been taking care of everything else around here. So, do you want candlelight, wine, rose petals?"

"Rose petals?"

"Duh, on the bed."

Max had a sudden visual of Andi lying naked in a pile of red rose petals. Nodding vigorously, he said, "Sure, yeah. Rose petals. Do that."

Krista laughed. "I am *so* loving this. Just keep her out of the penthouse from six until about seven-thirty and I'll have everything ready. I'm sure you can keep her busy . . . *somehow*."

"Mmmm, I'll think of something."

Krista stood up and put a file on his desk. "Here is what I have so far for the Labor Day festivities. Look it over and let me know what you think, okay?"

"Will do. Hey, Krista, when are you going to return my Travis Mackey CD?"

Krista paused at the doorway. "Oh, it slipped my mind. I'll get it back to you."

Max grinned. "What's your favorite song?"

"I don't *like* country music," she answered tightly, with a hint of a Southern twang that made her blush. "Or cowboys, for that matter." She turned on her heel and huffed her way out the door.

"Yeah, right," Max said with a chuckle as he opened up the file. He tried to concentrate. Really. But the thought of Andi sitting by the pool waiting for him was just too much. Besides, he thought, maybe he should buy something to give to her at dinner. With that in mind, he closed the file and headed over to the little jewelry boutique in the hotel lobby.

*   *   *

"Yes!" Andi said with the surge of joy that always came when she finished an article and knew that it was well done. She always strove to capture the feel of the destination and, dusting her hands together, she felt as if she had done Wild Ride Resort justice. She had even begun her piece with her preconceived notions about the resort and had dispelled them one by one. She did, however, explain that Max's Moonlight Madness carnival had to be experienced and no amount of description could quite capture the essence of being there.

"Now, to the pool," she said with a glance at the time on her laptop screen. She wanted to proofread the article one last time, but she was already late and didn't want to keep Max waiting. The thought seeped into her brain that she was leaving the next day, but she pushed it away, not wanting to spoil her last night with Max.

Her last night.

Andi took a deep, shaky breath. "You knew it would end," she whispered. But she hadn't had a clue as to how hard it would actually be. She could, of course, make up some lame excuse to have to stay a few more days. But she wouldn't. Staying longer would only make it that much more difficult to leave. Andi was so glad that she had fallen in love with the resort. Panning the place was something she would have hated to do.

But I would have, Andi thought as she headed to the bedroom to put on her bathing suit. As much as she loved Max, it wouldn't have changed her opinion.

Andi stopped in her tracks.

Loved Max.

The logical part of her brain brought that thought to a

screeching halt. But her heart started beating like a jackhammer.

"What am I going to do?" she wondered as she absently picked up her bathing suit. She shook her head at the skimpy royal blue bikini that was nowhere near the conservative style of the swimsuit she had packed. So much had changed in one short week. Closing her eyes, Andi remembered making love to Max last night on the deserted beach with wild abandon . . . doing things that would have made her blush to even think about until he had shown her how beautiful uninhibited sex could be. Total giving. With a hot shiver, Andi realized that she knew every glorious inch of his body; how he tasted, how he smelled, and the pleasure points that drove him crazy.

Andi also knew with certainty that it wasn't just about sex. It was about sex with *him,* because she had fallen deeply in love with the man. *Tell him,* a voice in her head demanded. "Oh, God, I can't," she whispered, thinking of a thousand *what if*s.

When Andi heard the sound of the door opening, her heart hammered even harder. After a few minutes of trying to muster the courage she finally opened the bedroom door. Still hesitating in the hallway, she decided not to be a weenie and to tell him how she felt. Inhaling a somewhat steadying breath, she marched into the living room.

"Krista?" Although Andi was surprised to see her, she smiled. "Where's Max?" Krista didn't return the smile, but that didn't really bother Andi at first. Max's sassy assistant was pretty much all business.

"I suspect he's at the pool where I thought you were as well."

Andi frowned at the unexpected bite in Krista's tone. "I

was finishing my article. I'm going to join him now." She frowned. "You've been reading the article?"

"How can you join him after you've trashed Wild Ride?"

"Trashed?"

Krista pointed down at the laptop on the coffee table and read the first lines of the article. "My anger mounted as the ferry swept me closer and closer to the once pristine Crystal Island. I wondered if the world needed another slick and sleazy all-inclusive resort." Krista looked up and shot Andi a look seething with anger.

Andi was about to defend herself, to tell Krista to read on, but a sudden thought flattened her joy like a steamroller. "So, Max sent you up here on a mission? Let me guess, while he kept me busy?"

"Ironically, yes, but—"

"Get out, Krista." Andi pointed to the door and was horrified that her finger was shaking. "What you did was despicable and has me rethinking my opinion of you, Max, and this resort."

"What do you mean, rethinking?" Her blue eyes rounded. "Wait, do I have it all wrong?"

Andi gave her a humorless smile. "I'm the one who has it all wrong. Now please leave."

"Andi, wait! The article was right there out in the open. Max did send me here, but—"

Andi walked toward her on rubber legs and opened the door. "It doesn't matter. Go. And by the way, tell Max he got what he wanted."

"Andi, I . . ." Krista tried again, but Andi closed the door in her face.

With a knuckle to her lips, Andi stubbornly refused to

cry. Being raised on a farm had made her a tough little cookie, she told herself. "And a naive little twit." With a shaky breath, she forced her legs to move. "I've got to get out of here," she mumbled. After shutting down her computer, she stuffed her laptop into her leather case. The only other thing she wanted was her purse. Max could have her new clothes and cosmetics. It was time to go back to being Andi Cooper from Indiana.

∽ chapter fourteen

Andi stood on the dock of the marina and felt like childishly stomping her foot. Okay, so the ferry wasn't running until the next day. There had to be a way off this island. "Aha." She hefted her laptop case to her shoulder when she spotted a guy hosing down his boat.

"Hello," Andi said with cheerfulness that she didn't feel.

The tanned and toned blond looked her way and with a flashy smile, turned off the hose. "The dolphin cruise isn't until tonight. You can purchase tickets at the hotel."

Andi kept her smile in place, hoping her yellow halter-top sundress scored her some points. "I really just wanted a ride to the mainland. Can you help me?"

"Well, I don't usually do that unless it's an emergency."

"It is."

He waited for her to elaborate.

Andi felt some of her goodwill evaporate. It was none of his business that her heart had just been ripped to shreds. "Look, I'll pay you double. Just get me the hell out of here."

His eyes narrowed. "Hey, wait a minute. Aren't you that reporter chick?"

"Yes . . ." Andi admitted slowly, not really sure if it was a good idea to admit that fact or not.

"Max is looking for you."

Her heart picked up speed. "I think you're mistaken."

"No, he called me and said that if you tried to leave the island that you should wait so that he could talk to you."

Think fast, Andi. "He's in an important meeting with Krista." The evil Krista. Andi hated having to drop her name. "I don't think you should bother them."

The shaggy blond ran his fingers through his hair. "I'll just give him a call anyway."

"Look, just forget the whole thing. I'll go find Max myself, okay?" Without waiting for him to answer, Andi headed in the opposite direction. God, she felt like a fugitive from the law.

When Andi heard him talking to Max on the phone she picked up her pace and found herself in line for the Dolphin. She was about to leave when she realized it was the perfect hideout. Max knew how much she feared riding roller coasters. He would never look for her here.

The line moved fairly quickly over a slightly uphill slope. Finally, she reached the last ramp, which was shaded by a roof. In a moment she was going to have to either get on the roller coaster or think of a reason to leave the line. Andi was so lost in thought that she didn't know that there was anything wrong until suddenly everyone was leaving the line. "What's up?" Andi asked the woman in front of her.

The woman shrugged. "Mechanical glitch. It's been shut down. Guess I'll have to walk to the hotel." She sighed. "What a pain."

"Oh, I'm sure it's just a simple safety precaution. Oliver Maxwell will have this baby up and running in no time. He's a perfectionist when it comes to the Dolphin. One little shimmy and he has to fix it." For some reason she felt compelled to defend him.

"You know him?"

Andi felt a lump form in her throat and could only nod.

The woman gave her a little nudge with her elbow. "I saw his picture in the brochure. Lucky you."

"Yeah, lucky me," Andi whispered. Now what? She had no place to stay, no way off the island. Max had people looking for her and now that the crowd was gone, she had no way of blending in. Andi sighed. No one was paying any attention to her, so she eased her way closer to the sleek blue roller coaster. The first car was shaped like the head of a dolphin. Andi counted four cars in between that looked like the body and then a car shaped like the tail. Up close, Andi could see the details. Water droplets were painted on the cars as if the dolphin were splashing through the ocean. It really was an awesome design and Andi suddenly wished she had mustered up the nerve to ride it.

Shading her eyes against the sunshine filtering in through the tall cypress trees Andi looked at the steep first hill and shook her head. "No way." Still undecided as to what in the world to do, she panicked when she spotted Max and a crew in the distance headed her way. Quickly, before they spotted her, she jumped into the first car of the Dolphin and ducked.

Luckily, the head-shaped car was roomy, long enough for her to scoot to the floor and stretch out her long legs. Pillowing her head on her laptop case, she listened and waited. If she hadn't been so depressed, Andi would have chuckled at her plight. In her world travels she had found herself in many a weird situation. She had been locked in a loo in London for over an hour. Then there was the time when in Paris when she had been given the key card to a room already occupied and had walked in on a couple in the throes of lovemaking. In Ireland she had gotten separated from the tour guide and became hopelessly lost in a castle . . . the list went on and on, but hiding out from her lover in the nose of a dolphin-shaped roller coaster pretty much topped them all.

Andi wiped away a tear, thinking that this was a really sucky way of ending what had been the best week of her life. Voices . . . very *close* voices brought her out of her musings. Her ears perked up when she heard the unmistakable sound of Max speaking to his crew.

"So what's the problem?" Max asked.

"The break run after the bunny hills is stopping with too much of a jerk," someone answered. "I've got a crew on it right now."

"How long are we talking?" Max asked.

"I'm guessing about twenty minutes to a half hour."

"Okay," Max answered. "Then I'll go on a test run."

A test run? Andi looked at her watch and made a mental note to make her escape as soon as possible. She wanted nothing to do with a test run. As soon as Max left, she was outta there. Max's cell phone rang and Andi went as still as a statue as she listened.

"No, Krista, I haven't found her," Max said and then

sighed. "It's a damned island. Where the hell could she be?" He paused for a moment and then said, "I know you tried. No, don't cry. No, I don't care about the fucking five stars. Krista, listen, it doesn't matter. Calm down. I'll call you if we find her."

Andi's heart hammered while thoughts bounced around in her head. Tough little Krista was crying? Max didn't care about the five stars? Maybe she should have given Max the chance to explain instead of running off half-cocked. Andi would have come out of hiding to confront Max, but she was too embarrassed that she had actually hidden in the roller coaster like a little kid. She decided to wait until he left and then come out. Then she would track him down and they could have a talk.

Andi took a deep breath. It was warm in the car, but because they were shaded in the woods it wasn't unbearable. With her head still resting on the laptop case, she shut her eyes and rehearsed in her head what she would say to Max . . .

A little jolt jarred Andi awake. Oh God, had she fallen asleep? Blinking, she found herself looking at two big running shoes. With horror, Andi realized that the roller coaster was going to take off but when she tried to move, she found that her shoe was snagged on something. In a panic she yelled, "Hey!" She latched onto an ankle and tugged.

"What the . . .?" Max's dark head leaned over and peered into the nose of the dolphin. "Andi?" His eyes widened. "What in the world are you doing? Hurry! Get out of there. We're about to take off!"

"I can't! A hook or something has snagged my shoe."

"Tug harder. Take it off or rip the damned thing!"

"I'm trying but I can't! It's a leather strap. Max, stop this thing!"

"There's no time," Max said and felt fingers of fear snake up his spine. Andi was going to be tossed around like a pinball down there. Since he had yet to lower the safety bar, he scooted from his seat and slid into the nose with her. The Dolphin was already beginning to ascend the first hill.

"Ohmigod," Andi whispered. "We're taking off!"

"Calm down," Max crooned into her ear. She was already trembling. Stretching his arm, he reached down and unhooked her sandal from where it was caught. "Listen carefully."

Her hazel eyes were wide with fear but she nodded.

"I'm going to flip over to my back and brace myself with my legs and hands. I want you to climb on top of me, put your arms around my neck, and hook your legs with mine."

She nodded again.

"Okay, hurry. We're halfway up the lift hill."

She scrambled on top of him, hooked her feet around his calves and wrapped her arms in a death grip around his neck. He could feel the rapid beat of her heart and her breath was coming in short gasps.

"Andi," he said softly. "It will be okay. I know every hill, every twist and turn of this ride. Just hold on and you'll be fine."

"I'm scared." She was breathing way too fast. Max knew she was going to hyperventilate and that could cause her to pass out. They were almost cresting the hill.

"Andi, think of something else. Anything."

"Can't."

"Kiss me."

"W-what?"

When they paused at the crest of the hill Max said, "Kiss me, Andi, and pretend that nothing else in the world exists except for my mouth and yours."

With closed eyes she nodded.

"Now!"

Max braced his palms against the ceiling of the car, pushing his back to the floor for leverage. Clinging to him, Andi kissed him as if her life depended upon it. Without the ability to see outside of the car it felt as if they were free-falling while kissing. The Dolphin dipped at the bottom of the hill and then swooped upward, creating airtime at the crest of the next hill. When Max felt Andi tremble he slanted his head, kissing her more deeply and wishing that he could wrap his arms around her. A half twist led into a loop, much like a dolphin's leap from the ocean and plunge back into the water.

Andi clung to Max, kissing him madly. The twisting, turning motion of the coaster had her moving against him until cold fear mixed with hot desire; it was a heady mix that made her want the ride to end and at the same time go on forever. The steely hardness of his erection pressed against the silky dress, making Andi long to have him buried deep inside her. She felt Max's muscles bunch and flex with each twist and turn. This was wild, crazy . . .

And then it was over.

"Wow," Andi said, breathing hard.

"Now that was a wild ride." Max wrapped his arms around her and asked, "Are you okay?"

"Well, my heart didn't explode from fear so I guess

so." It felt so good to be in his arms. With a sigh she laid her head in his chest. "Are . . . are we in the hotel lobby?" She started to unwrap herself from him but felt a sudden jolt. "Oh wait, it's . . . it's starting up again." Her grip around his neck tightened.

Max chuckled. "Don't worry. We're only circling around and coming to a stop."

"Oh."

"You sound disappointed. Weren't you scared to death?"

"Yeah," she admitted but then whispered in his ear, "I was also incredibly turned on."

Max chuckled while shaking his head. "Andi Cooper, what am I going to do with you?"

"I can give you a few ideas."

"Woman, you're going to be the death of me."

"Yeah, but you'll die happy."

"You've got me there. Now would you mind telling me why in the hell you were hiding in the Dolphin?" he asked as the roller coaster came to a final stop.

Andi rested her cheek against his chest. "I was hiding from you."

Max put his finger beneath her chin, tilting her face up so she had to look into his eyes. "You know you've got it all wrong."

"Are you telling me that Krista wasn't sneaking into the penthouse on some secret mission?"

"No, I'm not." He ran a fingertip down her cheek and over her bottom lip. "Andi, she was coming up there to set up a romantic dinner for us. I'm sorry, she had no right to even look at your computer, but she did. But please understand that Krista and I go way back. She's a

friend. She got the wrong idea and drew the wrong con-
clusions. Krista is protective of me like a sister and I'm
not defending what she did or what she said to you, just
explaining where she was coming from. But Andi, I don't
care about the damned five stars. I only care about you.
Surely you must know that. Feel that."

Andi gazed up at Max for a long speechless moment
because she knew with absolute certainty that he was
sincere.

"The article is finished," Max continued during Andi's
speechless moment, obviously thinking there was more
convincing on his part to be done. "I've got nothing to
gain and everything to lose. Come back with me to Wild
Ride and extend your stay. I want the opportunity to get
to learn everything about you. Your favorite food, the
music you listen to, your favorite movies, sports . . . *hey,*
have you heard anything I've said?"

Andi smiled and said, "Nothing past the 'I only care
about you' part. Why don't you just shut up and kiss
me?"

"You don't have to ask twice."

Andi's eyes fluttered shut at the touch of Max's mouth
to hers. She wrapped her arms around him, loving the feel
of his warm skin beneath the palms of her hands. "So?"
Andi began, a bit breathless from the kiss, "where do we
go from here?"

Max smiled. "In roller-coaster terms, we are at the top
of the first big hill, ready to take the plunge."

Andi arched an eyebrow. "Oh, really? Now you're
comparing our relationship with me to a roller-coaster
ride?"

"Oh, *yeah,* and I'm expecting some serious airtime."

"Hmmm, well, let's see. In travel writer–speak, I'll be expecting a five-star performance later this evening. Think you're up for it?"

Max chuckled. "I guess you'll have to come back with me to Wild Ride and find out."

"I guess I will."

ᕖ chapter fifteen

"**D**inner was exquisite," Andi said as she pat-ted her mouth with her white linen nap-kin. Wrinkling her nose, she looked past the candles at Max and added, "I guess I'll have to thank Krista."

"You two could be friends if you just give her a chance. Krista is . . . uh, complicated. But she has a good heart."

Andi nodded. "I'm sure she does. I promise to give her a chance. I find it amusing, though, that she included every aphrodisiac known to man."

Max grinned. "That was my doing. This whole five-star thing has me a bit nervous. I thought I could use all the help I could get."

Pursing her lips, Andi nodded. "You've got a point. I have very high standards." She hid her grin behind her napkin. Krista had instructed them to dress formally for dinner. Having Max seated across the dining-room table wearing a black tux had Andi as hot as a firecracker for him and it had nothing to do with raw oysters. "So what about dessert?" Andi tried to keep her voice casual. She didn't give a fig about dessert. She wanted *him* and nothing else would come close to satisfying her craving.

"I believe it's in the bedroom." Standing up, Max came over to her chair and helped her scoot away from the table. "By the way, have I told you how lovely you look in that dress?"

Andi smiled. "Three or four times. But you can tell me again. You're scoring big points." She should have felt uncomfortable in the barely-there black dress. The neckline plunged to her navel in the front and would have exposed her back to the top of her thong . . . if she had been wearing a thong. One little flick of his wrists and the dress would slither to the floor. Not wearing any underwear made her feel wicked and sexy and nearly out of her mind with wanting him.

"Wait here," Max said when they reached the closed door of the master bedroom. "Krista made me promise to go in and do a few things first."

"Oh, okay, take your time." *God, hurry.* Andi was tingling with curiosity. She hadn't been allowed to see the bedroom yet.

Max entered the room, closed the door, and smiled. His usually very masculine bedroom had been transformed into a haven for lovers. Candles of every shape and size were placed in every nook and cranny. Max began lighting them, stunned to see that his fingers were shaking slightly, but sitting through all of those damned courses at dinner had been sheer hell. Every move Andi made at dinner had caused the silky material of her dress to shift and move, revealing too much and then not nearly enough.

Soon the room glowed softly and the enticing scent of vanilla filled the room. Shadows flickered and danced on the walls. Red rose petals were scattered on the bed, champagne was chilled on ice, and Travis Mackey's CD was sitting next to the bed with a sticky note that read: PLAY NUMBER 7 AND NO THAT DOES NOT MEAN I LIKE COUNTRY MUSIC, JUST THIS ONE SULTRY SONG! Max chuckled. Krista had outdone herself, but then she usually went a little over the top.

Max slid the CD into the slot and a moment later Travis Mackey was singing a love song. *Okay,* he thought with a deep intake of breath. He was ready . . . *no, God,* more than ready. Max took quick long strides over to the door and swung it open.

Andi gave him a sexy-as-hell smile that trembled just a bit at the corners. As she entered the room her hazel eyes rounded, taking it all in. "This is beautiful," she said softly and sat down on the edge of the bed and brought a rose petal to her nose and inhaled deeply. With a shy smile she patted the bed and looked up at Max. "Come here."

"You don't have to ask twice," Max said, echoing his earlier statement. He leaned her back onto the mattress, kissing her deeply, thoroughly, loving the silky feel of the warm skin of her leg, her thigh. A heart-stopping moment later, he realized she wore nothing beneath her black dress and his hard-won control broke.

"God, Andi . . . you're driving me insane." He toed off his shoes, tugged at his tie, hopped around the room while trying to remove his clothes all at once.

Andi giggled, a low throaty sound that had Max pulling, yanking at his tux. "Damned tie!" he growled.

"Let me help," Andi offered. "Come here and I'll undress you."

Her nimble fingers shook, but made quick work of his clothes and then she stood up a second later and let her dress slide from her body and pool on the floor. Candlelight danced off her bare skin and as badly as Max wanted to make love to her, he paused for a long moment to just simply look.

Turning, Max scooped Andi up in his arms and laid her gently down on the rose petals. "Do you want some champagne?"

"No, I only want you."

That was all Max needed to hear.

Bright sunlight streaming into the room teased Max's heavy eyelids. With a groan, he opened his eyes a mere slit. Moving, however, was impossible for two reasons. First, he was exhausted. Depleted. *Marathon sex will do that to you,* he thought, too tired to even crack a smile. Second, one long leg entwined with his legs had him trapped.

Andi's head rested on his shoulder and her arm was wrapped around his chest. By the even sound of her breathing, Max thought Andi was still asleep, but then she murmured in his ear, "You got your five-star rating . . . again."

Max managed to chuckle and kissed the top of her head. A feeling of total contentment washed over him like a warm wave lapping over the sand. His heavy eyelids closed and he inhaled deeply, catching the scent of roses, vanilla, and warm, well-loved woman. Max thought he would fall right back asleep, but for a while he lay awake just listening to Andi breathe softly in his ear.

Krista was right. He was in love with Andi; he knew this with absolute certainty. The thought made his heart pound and he got the butterflies-in-his-stomach airtime feeling of plunging over the top of the first hill of a roller coaster. The weightless feeling should have scared the living daylights out of him, but it didn't. Max knew that loving Andi Cooper was going to be one hellava ride, but he wouldn't have it any other way.

Hold on Tight

∽ chapter one

Krista's breathing became reduced to short gasps, and her lungs burned, yet she ran faster. Her rubber-soled feet slapped against the hard-packed sand, sending water splashing when she hit the edge of the frothy surf. Perspiration soaked her sports bra, and she blinked at the salty sting of sweat dripping into her eyes, but she ran down the beach until her legs felt too heavy to lift. Finally she slowed, and then stopped running, dragging in deep breaths as she bent over, grabbing her knees for support.

Krista swayed, trying to blink away the darkness that threatened to envelop her, realizing that she had pushed her body too far, almost to the point of passing out. Sucking in a deep breath of sea-scented air, she willed away the urge to collapse and started walking, needing a cooldown so her muscles didn't cramp.

Although Krista ran almost every morning, it had been a while since she had pushed her body to the limit, but she had needed to relieve the stress that had been build-ing for the past two weeks. And today the reason for her frustration was going to arrive at Wild Ride Resort.

"Travis Mackey," Krista grumbled through gritted teeth, ruing the day that she had been talked into hiring *him* to be the headliner for the end of the summer Labor Day celebration on the island. *She* had wanted to go after the Beach Boys or maybe Jimmy Buffett, but *nooo*, Max had insisted on Travis Mackey, the rodeo superstar turned country singer. So, instead of fun-in-the-sun beach music, she had a frigging singing cowboy.

And to add insult to injury, the guy was a royal pain. Well, she hadn't had the displeasure of actually meeting Travis Mackey, but his manager had made so many de-mands for his client that Krista had no doubt that the singing cowboy was nothing but an arrogant jerk.

With a shake of her head that sent droplets of sweat flying, Krista headed back toward the hotel. She usually enjoyed her position as director of entertainment for the resort but from experience she knew that celebrities could push you to the limit. While she prided herself on keep-ing her self-control while bowing to the whims of pam-pered superstars, Travis Mackey had asked for the moon and then some. His demand for privacy rather than a suite in the hotel meant that Krista had to not only give up her own beach house to him, but she had to convert her guest bedroom to a workout center for his conven-ience. He had also insisted on a hot tub, but luckily she already had one on her back patio.

Krista let out a squeal of pure frustration and kicked her toe in the water. God, she was going to miss her house. Lo-cated to the left of the hotel, and mostly hidden by tall cypress trees yet with a crow's-nest view of the ocean, her home was her haven, her happy place at the end of the long days she put in at Wild Ride. Although Krista enjoyed her job and loved working for Oliver Maxwell, it was demanding. Her title might be director of entertainment, but she was really Max's right-hand man and her duties included much more than just booking the shows for the resort. She was constantly "on," basically keeping people happy and productive. But she always knew that at the end of the day she could escape to her home, pour a glass of wine, and soak away her stress in her hot tub.

If there had been any other way to accommodate Travis Mackey, Krista would have done it, but her little house was the only such animal on the private island. The college students that they hired during the summer rush stayed in the dormlike residence behind the hotel. Some of the other year-round employees, mostly retired friends of Max's from his carnival days, lived above the storefronts on Main Street and the rest of the employees commuted to the island via boat each morning or evening. Of course, Max had his penthouse, so Krista had no choice but to give her place up.

To make matters worse, Travis Mackey was arriving early for some rest before the Labor Day concert. Krista had been told that a recent bout with exhaustion coupled with complications from his bull-riding injuries had forced him to take a break from his grueling schedule. Just that morning Max had informed Krista that Travis Mackey was to be her first and only priority for his entire stay. Oh, but here was the kicker. Krista was supposed to pose as Travis Mackey's girlfriend to keep the women at the resort from hounding him.

Great. This was *so* not a part of her job description.

Still grumbling under her breath, Krista left the bright sunlight of the beach for the well-worn path through the woods that was a shortcut to the hotel. The tall, skinny cypress trees swayed slightly in the morning breeze, creaking and moaning while letting in filtered sunshine. She paused with a dramatic sigh to pout a little when she came to the clearing where her house stood. Sky blue with white trim, the house was pretty without being overly cute. If this were a normal day, she would head inside, put a pot of coffee on to brew, shower, and then come outside on the front porch and sip her mug of coffee while sitting in the swing suspended from the ceiling.

But this wasn't a normal day. This was the day Travis Mackey was due to arrive and turn her life upside down.

Krista sighed again, and she would have gone inside to torture herself, but she had just had the place cleaned from top to bottom and didn't want to track in any sand. The fridge had been stocked with Mackey's favorite beer, bottled water, and tons of staples. A variety of spices, most of which Krista had no clue as to the use of lined the countertop. In fact, the kitchen was about the only room in the house where Krista didn't spend much time, not being much of a chef, but Travis Mackey, she was told, would be doing most of his own cooking. This was unusual for a celebrity, but then Krista remembered reading somewhere in his bio that he loved to cook and had actually done some barbecuing on one of the Food Network shows. She had also read that Travis was in the process of putting his recipes in a cookbook that he was going to sell for charity.

Krista shrugged and muttered, "Whatever. Probably

needs a tax write-off." Okay, she knew she was being snarky, but she refused to have any warm and fuzzy feelings toward the person who was responsible for tossing her from her own home. Of course, he probably didn't know that he was doing it, but that was beside the point. Krista did admit to having a little bit of admiration for a guy who had reinvented himself after a near fatal bull-riding accident that had permanently taken him off the professional circuit. She also knew, however, that Travis Mackey had been a three-time Professional Bull Riding World Champion because he was basically fearless, leading a wild lifestyle that had finally caught up to him big-time.

Women, Krista knew, found reckless bad boy Travis Mackey irresistible, following him from the PBR circuit to country music in droves. Luckily, there was nothing about Travis Mackey that she found attractive. Sure, he was sexy in that rough-and-ready cowboy kind of way, if you went for that sort of thing, which she didn't. Krista was into designer suits, not Wrangler jeans.

Krista valued her independence above and beyond everything else, but if she ever did consider getting married, it would be to someone who enjoyed cool jazz and a bottle of good wine, not country music and longneck bottles of beer. Krista's thoughts skittered to a halt. *Married?* Now where in the world did that off-the-wall thought come from? Marriage was definitely not in her short- or long-range plans. "No, no, *no!*" Krista shook her head, thinking that she must be in dire need of caffeine or carbs or *something.*

She had spent her childhood in Alabama watching her father live his life trapped in the lyrics of a you-done me-wrong country song. Her flighty, artsy mother hadn't been cut out for domestic life and had left her father the job of raising her, swinging in and out of their lives like a revolving door, mostly when she needed money, and her father had been fool enough to put up with it.

Krista shook her head at the memory. Her daddy had always taken her mother back and then he would be sad and sulky for weeks after she took off again. Not that he was ever mean or abusive, just in her view pathetic. When Krista had asked her daddy point-blank why in the hell he put up with that treatment and didn't just divorce her mother, her daddy had said that he loved her beyond all reason and was grateful for the time he had with her.

"Your mama's a free spirit. She's an artist, Krista," her daddy had once told her. "She needs to have her wings to survive. I knew that from the beginning and I can't ever take that from her. I love her enough to let her go here and there to paint and then to open my arms when she walks back through the door. She loves us, too, Krista. That's why she always comes back. It's just her way." He had smiled and said to her, "I see a lot of your mama in you. Maybe someday you'll understand."

Krista had thought that was a crock then, and she still did. "I'm nothing like her," Krista firmly said to herself and then wondered why in the world she was even thinking about all of this. Marriage and her mother were two subjects she liked to avoid thinking about. Things could be worse. At least she didn't have a mother hovering over her begging for a grandchild.

Krista had vowed a long time ago never to let someone have that kind of hold over her. She did, though, feel a little twinge of longing for what Max and Andi shared.

They were so into each other and although Krista acted like it gagged her, she was just a teeny bit envious. Okay, a lot envious. Deep down, she wanted forever, but was too damned scared to go after it. It was so much safer to just be a tough, cold-as-ice blond, aloof, and a little bit bitchy. She supposed she had just enough of both her parents' personalities to be a walking, talking contradiction, needing what she claimed she didn't want, pretending to be what she wasn't.

It pretty much sucked. At least her parents were honest and true to themselves.

So Krista kept her guard up most of the time. The only one who was able to get her riled, to get her to let her hair down and allow her redneck roots bubble to the surface, was Max. But now Max had Andi and although he didn't mean to ignore her, he pretty much did.

Lately, Krista had been so lonely that it hurt. She felt unaccustomed emotion well up in her throat. What in the world has wrong with her, she wondered, swiping at a damned teardrop. She never cried! It was probably just the emotion of having her house yanked away from her, she thought, feeling a flash of anger toward Travis Mackey. This was entirely his damned fault!

With that thought still buzzing around in her brain like an angry bee, Krista stormed into the hotel lobby. The air-conditioning cooled her overheated body, making her shiver in her damp clothing, but as much as she wanted to hightail it to her suite and peel off her spandex for a long, muscle-soothing shower, she decided to pause and remind Paul Timmer at the front desk that Travis Mackey would be arriving later that day. Because of the early hour, the lobby was empty and almost eerily quiet except for the faint clanking and tinkling sounds of plates being set up for breakfast in the hotel restaurant.

"Hey Paul," Krista said, leaning her elbows on the cold, shiny black countertop. She grabbed a Red Delicious apple from a crystal bowl. "I just want to remind you that my singing cowboy will be *moseying* on over here later today."

Paul gave her a little flip of his fingers. "It's funny that you should say that because—"

Krista raised one hand in the air. "I know you're on top of things, Paul. Let's just keep our little ol' cowpoke happy since we're going to have to put up with him for an eternity."

"Uh, Krista . . ."

"I know you are probably into country music just about as much as I am—"

"I love it! Love it. *Love it!*" he said, eyes widening, he gave a dramatic sweep of his hand, almost taking the bowl of apples with it. "Country music . . . is . . . uh, the *bomb!* I know *you* absolutely love it too!"

"Oh come on, Paul, you know that I hate . . ." she paused when Paul started moving his head in a slight sideways motion. *Oh, damn.* Krista swallowed and mouthed, "He's standing right behind me, isn't he?"

Paul gave her a barely perceptible nod.

"What I mean is that I hate, um, rap music. But country music is . . . uh . . ."

"The bomb," a deep voice finished for her, laced with way too much humor.

Taking a deep breath, Krista pasted a Julia Roberts smile on her face and turned around.

chapter
two

Travis lifted his gaze from the little blond's ass just in time when she pivoted around to face him. Shoving his hands into his front pockets of his jeans, he tried to look good-ol'-boy innocent. He almost burst into a fit of laughter while she tried to compose herself but then he just about swallowed his tongue at the sight of her very fine breasts clearly outlined in the damp sports bra that was molded to her body like shrink-wrap . . . and *hot damn,* he'd bet the farm that those puppies were real. Her nipples strained against the white cotton, and he had an instant reaction that he really needed to control in his tight Wranglers or he was going to be the one with the red face.

"Hello, Mr. Mackey," she said coolly, offering her slim hand. "I'm Krista Ross, director of entertainment. Welcome to Wild Ride Resort."

Carefully keeping his gaze on her face, Travis grasped her hand, which felt as delicate as a baby chick in his big, calloused grip. Krista had a where-in-the-hell-did-you-come-from look in her light blue eyes, but she gave him one of those practiced, professional smiles that he despised. Nick Tackett, his manager, had said that Krista Ross was as cool as a cucumber and even though she was sending him I'm-not-impressed-by-you vibes, Travis was intrigued. Or maybe that was why he was intrigued. He thought of the Shania Twain song "That Don't Impress Me Much" and grinned. That was just fine with him. After a meteoric climb to the top of the country-music charts and a recent Best New Artist award at the Country Music Awards, Travis was damned tired of having to impress people. Not that he wasn't grateful for his success, because he had worked hard to get there, but after his last road stand, he was just plumb wore out and had an emergency hospital stay to prove it.

"Why, thank you for the warm welcome," Travis said with a tip of his black Stetson, purposely accentuating his Texas drawl. "I didn't mean to startle y'all, but I was in the *little ol' cowboy's* room." He jammed a thumb in the direction of the bathroom, directly behind him.

One delicately arched blond eyebrow raised just a fraction, letting Travis know that she knew that he was mocking her. "Oh, that's quite all right," she responded smoothly. "I just wasn't expecting you until later. I apologize for my appearance. As you might have guessed, I've just gotten back from my morning run."

"No apology needed." Travis rocked back on the heels of his boots, jamming his hands back into his pockets once again. "I just wanted to slip in unnoticed. I'm counting on you keeping my early arrival here on the down-low."

"Oh, certainly, I understand." She angled her head, causing the bottom of her blond ponytail to flip over her shoulder.

Damn, Travis thought, her hair must go halfway down her back. She was a little bitty thing, and way too snooty for his taste, but sexy as hell. She lifted her chin a notch, trying her best to look like a tough cookie, but she had a vulnerable set to her mouth that told Travis that she wasn't nearly as sure of herself as she pretended to be. He'd be willing to bet that she was one hot mama beneath her cool-as-you-please demeanor.

"Where's the rest of your crew?" She had a nervous little edge to her voice.

"Oh, it's okay if you're not ready for them. They won't arrive until later next week when we start rehearsing for the concert," Travis said. "I've been a little under the weather and needed some time off."

"Oh, I'm sorry to hear that. I hope your stay here will help you recover." The smile she gave him seemed genuine.

Now this smile he liked. "I'll be fine. So," he said slowly, "you think country music is . . . *the bomb?*" Travis was willing to bet that Krista had never used that phrase in her life. Her cheeks turned a pretty shade of pink and behind the counter Paul coughed.

"Uh, yes, sure. The bomb."

"Who is your favorite country artist?"

She turned a little pinker and shifted from one running shoe to the other. "Why *you,* of course."

Travis was only teasing, but her fake smile returned, making him a little annoyed. He was so tired of fake flattery. "Really? What's your favorite song?" he asked, knowing he had her. She raised her face so she could look him straight in the eye and Travis thought she was going to confess that she didn't have a clue. Uppity chicks like her didn't usually listen to country music or at least admit to it. He was ready to tell her to just come clean and tell him that she hated his music when she frowned and put her finger thoughtfully by her chin.

"Um, well, number three on your CD *New Beginnings,* 'Test of Faith' is probably my favorite. I love the gospel roots and I think just about everybody could relate to the lyrics. I suppose everyone has had a test of faith at one point or another, don't you? Oh, no wait, 'On The Other Side' is so soulful, hmm, but wait a minute, number seven, 'Love Me' showcases your voice." She nodded, "Yes, 'Love Me' is my top pick. I know I didn't choose the most popular song, 'Watch Out,' your first big hit, but you-done-me-wrong songs aren't my cup of tea."

Travis closed his mouth, since it was hanging open. She smiled up at him, a bit smug. He would have chalked it up to her just doing her homework, but in the midst of her answer, he detected some honesty and it pleased him more than it should have. He had millions of fans, so why should it matter if cool little Krista Ross liked his music? It was a little unnerving, too, that she had managed to choose *his* favorite songs. Travis shrugged it off. He must have divulged his personal favorites in an interview but he couldn't help but ask, "Did you know that those were my three favorites, Krista?" He smiled, thinking he had her this time.

Her blue eyes widened in obvious surprise and she answered, "No. No, I didn't. Honestly."

Travis nodded. He believed her. "Good. People kiss my ass with dishonesty all the time. I hate it."

"It's my job to kiss your ass, Mr. Mackey," she responded drily.

Paul coughed in the background.

Travis grinned, liking her a bit more. "Now that was honest."

She flushed a bit pink again. "Honest, but inappropriate. Forgive me."

Travis chuckled. "See, now being inappropriate sits just fine with me since I'm more often than not on that particular side of the fence. Ms. Ross, just be honest and be yourself and we'll get along just fine and dandy."

When Travis gave her a smile that showed off a dimple in his left cheek, Krista softened just a little. She had to admit that he was charming in a good-ol'-boy kinda way and even better looking in person than on his CD cover, if you went for that broad-shouldered rough-around-the-edges look, that is. Some women, *not her of course,* might wonder what that scruffy stubble darkening his cheeks would feel like rubbing against their skin . . . *oh,* he had just asked her something. Krista blinked and said, "Excuse me?"

"I was wondering if you could show me where I'm staying?"

"Oh, I had planned on showing you to your house and then taking you on a tour of the resort, but would you mind if I showered and changed? Paul can take you over to the restaurant for breakfast and by the time you've eaten, I'll be ready to show you around. If that's okay, of course."

Travis nodded. "Sounds like a winner. I realize that I'm here early. Besides, I could use a cup of joe."

Oh, there was that dimple again. Krista was a bit

stunned when her stomach did a little flip-flop thing. How stupid, she thought, annoyed at herself. Must have been hunger pangs. "I'll meet you in thirty minutes," she said crisply, trying to sound businesslike.

"That's fine. Don't hurry on my account." With a tip of his black hat, he turned to follow Paul toward the restaurant. Wranglers were so *not* her thing, but she sneaked a peek at his butt, just to check him out as she knew he had been checking her out. Tit for tat or whatever. *Nice,* she conceded with a little grin, but her smile faded when she noticed a slight hitch in Travis' walk. She remembered reading about the horrible incident when he had been thrown from a bucking bull and repeatedly stomped on, the hoofs nearly crushing his right leg and injuring his shoulder. There had been talk that he'd never walk again, but he had proven the doctors wrong, she supposed with the same steely determination that enabled him to stay on a wild bull for the required eight seconds.

"Stupid sport," Krista muttered as she headed to her suite, but she couldn't help but wonder if Travis was in pain. She realized with a little guilty pang that he had probably requested the hot tub and workout machines for pain relief and physical therapy, not to keep buff and seduce women. Krista felt a little rotten about prejudging Travis Mackey. She had done the same thing with Andi Cooper and had been dead wrong. She was still miffed about having to give up her house and pose as his girlfriend but maybe she should give the guy a chance. He was much more likeable than she had expected and the fact that he had arrived quietly, instead of with the customary entourage, was impressive in her view.

Thank goodness Max had lent her Travis's CD. Although she had returned it, Krista had secretly burned a copy, liking Travis Mackey's whiskey-rough voice more than she cared to admit. "So what?" Krista muttered as she entered her suite and made a beeline for the shower. She wasn't about to let one charming cowboy strip away the polished surface she had worked so hard to achieve to find her carefully hidden redneck roots. Krista sighed as she peeled off her workout clothes and turned on the shower, thinking that she had reached a level of sophistication that no longer included country music, tractor pulls, moon pies, cheesy grits, or smooth-talkin' cowboys.

And she didn't miss any of it one doggone bit. Really, she didn't.

⤜ chapter
three

Travis watched Krista enter the dining room from over the rim of his coffee cup. Dressed in a pale, peach-colored sleeveless dress with her long blond hair clipped back at the nape of her neck, she had that classy appearance that made her look as if she belonged on the arm of a Kennedy. *Not my type at all,* Travis thought with a pang of disappointment. He preferred his women in worn, hip-hugging jeans and tiny white tank tops and yet there was something about Krista Ross that stirred his blood.

She approached his table with one of her cool smiles and Travis thought again that perhaps part of her appeal was that she seemed so completely unaffected by him. Travis was used to women fawning all over him and although he was certain that she would provide him with whatever he asked for, she wasn't going to ask him to autograph her ass, a request that he had gotten more times than he cared to count. Not that he would mind autographing hers . . .

132

"Ready?" she asked, with another no-nonsense smile that was at odds with the shiny, peach-colored stuff on her lips that made them look just-kissed. For God's sake, Little Miss Priss was turning him on something fierce.

"Uh, just let me finish the rest of my coffee," he said, stalling while the embarrassing tent in his pants subsided.

"Okay," she said with a short nod and then busied herself checking off things on her Palm Pilot.

It irritated Travis that she was so composed, all business, and that she clearly wanted to check him off of her to-do list . . . *when she was at the very top on his to-do list.* Travis chuckled at the thought and her head snapped up.

"Oh, did I miss something?" A little frown furrowed her smooth brow. "I'm sorry, I was concentrating . . ."

"On your to-do list?"

She shrugged her slim shoulders. "My boss is busy planning his wedding, leaving me a little frazzled."

Travis pushed back from the table. "I get it. You're in a hurry to scratch me off and move on to the next item."

"I'm sorry. I didn't mean it that way, Mr. Mackey."

"Quit being so damned polite. I hate it when people patronize me. Call me Travis."

Her light blue eyes widened a fraction and Travis saw a flicker of anger. Ahh, so she was human after all. But then she gave him that damned polite smile. For some reason, he wanted to see her lose her cool, but he decided to do the nice thing being the good ol' boy that he was, and just get out of her hair and let her go onto whatever the hell else she so desperately needed to do, and it sure wasn't him. Standing up, Travis tipped his Stetson back with his thumb, and then said, "Look, just point me in the direction of the house. You don't need to babysit me. I'll be fine."

"But—"

"No, really, I'll be okay."

"Mr. Mackey . . . *Travis*, there are some things I'd like to show you."

Travis took off his hat and scratched his head. "I think I can figure out all I need to know. I'm smarter than I look."

"Have I done something to offend you?"

Aw, damn. Krista looked so stricken that she might have screwed up that he felt like a horse's ass. She tipped her head to the side and her long hair slipped over her shoulder and it was all he could do not to reach over and run his fingers through the long tresses just to see if it would feel as silky as it looked. "Hey," he said gently, "I'm sorry for being a jerk. I guess I'm just tired after the long road tour and I probably have jet lag from the flight followed by the bumpy boat ride to the island. Let's just chalk it up to my all-around fatigue. Look, you're busy, so just cross kissing my ass off of your to-do list."

Krista turned her Palm Pilot around so he could see the blank screen. "Actually, I had just cleared my schedule so I can be with you all day long. You, Mr. Mackey, are the only thing left on my to-do list."

Travis chuckled. "Well, then, since you put it that way, I guess I just have to let you *do* me."

"I didn't mean it *that* way," she said and primly pursed her lips. She was so damned sexy, though, that she just wasn't pulling it off. Plus, Travis had a sneaking suspicion that she wanted to laugh but was refraining. Just like that, she was all business once again. "I'm sorry. I don't know what's getting into me."

"I know," he said with a long dramatic sigh. "And my comment was probably sexual harassment and politically incorrect, which I unfortunately tend to be, so forget I said it. But a guy can dream, can't he?"

One delicate eyebrow arched. "Oh, come on, Mr. Mackey. You can get any woman you want on this island, so don't give me that."

"Any woman?" He gave her his best grin.

"Almost."

"Hey, call me *Travis*."

"Since I'm supposed to be your girlfriend I guess I'll have to."

"My girlfriend? Sugar, you've lost me."

Krista gave him a confused frown. "I was told that I was supposed to pose as your girlfriend to keep the women at Wild Ride from bugging you."

Although hot little Krista had a smile pasted on her face, he could tell she was none too pleased at the prospect of pretending to be his girlfriend. For some reason this amused him. "So, let me get this straight. You're going to be my arm candy and fawn all over me?"

"That's right," she said with a tight smile.

"Hang out with me by the pool and rub lotion on my back?"

"If that's what it takes."

After having so many women throw their panties at him for the past year this would be a welcome change. He had no idea who had requested that she do this but it sounded like a plan. "Works for me. I've been ordered to take it easy for a while." He fell into step beside her, but was having a bit of trouble keeping up with her brisk pace. Rather than embarrass himself by asking her to slow down Travis said, "You know, a kiss now and then would be pretty convincing."

That stopped her in her tracks. "Mr. Mackey. While I'm willing to go above and beyond my professional duties you're—"

"Pushing my luck?"

"With all due respect, yes."

He shrugged while giving her a cocky grin that he knew would piss her off. "I tend to push my luck." He let his gaze travel to her mouth. She pursed her lips as if she'd rather kiss a toad then pucker up to him. Travis was hard pressed not to grab Miss Priss and kiss her right then and there just to show her a thing or two but he had a sneaking suspicion that it might land him a knee to the groin. Since his shoulder and his leg already ached, he decided *not* to push his luck . . . for now. Instead, he filed her rebuff away as a challenge and if there was anything Travis loved, it was a challenge.

With a haughty lift of her chin she took off down the sandy path. Travis didn't even try to keep up, but sure enjoyed the sight of her tight little ass swaying back and forth even though her back was ramrod straight. Little did she know that he found her don't-mess-with-me attitude not only a challenge, but sexy as hell.

"Here you go," she said briskly, holding the door open for him to enter. "Follow me and I'll show you around. If you have any questions, just let me know as we go." The professional smile was back in place, but perhaps a little strained around the edges. With a sweeping gesture she said, "This is the living room." Flicking on an overhead paddle fan, she then pulled open the double doors of an entertainment center. "You have satellite television, a DVD player, and surround sound."

"Nice," Travis commented, but she kept right on going a million miles a minute without looking at him. He wanted to grab her and tell her to just *relax,* but she was already acting so skittish, he thought better of it.

She closed the doors with a quiet click and walked into the adjoining dining area. "Your dining room and kitchen," she said with another gesture like that of a game-show hostess, and walked quickly into the kitchen. "I had it stocked with everything you requested. If there is anything at all that you need just let me know and we'll get it as quickly as possible." She gave him a cordial smile. "I understand you are quite the cook."

"I try." Travis shrugged, getting a little irritated at her polite demeanor which, of course, was unfair on his part. She was only trying to do her job in a professional manner. He absently began rubbing his shoulder, which was beginning to ache even more. As if on the same wavelength, his leg started to stiffen up on him. He concentrated on the spice rack, trying to ignore that dull pain that was a part of his daily life.

"You okay?"

"Fine," he said a little too sharply. He really wanted her to leave before she saw the pain get worse, which he knew it would. He hated this damned weakness that he couldn't control. "Listen, I can take it from here. You're officially off the hook."

chapter four

Even though Travis had successfully ticked her off, Krista wasn't about to leave him. Not when he had brackets of pain around his mouth and had gone a bit pale beneath his tan. "Sit down, Travis," she said firmly and gestured toward a cane-backed chair at the small table in the breakfast nook.

"You're awfully bossy," he grumbled but plopped his long frame down on the chair and tried to grin.

"Now, what do you want me to do?"

"Now that's a loaded question, sugar."

"Don't call me sugar."

"Now, just why not? Oh, right, not the politically correct thing."

"Right!" Krista tentatively touched the shoulder he had been rubbing. "Okay, now what?"

"Your bedside manner leaves a bit to be desired," he grumbled with a sigh. Oh damn, that made him picture her *in* bed full of desire. "Massage it with both hands," he said tightly while wishing he meant something entirely different.

"Like this?"

"Harder."

"I don't want to hurt you."

"You couldn't possibly make it any worse." Taking off his hat, Travis angled his head to the side to give her better access to his shoulder. "Harder."

"Okay." She massaged a bit deeper, wincing at the pain etched on his handsome face. "Travis, am I hurting you?"

"Yeah, but don't stop. It will get better in a minute." He groaned and then closed his eyes. "Kinda like no pain, no gain."

Krista swallowed as she moved her fingers over his shoulder and biceps. Her fingers were tiring, but she wasn't about to quit. "Is this from that damned bull stomping all over you?"

Travis chuckled at the fire in her statement. "Yep. Mmmm, you have magic fingers. Just the right touch."

"Getting better?"

"Yes." He rolled his shoulder, but she noticed that his jaw was still clenched.

"Relax," she crooned in his ear, trying to sound like her Pilates instructor. "Take a deep breath. That's it. Again." She was rewarded when she felt the tense muscles soften a fraction beneath her touch. His eyes were still closed . . . *wow*, he had impossibly long lashes at odds with the dark stubble on his chin. His hair was a rich, chestnut brown, tousled and a bit on the long side, curling over his ears. His chest rose and fell with deep breaths, stretching the snug black T-shirt to the limit. Krista could see the outline of his pectoral muscles. He

was lean and hard-bodied without too much bulk . . .
whipcord strength.

Krista had the almost uncontrollable urge to ease her
arms around his neck and to flatten her palms over his
chest. What would he do if she nuzzled his exposed neck
and then came around to straddle him on the chair?
Good God, she thought and gave herself a mental shake.
"Better?" she asked gently, a bit embarrassed that her
voice shook slightly.

His eyelashes flickered. "Much." Opening his eyes, he
looked up over his shoulder at her. "Thank you. By the
way, your bedside manner is getting better."

Krista shook her head at his suggestive tone but then
smiled and actually gave in to an odd urge to ruffle his
hair . . . ohhh, baby-soft. She suddenly longed to sink her
fingers in and let his hair curl around her fingers, but
pulled away, wondering again what in the world was getting into her. "Good. Well, then, I should be going," she
said briskly. *Before I do something stupid.*

Travis twisted in the seat. "I thought I had you all to
myself for the day."

"Well, you seem like you need some rest. I don't want
to intrude."

"I do need some rest and I just bet you do, too. How
about this? Go on back to your place. Get out of that
fancy dress and come back here in your favorite jeans.
We'll hang out. Be slugs all day. Watch movies and eat
junk food before my trainer gets here and watches everything that goes into my mouth."

"I . . ."

"Oh, come on. When was the last time you were a slug
all day?"

"Well . . ."

"I'm guessing never."

"It's been a while," she said a bit defensively.

Travis gave her a slow smile that did crazy things to her insides. "Come on back and I'll teach you the fine art of being a slug."

"Do *you* really know how, Mr. Mackey?"

"I'll admit that it's been a long time since I've done a whole bunch of nothin' but I think I can remember how. Are you game?"

Krista caught her bottom lip between her teeth for a second. She was torn between doing her job and putting some distance between herself and the sexy, singing cowboy. He was making her want things she hadn't wanted in a long time. Krista knew it wasn't logical thinking, but Travis Mackey, with his Texas twang and his good-ol'-boy demeanor, reminded her of everything she had left behind and missed so very much. "I still think it would be better if you rested. I'd just be in your way."

"Really . . ." Travis said slowly, trying not to sound too irritated. Miss Priss was making it quite clear that she didn't want to spend one more minute with him. Travis would have let it slide even though it *was* her job to do whatever the hell he wanted. It was her uppity attitude that ticked him off and at the same time amused him. "You know, I think that I just might like to spend the afternoon by the pool catchin' some rays and tossing back frozen drinks with those little umbrellas in them." He had never had a frozen drink in his life. His band, especially Brody, would laugh their asses off if they saw him with a girlie drink.

"Oh." She frowned at him, clearly not warming up to

the idea. "That might bring you some unwanted attention."

"Well, sugar, that's where *you* come in. You need to sit there and fawn all over me while fending off fans."

"Certainly," she answered in a businesslike manner but Travis saw an angry little tic in her left eye. Her brisk tone indicated that she considered this her job and nothing else. Maybe his ego was getting in the way, Travis thought. After all, Miss Priss was the first woman in a long time to want to run away instead of throwing herself at him. Even during his bull-riding days there had been endless supplies of buckle bunnies wanting to jump in the sack with him. Travis thought of Brad Paisley's music video about spoiled celebrities and had to shake his head. The last thing Travis wanted was to become a pain in the ass, maybe he needed a good dose of humility.

"Is there something wrong Mr. Mackey?"

"Hmm?" Her question brought him back to reality.

"You were shaking your head at me."

No, I was shaking my head at me. "Oh. No, everything's fine."

"Good," she said, but he knew she really didn't mean it. "Give me half an hour to change and then meet me by the tiki bar at the pool, okay?"

"Sure."

With a tight little nod she turned to go.

"Oh, Krista?"

She stopped and slowly turned back around to face him.

"Wear a bikini, okay?"

For a moment Krista couldn't trust her voice not to come out a screech. Deep down she knew he was only teasing but he had her tied in so many emotional knots that she just snapped. "Cowboy, don't get *anything* up but your hopes." With that parting comment, she spun on her heel and marched out of the house.

His laughter had Krista muttering and sputtering under her breath as she wound her way down the sandy path leading to the hotel. Still fuming, she barely refrained from slamming shut the door to her suite just to let off some steam. "Wear a bikini," she hissed, mimicking his Texas twang, fully wishing that she could wear a turtle-neck and long pants to the pool . . . *ahhh,* but then another tactic entered her brain.

Marching over to her closet, she found the skimpiest bikini she owned and shimmied into it. Ha! A vibrant, shiny light blue, the string bikini showed off her cleavage and trim, athletic shape. She slipped on a toe ring and a gold ankle bracelet and then piled her long blond hair up in a sexy, sloppy ponytail instead of using the conservative gold clip that she usually wore. She located a silky beach cover-up and jewel-encrusted sandals to top off her sex-kitten attire. After tossing sunscreen and some coconut-scented tanning oil in a beach bag, she walked out the door. Krista fully intended to be a total tease, playing up her fawning-girlfriend role until Travis wanted to drown himself. She smiled as she headed to the pool.

This was going to be fun.

Krista hurried over to the tiki bar hoping to beat Travis there. "Hi, Danny," she said with a smile for her favorite bartender. Big and brawny, he was of Hawaiian descent with an easy smile and laid-back island demeanor. He did, however, keep an eye on things and wouldn't hesitate to muscle someone out of the bar if need be.

"Wow, look at you," he said with a confused grin. "Did Max finally get you to take a day off?"

"Not exactly. I'm babysitting," she grumbled and slid onto a cane-backed bar stool, ignoring a couple of admiring glances. Since it was early by vacation standards, most everyone was sleeping off the night before. Max had informed her that Moonlight Madness had been a bit crazy last night so the pool crowd would probably be a bit thin.

"Who are you babysitting?"

Krista crooked a finger for Danny to come closer. "Travis Mackey."

"The country singer?"

Krista nodded but put a finger to her lips. Leaning in, she said, "Keep it on the down-low. He's here for a little R & R before his band arrives. I'm posing as his girlfriend to keep the women at bay. Hopefully, he's smart enough to leave the cowboy hat off and hide his face with a ball cap and sunglasses or something."

"Gotcha covered," Danny said. "But he's pretty big time. I'm surprised he doesn't have a slew of bodyguards hanging around."

"His crew arrives next week. Max beefed up security and Mackey's manager has a couple of people here as well. Even though he doesn't know it, he's being watched. But still, keep your eyes open, okay?"

"Sure."

Krista smiled. "Thanks. Now, could you whip up a couple of piña coladas? Oh, and put a big, pink umbrella in Mackey's."

Danny's dark eyebrows shot up. "Is he . . . ?"

Krista smiled. "No, he's not gay. He'd much rather have a frosty beer, I'm quite sure."

"You've lost me."

"Just a little payback."

Danny started pouring ingredients into a big blender. "Whatever. Two piña coladas coming right up."

"Make them stiff, Danny. I'm going to need it to pull this off."

Danny grinned. "You got it."

*chapter
five*

A fter a brief soak in the hot tub to relax his stiffened leg muscles, Travis towel-dried off and slipped on some flip-flops, a blue baseball cap turned backward, and his favorite Oakleys. Glancing over at the sofa, he realized that he really was beat. The smart thing would have been to take a long afternoon nap, but he supposed he hadn't exactly been thinking with his brain. Travis had half a notion to call the whole damned thing off, but the urge to see Krista won out over a nap, and that was saying something since he felt bone-weary.

Travis walked down the path paved with sand and pine needles, smiling when a little green lizard scurried for cover. The sea-scented air was heavy with humidity, making sweat trickle down his back. A frosty beer and a dip in the pool suddenly sounded pretty good. He hoped that he blended in with the other tourists and since this was such an upscale resort he thought it was likely that not too many people would recognize him. Although the country-music audience was growing, these rich yuppies weren't exactly his fan base. While his agent had been thrilled to score this gig, Travis was a little nervous that his music wouldn't go over with the designer-wearing, imported-beer-drinking crowd. While Travis loved a challenge, he hoped he wouldn't get booed off the damned stage.

"Don't even think about it," he mumbled under his breath. He had a few days to just chill and that's what he was going to do . . . *if* he could remember how. The past year had been a crazy, meteoric rise to the top of the country-music charts and in truth he hadn't been physically ready for it. After his bull-riding wreck, playing his guitar and writing songs had kept him sane throughout the months of grueling physical therapy. When his agent from his PBR days, Nick Tackett, insisted on sending out demo tapes Travis had agreed, never imagining that he would land a recording contract or that his first CD would go double platinum. Having a crowd of screaming fans singing along to songs he had written was still a surreal feeling. While it wasn't quite the adrenaline rush he felt when sitting on the back of a muscle-bound bull as the chute opened, it was pretty damned amazing, but also exhausting.

Travis entered the huge courtyard and paused to admire the glistening beach-entry pool. Sunbathers were quickly snatching white lounge chairs surrounding the pool in neat rows. Piped-in calypso music played softly in the background and the smell of coconut-scented lotion mixed with the balmy sea breeze. Cabana boys scurried here and there with drink-laden trays.

Travis smiled. Maybe this was a good idea after all.

Looking around, he spotted the thatched roof of the tiki bar and headed that way. *Ahh,* a cold beer was calling his name. A big Hawaiian bartender gave him a nod before turning to pour rum into a big blender with a delicate flourish at odds with his size.

Glancing around, Travis took a moment to realize that the blond sitting at the bar was Krista. She sipped a huge frozen drink from a bent straw while being chatted up by some GQ-looking dude. Sitting sideways on the bar stool, she looked sexy as hell with her hair pulled back in a messy ponytail. She wore some silky-looking cover-up that was belted around her waist but that gaped to show off her tanned legs. GQ dude leaned in close and said something in her ear that made her smile.

With his tattered baseball cap, worn board shorts, and necklace of vintage puka shells, Travis felt like a bum next to Mr. Smooth Talker. With a tired sigh, he sorely wished he had just stayed back at the beach house and napped. He didn't need this, he decided, and turned to go, thinking he should call Nick Tackett and tell him to get him the hell off this island of yuppie jackasses. The fact that it bothered him to see Krista with another man bugged the crap out of him as well. He barely knew the woman and he had the sudden jealous urge to march over there and jack Smooth Talker's jaw. He was just about to make his exit before he did something really stupid when he heard Krista call out to him.

"Hey!" Krista spotted Travis out of the corner of her eye. She had started to think she had been stood up and was really glad to see him. This dude with his worn-out pickup lines was getting on her nerves. Funny because he was actually her usual type but somehow seemed so smarmy compared to Travis. *Why* she was comparing him to Travis bothered her a bit but she shook it off. "Come on over!" Krista called with a wave, not wanting to use his name. He clearly hesitated, which made her stomach do a crazy little disappointed lunge, but then came walking her way.

Krista tried to look cool and collected but Travis made her heart race as he approached. There was nothing smooth about Travis Mackey. His blue ball cap was a bit battered and he had dark stubble shadowing his jaw. His board shorts, with a blue-and-white surf pattern, were frayed at the hem and slung low on his lean hips. With his linebacker shoulders and the dark hair on his chest, the pretty boys at the bar paled in comparison. Oh no, Travis Mackey looked rough and ready, definitely all male . . .

Which is why it delighted her to hand him the frozen piña colada in the curvy hurricane glass sporting a pink umbrella and a big hunk of pineapple hooked on the side for garnish. "Here you go," she cooed. "Just what you ordered up."

He looked at the glass as if she had just handed him a snake and it was all Krista could do not to laugh. She wished she could see his eyes behind his dark sunglasses. She knew, however, that although the drink looked harmless, Danny had loaded it with rum. Krista had consumed most of hers, which had made her feel uncharacteristically mellow but had also made her itch to have a little fun. "Aren't you going to take a sip?" She sucked on her pineapple wedge and gave him an innocent lift of her eyebrows.

"Sure," Travis chased the straw with his tongue and the paper umbrella poked at his sunglasses but he finally managed a swallow. He coughed and then said with a good-natured grin, "Now that's a damned fine drink."

GQ dude gave Krista a curious look and asked, "Uh, are you with *him?*" He gave Travis a sidelong glance and turned back to Krista with a you've-got-to-be-kidding twist of his lips.

Krista almost laughed out loud. While this guy was the typical successful executive type who frequented Wild Ride, he still probably made only a fraction of the money that Travis raked in. Oh, how she wished she could say who Travis really was.

"You *sure* you wouldn't like to hook up later?" He looked at Travis and then back at her with a confident grin.

"She's sure so y'all just better back off," Travis said firmly.

GQ dude raised one eyebrow at Travis. "I wasn't asking *you.*"

Krista swallowed. This wasn't good. Even holding the piña colada Travis looked ready to deck the guy, not that she could blame him. She flicked Danny a glance and was relieved to see that he was standing with his hands on the bar, poised to intervene. But even though Danny could handle the situation Krista didn't want it to come to that. She took two steps toward Travis, closing the gap between them, while trying to think of a distraction. In a moment of inspiration, she wrapped her arms around his waist, rose up on tiptoe, and kissed him.

The instant sizzle surprised her, starting where her mouth met his mouth and curling slowly to her toes. Travis tasted of pineapple and coconut . . . sweet heat and temptation. Krista had the urge to lean in and rub her body sensuously against his but she suddenly remembered she was standing in the middle of the tiki bar surrounded by people and pulled back. She turned to Danny and raised her glass. "Keep them coming. We're going to chill by the pool."

"I'm on it," Danny said with a nod.

After slinging her beach bag over her shoulder, Krista gave GQ dude a dismissive little wave of her fingers. "Follow me," she said to Travis, who was discreetly trying to leave his drink on the bar. "Oh, do bring your drink. It's starting to really heat up." Without waiting for an answer Krista found two vacant lounge chairs and tossed a towel on each chair. "How's this?"

"Fine, I guess," Travis said and sat down on the lounge chair. He looked a little uneasy holding the piña colada but then took a long pull on the straw. "So just what was that all about back there?"

"What?" Her heart skipped a beat and she spent way too long arranging her towel on the chair.

"The kiss, Krista."

"Oh, *that*. I was just performing my job, nothing more. Don't read anything more into it, okay?"

"Okay," he said but his slow nod and the slight twitch of his lips said that he didn't quite believe her.

Krista narrowed her eyes at him, deciding that it was time to put her plan into action. She reminded herself that her game plan was to be a tease while playing up the gushing-girlfriend routine, but now that it was time to drop her cover-up she was feeling self-conscious about the teeny bikini. She didn't really know why. The resort was full of bikini-clad women so she hardly stood out. But still, she was thinking she would leave her cover-up on for a while when she noticed Travis eyeballing a tall redhead in a thong.

Downing the rest of her slushy drink she waited for Travis to tear his gaze from the woman's ass and decided it was time to kick her plan into high gear. She needed to teach this arrogant cowboy a lesson. What lesson she wasn't quite sure but he needed to be taught . . . *something*.

Travis had been battling brain freeze from sucking down his girlie drink hoping there was enough rum in it to calm his nerves. He was already onto Krista's plan. Her parting comment about not getting anything up but his hopes meant that she was probably going to tease him until he was begging for mercy . . . not that he didn't deserve it. This whole posing-as-his-girlfriend scenario was a bit demeaning and uncalled-for and he should have put an end to it before it even began. God, and *then* he had to make the stupid bikini comment. Yeah, he deserved whatever she was going to dish out . . . he just wasn't sure if he was going to be able to take it. One little ol' kiss had just about buckled his damned knees. Maybe he should just stop staring off into space and apologize.

After taking a deep breath, Travis turned to face her but whatever he was going to say melted from his still half-frozen brain. Okay, there were women everywhere in itty-bitty bikinis, but somehow the sight of *her* in one rendered him speechless. She was petite but had the type of slim, feminine figure that totally turned him on. Miss Priss had somehow morphed into his ultimate fantasy.

"Would you mind doing my back?" she asked in a sex-kitten purr.

"Sure," Travis answered, trying to sound bored. Her

voice might be soft and sexy but the straight set of her back screamed that she was trying to turn him on so she could turn him down. She sat down in front of him on the lounge chair and bent forward.

"Won't this oil make you fry?"

"It's got sunscreen in it and it makes my skin supple and soft. Be generous, now. Don't you just love the smell?"

"Yeah," Travis said absently. He'd let her try but he wasn't about to let her win this little game. The harder she tried to turn him on the less interested he would pretend to be . . . but *God,* if he could pull this off he deserved an Oscar instead of a Grammy.

He squirted some of the sun-warmed, coconut-scented oil into the palms of his hands and rubbed it onto her shoulders. Her skin *was* supple and soft and although she might have some curves, she was toned and firm with a golden touch-me tan. He moved his oiled hands down her back, loving the slick feel of his hands on her body, but made quick work of it, wanting her to think that he was totally unaffected when he was anything but. The feminine curve of her back and the flare of her hips had Travis counting back from one hundred in his head in a huge effort not to press his mouth to her neck and reach around to cup her breasts.

"Thanks." She reached for the bottle but instead of moving to her own lounge chair she remained between his thighs and began slathering oil onto her legs and then her arms. Mesmerized, Travis watched her golden skin begin to glisten. He sucked in his breath when she leaned back to do her torso, bringing the delicate curve of her neck *so* very close to his mouth. Inching forward, Travis almost gave in to the urge to wrap his arms around her, but she suddenly got up from the chair and turned to him with a smile that made him swallow. He just knew that the torture was far from being over.

"Okay, your turn. Scoot up so I can get behind you and do your back."

"I'm fine. I don't burn."

Krista clicked her tongue. "You don't want to ruin that nice tan of yours by burning and peeling. Come on. Scoot."

With a sigh, Travis moved forward, giving her room to straddle the chair behind him. When she began spreading the warm oil over his shoulders he had to hold back a moan. Of course, whereas *he* had done his job quickly, Krista lingered, moving her hands slowly over his shoulders and down his biceps. She took her sweet time on his back, moving up and down until he was gritting his teeth. Travis picked up the rest of his girlie drink and chugged it, hoping to cool off his overheated body.

No such luck.

Her hands suddenly stilled at the bottom of his back. "My God, what happened to you?"

Travis felt her trace the jagged scar with her fingertip. "Barbosa got me."

"I'm guessing Barbosa is a bull."

Travis chuckled. "Yeah, a damned mean one."

"I thought you guys wore vests."

Travis nodded and said over his shoulder, "We do, but they don't always get the job done. Barbosa threw me after about three seconds. I landed facedown in the dirt and had the wind knocked out of me so I wasn't able to immediately get the hell out of there like you're supposed to do. Before the bullfighter could run him off he somehow gouged me beneath my vest. Then, to add insult to injury, he tossed me in the air about fifteen feet."

"Good God!" She traced the scar again. "How many stitches did you get?"

"Twenty-eight stitches, a concussion, and a dislocated right shoulder."

"Didn't you wear a helmet?"

Travis shook his head.

Krista sucked in a breath. "Well, just why not?"

"I'm a cowboy. I wear a cowboy hat." Travis was glad the she couldn't see his grin. A little bit of a Southern twang had crept into her voice. She was letting her guard down and he liked it. "It's a tradition to toss your hat into the air if you cover the bull."

"Cover?"

"Hang on for the required eight seconds. Tossing a helmet in the air just isn't the same."

"Yeah, but a lot safer." She rubbed more oil on his back even though he was more than greased up.

Travis shrugged again. "It's part of the allure. People come to watch for the element of danger. They don't call it the toughest sport on dirt for nothin'."

"Is that why you did it? For the rush?"

"I did it to save my father's ranch. Only the top bull riders make good money," he answered and then wondered why he admitted that little-known fact. He supposed that he didn't want her to think he was just some hotshot trying to impress people, the way most people thought he was. His badass reputation had made him a PBR champion and had gotten him a sponsor and endorsements but it was just an act. Travis sighed. When was the last time he had just been himself?

Her hands went still once again. "Weren't you scared?" she asked softly.

Travis was about to give her one of the cocky answers that he had perfected over the years, but instead he swung his leg over the lounge chair to face her. "Yeah, climbing on the back of a big bull used to scare the hell out of me but nothing compares to getting up and singing in front of a screaming crowd of people. I just about toss my cookies before each concert."

"You're kidding."

"I have no idea why I just told you that but it's the God's honest truth. Now that you know that I'm a big wuss, I think I'll just go do a big cannonball into the pool."

Krista put a hand on his shoulder. "Being afraid and doing something anyway is called bravery, Travis."

Not knowing what to say, Travis just shrugged his shoulders. He had always been uncomfortable with admiration or flattery and yet it somehow pleased him that she thought something good of him. "Have I finally impressed you, Krista?"

She angled her head at him and then gave him a real smile. "A little."

Travis grinned. "Just get a load of this cannonball and you'll really be impressed." Taking off his ball cap and sunglasses, Travis jogged over to the deep end of the pool and jumped in with his legs tucked beneath him, creating a huge splash. But when he looked at Krista, hoping for a laugh, her head was bent while she talked on her cell phone. He noticed her look around a bit frantically and then she hurried over to the pool and dove in.

Travis waited by the side of the pool for her to swim over to him. "Something wrong?" he asked with a frown.

She pushed wet hair from her face and then said, "Danny called my cell and said that a group of women think that they may have spotted you and the word is spreading like wildfire."

"Okay, now what?"

"Quick! Follow me. I have a hiding place."

❧ chapter six

Krista swiftly swam over to a small waterfall at the far corner of the pool. The water spilled over from an upper-level fountain that fed into the main swimming pool. Grabbing Travis's hand she dove beneath the water and surfaced behind the cascade. Barely enough room for two people, it was the perfect hiding spot.

"We can stay here for a while," she said over the hiss and gurgle of the water.

"Can you stand?" Travis asked.

Krista shook her head while treading water. The depth was over her five-foot-three-inch height.

"Well, then hang on to me," he said into her ear.

Krista wrapped her arms around his neck. "Sorry, it sucks to be short."

"I'm not complaining," he answered close to her ear.

Neither was she. She had to admit that it felt good to be in his arms. Sunlight shimmered through the cascading water but the shaded little cocoon provided welcome relief from the tropical heat. Water lapped against them, causing Krista to sway sensuously against Travis. "Sorry."

"I'm still not complaining."

"We shouldn't have to—" she began just as he turned his head to say something. Her mouth grazed across the rough stubble on his cheek and then brushed against the contrasting softness of his mouth.

"Sorry," he said gruffly.

"I'm not complaining," she said with a shy smile.

He grinned back. Water made his lashes spiky and his wet hair curled over his ears. His grin faded and he looked into her eyes. "Kiss me, Krista."

Krista somehow knew that kissing this cowboy again would send her over the edge of reason and yet she couldn't help herself. Wrapping her legs around his waist, she dipped her head and pressed her lips to his, intending a soft, sweet kiss, but the touch of his tongue to hers sent a jolt of white-hot desire through her veins that had her wanting much more. With a little moan Krista opened her mouth and kissed him deeply.

His lips were soft and yet firm and his mouth was hot and hungry. Threading her fingers through his wet hair, Krista melted against him, loving the feel of her barely covered breasts pressed to the firmness of his chest. The water lapped over her shoulders, sliding over her oil-covered skin. Travis licked her bottom lip and then moved his mouth to her neck where he kissed and nibbled until Krista arched her back, offering him more bare skin.

"God . . . Krista." With his teeth he tugged on the bow tied around her neck and her breasts tumbled free. Scooting her up higher on his waist, Travis braced her back with his hands and then watched the spray from the waterfall sluice over her bare breasts. He licked one breast and then the other before taking one nipple into his mouth, where he teased it with the tip of his tongue. God, how he wanted Krista completely naked so he could taste her *everywhere* and then bury himself deep. But he reminded himself that although they were hidden from view, they were in a public place and could conceivably be caught any moment now. With that thought in mind he reluctantly removed his mouth. "Krista," he said gruffly in her ear, "we've got to stop before I'm out of control. You're driving me wild."

Krista pulled back and suddenly gave him an oh-God-what-am-I-doing look. She yanked her swimsuit back into place. "Wow, how did we let things go so far? There are people just a few feet away." She avoided his eyes while retying the knot around her neck.

"It's okay to get caught up in the moment. To let yourself go."

She flashed him a look. "I like to be in control."

Travis sighed. Her guard was right back in place but the slight tremble of her fingers told him that she wasn't nearly as in control as she wanted to be.

"I'm going to go out and see if the coast is clear. I'll be back."

"Krista—" he began, but she slipped from his grasp, dove into the water, and disappeared. Travis smacked the water with this fist, thinking that he didn't need this kind of distraction or complication in a life that was already too damned complicated.

After waiting a few minutes for Krista to return, Travis finally muttered, "Screw it." He decided to just swim out

of there and hightail it back to the beach house to rest as
he should have done in the first place. Taking a deep
breath, he dove beneath the waterfall and surfaced in the
pool.

"There he is!" A bikini-clad female pointed in his direction, drawing the attention of several others who
shrieked and jumped into the pool.

"Holy shit." Travis dove beneath the surface and
swiftly swam back to the waterfall so that he disappeared
from view. A moment later Krista popped up next to him.

"I told you to stay put!" She trod water next to him,
glaring.

"You were gone forever!"

"Hellooow! That's because we have a bit of a situation
on our hands. Danny alerted me that you had been spotted and let me tell you, cowboy, it's creating quite a stir."

"Okay, so, now what?"

"We chill here for a few minutes and hope that no one
discovers us. Danny is going to create a diversion and
then we'll make our escape." She frowned at him and
asked, "Does this, like, happen a lot?"

"All the time," he lied.

She rolled her eyes.

"Okay, not *all* the time."

"They were screaming. God, what an embarrassment
to my gender."

"Oh yeah? I bet I could make you scream."

"In your dreams, cowboy."

Travis chuckled. "Are you going to tread water forever
or come over here and hold on to me?"

"Tread water forever."

"Don't be stupid," he said and pulled her over to him.

Krista put her arms around his neck but remained as stiff as a board. After a moment of awkward silence she said, "About what happened before, it was—"

"Spontaneous and amazing?"

"I was going to say *unprofessional*."

"Okay, unprofessional and amazing."

"Unprofessional and not going to happen again. I'm just going to perform my job from now on."

"I'd rather that you'd kiss my mouth than kiss my ass."

She narrowed her eyes at him.

"Okay, you can kiss me wherever you like."

Krista splashed him. "I'm serious, Travis."

"Well, don't be. Let's just kick back and have some fun."

"Mr. Mackey," she began in a prim little voice, "I know that you're probably used to getting whatever you want from women but I'm not about to be your booty call while you're on this island. There are plenty of other women more than willing to kick back and have some *fun* with you. I'm serious when I say that we need to keep our relationship on a professional level."

Given the fact that they were beneath a waterfall with her arms and legs wrapped around him, Travis found her speech rather amusing. Knowing that she'd get ticked, he tried to hold back a smile but failed.

"You're laughing at me," she said and pushed at his shoulders.

"Sorry, but the whole booty-call phrase got me."

"I was trying to make a point," Krista said with a lift of her chin. If she *were* to be honest she would have to admit that the situation that they were in was rather comical. But being honest with herself would mean acknowledging that she wanted to lean in and close the mere inches that separated her mouth from his.

"You want to kiss me," he said in her ear, as if reading her thoughts.

"You are so full of yourself, cowboy."

Travis was about to make a flippant reply when he suddenly wondered if there was some truth to her accusation. "You're right, maybe I am." Although he was trying his damnedest to stay grounded, it was getting harder and harder not to get swept up in the whole celebrity thing. Fatigue suddenly washed over him and he sighed.

Krista angled her head, giving him a curious look. "Listen, I was out of line with that comment."

Travis shook his head. "No, you weren't. I shouldn't be hitting on you and making a general jackass out of myself."

Krista nodded. "I wasn't behaving the way I should have either. What do you say we call a truce and start over?" She unhooked one arm from around his neck and offered her hand. "Deal?"

Travis nodded and grasped her hand. "Here's to total professionalism."

"Great," she said brightly. "I'm glad we got that out in the open. Things will be so much easier this way. Really they will. You just wait and see." She pumped his hand so hard that she was splashing water all over the place while protesting a thousand times too much to be believable. Miss Priss was way more attracted to him than she wanted to admit. But Travis was a man of his word, so he would keep their relationship strictly business if that's what she wanted. It wasn't going to be easy but neither was riding a bull or singing for thousands of people. He could do this. Really, he could . . . but not with her cling-ing to him in a tiny bikini beneath a waterfall.

"We should make a run for it," Travis said.

"You mean a swim for it?" she asked with a smile that made him want to kiss her all over again. "Okay, Danny is probably creating some commotion as we speak over at the tiki bar so we need to go in the opposite direction. I know a shortcut through the woods to the beach house. Are you ready?"

Travis nodded. Oh, he was more than ready. One more second and he would have to kiss her and he had just promised to keep his hands to himself. "Let's go."

"Okay, follow me."

Travis dove beneath the water and followed Krista to the opposite edge of the pool. Some shouts over by the tiki bar indicated that Danny was indeed creating a diversion.

"This way," Krista whispered and grabbed his hand. They jogged over to the woods leading to the beach house and hurried down the sandy path. She giggled as they ran and Travis loved the sound of her carefree laughter. When they arrived at the house they were both breathless and laughing.

"Would you like to come inside for some lunch?" Travis asked when they reached the back steps.

"I should go."

Disappointment smacked him in the gut but he nod-ded. "Okay."

"But if there is anything that you need, just call my cell."

"Okay," he repeated.

She turned to go but then turned back to him with a grin. "Sorry I made you drink the piña colada."

Travis smiled. "Don't tell anyone but I kinda liked that girlie drink."

"Well, I should go."

"Krista . . ." He took a step closer.

"Don't, Travis." She put a hand on his chest. "There are so many reasons why we shouldn't get something started."

He nodded, "Yeah, but none of them seem to matter right now." He put a finger beneath her chin, forcing her to meet his gaze. "Besides, we've already got something started, like it or not. I know you feel it too."

"I won't deny that, Travis." Her bottom lip trembled. "But you'll be leaving here in a few weeks. And then what?"

He shrugged. "I have breaks in my schedule. You could—"

"Stop." She put a finger to his lips. "I know what it feels like when someone you love walks in and out of your life because something else means more. Music is your life, Travis. I could never compete with that."

Travis closed his eyes and swallowed. "I'm not lookin' for, what did you call it?"

"A booty call?" Her laughter gurgled with unshed tears. "I know. It would be easier if you were. We need to end this before we both get hurt."

Travis nodded. He already cared too much about her to hurt her. "Okay."

She gave him another trembling smile that tore at his heart and then turned and walked away. He watched her go until she disappeared from his line of vision. With a tired sigh he walked up the steps and into the cool interior of the beach house, feeling such a sense of loss that he wondered if it was all worth it.

chapter
seven

A foul mood hovered over Travis like smoke in a honky-tonk bar, making him tired and more than a little cranky. The rehearsal seemed to last a lifetime and to make matters worse, it was hotter than blue blazes and it wasn't yet noon. His T-shirt was plastered to his sunburned back, his shoulder had started to throb, and he had the mother of all hangovers from drinking too much of some rum concoction with his band over in Max's Moonlight Madness last night. Not that he hadn't had fun, but he was paying the price, big time.

Looking around, he noticed several of his band members looking a little green around the gills. "Hey boys, let's take a break. We know this damned show inside out anyway."

"I won't argue that," said Brody Baker, his wild and crazy bass player. Brody was hell on wheels both on and off the stage, but even he was under the weather. "I'm going to snag one of those sub sandwiches that pretty little Krista brought over a little while ago. Damn, that woman is super-fine."

"Stay away from her," Travis growled as he sat down on the edge of the stage with an icy-cold bottle of water.

Brody raised both palms in the air. "Whoa there, big boy. You got dibs on her?"

"Just leave her the hell alone." Travis put the plastic bottle to his lips and guzzled most of the water.

Brody unscrewed his own bottle of water while eyeing Travis. "We're all hung over, but damn, who pissed in your Cheerios?"

Travis flipped Brody the bird just as Krista arrived driving a golf cart. After bringing the cart to a smooth stop she looked his way while his middle finger was still directed at Brody. Quickly lowering his hand, Travis was embarrassed as hell, but Krista only spared him a brief glance before going about her task of tossing bottles of water into a huge cooler. He angled his head, watching as she bent over, admiring her cute butt. She looked cool and beautiful in cuffed white shorts and a lime green halter top. Her golden hair was pulled back into a ponytail, reminding him of how her hair had felt brushing over his bare chest. Travis glared at Brody, who looked ready to swallow his tongue.

"Hey, I'm only lookin'," Brody protested. "You into this chick?"

He shrugged. "She's off-limits."

Brody chuckled. "Oh, did the mighty Travis Mackey get turned down? I'm lovin' it."

Travis flipped him off again just as Krista looked their way. She gave him a disapproving frown. "Dammit, Brody. I oughta kick your ass."

Brody laughed as he walked over to a table laden with food. "Come on over and eat. You'll feel better."

"In a minute," Travis answered, trying to decide whether to approach Krista or not. She had been on his brain nonstop for the past couple of days. By the time he had decided to approach her she had turned away and hopped back into the golf cart. "Well, damn."

Brody plopped down next to him and handed him a sandwich. "Ham and cheese. Eat it."

Travis nodded glumly and unwrapped the sub. He took a big bite while watching Krista drive past them. She gave him an abstract wave that had Travis wanting to torpedo his sandwich at her.

"If you want her, why don't you go after her?" Brody asked.

Travis shrugged. "She made it crystal-clear that she doesn't want to get something started."

"And you're letting that lame proclamation stop you?"

"Aw, come on, Brody. Krista is one of those uppity chicks who turns her nose up at country music and washed-up bull riders," he lied. "You know me. I like a woman who will ride on the back of a Harley with me. Krista Ross on the back of a bike? She might break a nail," he scoffed, but the thought of her arms wrapped around his waist while they rode down a long, winding country road almost made him moan.

Brody scratched at his three-day blond stubble. "You just might be underestimating her. I think she's tougher than she looks. *Damn* she's hot. You know, I'll give you another day and if you don't make a move, I'm gonna be all over her."

"The hell you will."

"You afraid she might not turn Brody Baker down? You might be the lead singer, but chicks dig bass players."

"I'm warning you, Brody."

"Then get up off your sorry ass and go after her."

Travis took a long pull from his water bottle and said, "There's lots of women on this island. I don't need the kind of complications being with her would cause me."

Brody frowned. "I thought maybe this was a business-and-pleasure conflict. I sense something more than that. Spill."

"I don't want to go into it." Travis slapped his thigh. "This is damned stupid. I've got a show to perform in a few days and a photo shoot on the beach. You know how I hate those damned things. I don't need or want any distractions. I came here to end the tour and then chill for a few weeks so I could write some songs before starting the whole process over again. End of story."

Brody ran his fingers through his choppy shoulder-length blond hair while eyeing Travis.

"What?" Travis barked.

"Maybe you do need a distraction. You know, bro, the past couple of years have been tough. A little TLC might be just what the doctor ordered. Seriously, Travis, you push yourself too hard sometimes. If you dig this Krista chick, then go for it." Brody wagged his eyebrows. "I've seen her checking you out."

"Liar," he growled but his stomach did a little flip-flop that had nothing to do with being hung over.

Brody shrugged as he polished off his sandwich. "I know what I see and she was checkin' you out."

"Really?" Travis was ridiculously pleased at the thought.

"I'm tellin' ya," he said around his mouthful of sandwich. "I know this because I've been checkin' *her* out."

Travis gave him a glare of warning.

"She only has eyes for you, bro. The two of you should quit your pussyfootin' around and hop in the sack."

"Krista's not a one-night-stand kind of girl."

"And you know this how?"

"Some things you just know."

Brody grinned. "I wasn't talkin' about just one night. You're gonna be here for a while. Give it a whirl."

Travis shook his head. "She's not going to get involved with the likes of me."

"The likes of you? You're fucking rich and famous."

Travis shrugged. "Does she seem impressed?"

Brody tossed his water bottle into the trash and then shook his head at Travis. "You haven't been listening to me. She looks at you like you're a hot-fudge sundae."

Travis laughed. "A hot-fudge sundae?"

"Hey, I'm hung over too. It's the best my brain can do."

Travis plucked at his shirt while wiggling his shoulders.

"Why are you so doggone twitchy?"

"Damned sunburn."

"You'd better put somethin' on that."

Travis pushed up to his feet. "It's kind of hard to put lotion on your own back. And no, I'm not letting you."

"I wasn't offerin'." Brody scratched his chin and said, "I think maybe that's a job for pretty little Krista. Don't ya think? You'd have to take off your shirt. Flex them muscles that all the girls go goo-goo over."

"Like you don't work out."

"Only because that trainer from hell who follows us

everywhere makes me. Damn, he caught me with a Snickers last night and grabbed the doggone thing right out of my mouth. I would've fought him for it, but he's built like a frigging refrigerator."

Travis grimaced. "Ah, you had to remind me. I've got a session with Victor when we're finished. I have rehab plus a workout, so don't complain." He rubbed his shoulder just thinking about the pain he was about to endure. The workouts he didn't mind, but the rehab sucked. "Come on, let's get this rehearsal over with."

By the end of the day Travis was totally beat and his grumpiness had taken a turn for the worse. Victor had worked him like a dog while chastising him for the excessive drinking the night before, asking him why he would want to pollute his body like that. At six foot six, Victor looked like a middle linebacker for the NFL and was also as gay as you could get. Victor believed that his body was his temple and never put anything unhealthy past his lips and fully expected the band to do the same. While Travis understood that being a country star involved more than just the music, he felt compelled to indulge in some pure decadence once in a while.

After a long hot shower, Travis tugged on a pair of worn gray sweatpants, leaving off his shirt since his sunburned back felt tight and itchy. Too tired to cook, he tossed a salad and then sat down at the small kitchen table. He was munching on the greens halfheartedly when he heard a soft knock at the door. He dabbed at his mouth with a paper napkin as he scooted back from the table, hoping that the visitor wasn't a fan. Most guys in his position would have a bodyguard staying with them, but Travis refused, wanting his privacy. Krista had promised to keep his whereabouts secret, but that information had a way of getting out.

Padding across the cool tiled floor on bare feet, he opened the door. "Krista?" He blinked at her in surprise.

Thrusting a plastic bottle at him, she said, "I was told that you needed some aloe for a sunburn."

"Oh, uh, thanks." Brody. Travis didn't know whether to be grateful or ticked at his friend's interference.

She nodded and gave him a cool smile. "Well, if there's nothing else . . ."

"Well, actually, uh, would you mind putting it on my back?" He turned around in the doorway for her to see the pink skin. "It hurts. Makes it hard to sleep."

"Why didn't you use sunscreen?"

"I did. I just couldn't reach my back." He jammed a thumb over his shoulder. "Would you, please?"

She stood there for a long moment and Travis thought she was going to refuse but then she gave him a jerky nod.

"Thanks. You're an angel." Travis gave her his best grin and suddenly started to perk up. With a wave of his hand he said, "Come in."

She breezed by him, leaving a light, floral scent in her wake. Travis inhaled and it suddenly dawned on him that he was living in *her* house. A hint of that same perfume was in the bed where he slept, in the bathroom. "This is your place, isn't it?"

Krista whirled around with an expression of surprise.

"It smells like you," he explained, his voice more husky than it should have been. "I'm sorry I kicked you out of your home."

She shrugged. "No problem."

"I can move into the hotel."

She smiled then. It was a genuine smile that took his breath away. Then she said, "You're a nice guy, Travis, but no thank you. I've got a suite in the hotel."

Travis took a step toward her. "If I'm so nice, then why are you avoiding me?"

"You know why. Let's not go there, Travis. Now turn around and let me do your back," Krista said, trying not to be affected by him. *This is business. Keep it that way.* "This will be cold, but will help. It's pure aloe." She squirted a dollop into her hand and gently smoothed the sticky gel onto his back.

"God almighty!" Travis arched his back. "That feels like an ice cube."

"Don't be a baby," she scoffed but had to grin. "I'll try to warm it up in my hands."

"Ahh!" He shivered. "This is torture."

"You should have used sunscreen! I'm sure you could have found a more-than-willing female to rub you down with lotion."

He turned around to face her. "The only woman on my mind is you. Krista, I can't get you out of my head."

"Sounds like you're quoting lyrics from one of your songs," she said, trying to sound flip, but her insides were turning to warm jelly.

"I'm not handing you a line."

She crooked an eyebrow at him.

"Well, maybe I am. Is it working?"

Like a charm. "No, I'm afraid not." Krista turned away from him and walked into the kitchen to wash the sticky aloe off her hands. She could feel that he was watching her and it made her feel jittery. Warm. She could have sent someone else over with the lotion, *should* have sent someone else over. But the sad truth was that she had wanted to see him, no, *needed* to see him. Krista took her time drying her hands and then inhaled a steadying breath before turning around.

Travis stood in the kitchen doorway with one shoulder leaning against the door frame. His arms were crossed and his bare feet were hooked at the ankles. He looked casual, relaxed. His worn gray sweatpants were slung low on his hips, several inches below his belly button leaving her no doubt that he wasn't wearing any underwear. One little tug on the drawstring and . . .

"Come here."

Krista shook her head. "I should go."

He sighed deeply. "Okay," he said softly.

"Travis," she began, but he held up his hand and she stopped talking. It was then that she noticed the faint dark smudges beneath his eyes. He looked weary. Worn out. And why not? He had barely recovered from his near-death bull-riding wreck before throwing himself into a singing career. Krista suddenly understood. She knew the feeling of going full throttle, never looking back . . . pushing . . . needing to succeed or maybe to prove something. But as she gazed over at him, she thought that maybe, just maybe it was time to ditch her childhood baggage, throw caution to the wind, and allow herself to fall in love.

Travis represented so much of what she had left behind, so much of what she missed. Dammit, she *did* like country music, wearing jeans, and eating moon pies. Krista grinned. And she sure liked cowboys.

Travis reached up and absently massaged his shoulder.

"You want me to rub that for you?"

He gave her a ghost of a grin.

"Your shoulder," Krista said, feeling her cheeks glow.

His smile faded. "I knew what you meant. You've made yourself quite clear where I'm concerned." He inclined his head and stared at his feet. "I'm sorry that I keep pushing. From now on, I'll back off."

Travis made his quiet promise without looking at her. She should just walk past him and out the door, but Krista was suddenly fed up with doing what she should do and she made a decision that had her heart beating like the wings of a hummingbird. "I could have had Paul bring the aloe over."

Travis's head snapped up.

Krista grinned. "He offered."

Travis blinked over at her, looking confused. "So why didn't you?"

Krista gazed over at Travis, feeling as if she were cresting the first hill of the Dolphin. *Don't look down and hold on tight.*

chapter eight

Travis kept his nonchalant pose of leaning against the doorjamb even though it was uncomfortable. His heart was beating like a snare-drum solo while he waited for Krista to answer. She looked as if she were ready to toss her cookies, but then her chin raised a notch and by God she started walking slowly toward him. Travis let his arms drop to his sides and he straightened up as she came closer . . . and closer. She stopped mere inches from him and tilted her face up.

"I have a confession," she said with a slow smile that turned him inside out.

Travis tried to think of a clever comeback, but he wasn't quite sure where she was going with this. So he merely raised one eyebrow in question.

"I burned your CD."

Okay, that was unexpected.

"And I listen to it all the time."

"All the time?" What was going on here? Was she flirting with him?

She nodded and placed her hands on his chest. "You've been singing me to sleep, Travis."

Okay, she *was* flirting. This was good. Very good. "You know burning CDs is against the law," he said in a mock-stern voice.

"Are you going to turn me in?" She caught her bottom lip between her teeth.

"I just might have to take the law into my own two hands."

She swirled one fingertip down his chest and over his abs, making his muscles quiver in response. "Go easy on me, okay?"

"Not a chance. You're gonna pay, big time, for your crime." He put a fake frown on his face and wrapped his hands around her waist, pulling her against him. The perfume that had been driving him nuts filled his head. "A kiss might soften me up a bit."

Krista had to come up on tiptoe to reach his mouth. Travis helped by bending his head toward hers. He threaded his fingers through her hair, cradling her head with the palm of his hand. Her lips were soft and pliant, warm and inviting. Travis teased her bottom lip with the tip of his tongue, going slow, savoring the taste of her. He slanted his head to the side, covering her mouth fully, deepening the tender kiss. When Krista wrapped her arms around his neck and leaned against him, desire flared, hot and potent.

Still kissing, they somehow stumbled from the kitchen into the living room and found their way to the sofa, nearly knocking over a lamp. Krista giggled as she all but fell on top of him, but then gasped, "Oh Travis, your shoulder!"

"My shoulder is fine," he assured her, running a fingertip down her cheek. "Unclip your hair," Travis said, half propped against the plump cushions.

Krista reached up and unhooked the barrette, letting her hair fall forward. Travis reached up and fingered a few strands. "Soft," he murmured, "and beautiful. Krista, kiss me again."

"Mmm, okay." She kissed his cheek and then his chin, loving the texture of his rough stubble against her tongue, the way it made his lips seem even more soft when she finally pressed her mouth to his. He groaned deep in his throat and wrapped his arms around her. Krista could feel the steely hardness of his arousal, and desire, sharp and intense, made her suck in a breath. Travis cupped her bottom, pressing her against him.

"Krista . . ."

"I want this, Travis. I want you."

He closed his eyes and swallowed. "You're sure?"

Krista pushed up from his chest. "I don't want this to be a casual thing. I'm not asking for a commitment, just for this to mean something to you."

"I'm not like that, Krista. The whole celebrity thing is bullshit. God, I hope you know that."

"I feel it." She ran her fingertip across his bottom lip. "I want to please you, but it's been a long time . . ." She felt unsure, shy.

"Krista, I think it's safe to say that you're going to please me. Just having you here pleases me."

Krista gave him a peck on the mouth. "You are such a good guy."

Travis rolled his eyes. "You make me sound pretty boring."

Krista chuckled. "Oh, I don't think you're boring. I'm just surprised at how down-to-earth you are. I fully expected you to be cocky, arrogant."

"I used to be. It's funny how almost getting trampled to death gives you a different perspective on life. I've been given a second chance, Krista. I don't take that lightly."

"You've worked hard to get where you are."

Travis nodded. "True. But I'm no longer reckless and I sure as hell don't take simple things like walking for granted. It's been a grueling, uphill climb, but I appreciate what I've got." He grinned. "That damned bull made me a better person."

"I'd still like to punch it in the nose," Krista said hotly.

Travis laughed. Her Southern drawl was bubbling to the surface. She was letting her guard down and he liked what he saw just as he'd known he would. He was going to make love to her slow and easy, like there was no tomorrow. He hadn't been joking when he said that he no longer took things for granted. He believed that everything happened for a reason. Travis was going to chase the wariness from her blue eyes . . . make her laugh, make her sigh. Krista Ross needed him; he felt it in his bones.

"I want to make love to you beneath the waterfall where we hid in the pool, Krista."

She nodded and then pushed up from his chest. When he stood up, she leaned against him and said shyly, "The pool is closed and everyone will be over at Moonlight Madness so we'll have privacy."

"Perfect. I've fantasized about making love to you there." He scooped her up into his arms.

"Travis, put me down! Your shoulder!"

"To hell with my shoulder. I want to carry you. Besides you don't weigh a thing."

"I do too!"

"Yeah, about a hundred pounds dripping wet." Okay, *that* was an image he really didn't need about now.

"Put me down, I mean it!" She wiggled in his arms until he relented.

"You're a bossy little thing," he said but leaned in for a quick kiss.

They hurried through the woods holding hands and laughing but when they arrived at the end of the path Krista tugged on his hand. "I don't think I can do this."

"The pool is closed, Krista."

She put her hands to her cheeks.

"Chicken," Travis taunted with a lift of one eyebrow.

"I'm *not* a chicken!"

He flapped his arms like wings.

"Stop!"

He bent his legs and did an imitation of a chicken walking.

Krista narrowed her eyes at him and then suddenly took off running. "Last one in is a rotten egg!" she called over her shoulder. She kicked off her sandals and dove into the deep end of the pool fully clothed. With a whoop, Travis followed, ignoring the pain in his leg as he ran after her.

They surfaced together just beyond the edge of the waterfall. Krista's laughter mingled with the sound of the rushing water. She wrapped her legs around his waist and asked, "How did you know calling me a chicken would work?"

Travis grinned and pushed wet hair out of her eyes. "Because you're feisty and stubborn and deep down you really wanted to do this."

"You mean *this?*," She slipped her arms around his neck and kissed him deeply while rocking her hips suggestively against his erection. He was still reeling from the kiss when she continued with a throaty, "And this?" She surprised him by sinking beneath the surface and tugged his sweatpants down to his ankles. He lifted his feet, allowing her to slip the heavy pants all the way off. She surfaced once and took a deep breath before slipping beneath the water again. Travis sucked in a breath when she hooked her legs through his, cupped her hands on his ass, and took his penis in her hot mouth.

Her blond hair fanned out in the water that glowed softly from an underwater light. Travis gripped the side of the pool. His heart pounded in his ears and his breath became deep and ragged as the pleasure built. The water rippled and lapped over his shoulders. She resurfaced once for air and then returned to work her magic until intense pleasure rolled over him like waves lapping to the shore.

Krista came up gasping for air.

"That was . . . incredible," Travis said with a weak laugh. *"You* are incredible."

With a shaky little laugh she said, "I can't believe I just did that. Cowboy, you are bringing out a naughty side of me that I never knew existed."

"Glad to be of service." After taking a deep, recovering breath, Travis said, "Hang on to the side of the pool."

Nodding, Krista did as he asked. While she bobbed in the water he peeled her wet shorts from her body and let them float away. While kissing her he toyed with her thong, slipping his finger over the tiny triangle of satin until she began to pant softly in his ear. Her green silk halter top molded to her body like second skin.

"You are so beautiful," he murmured, cupping her breasts with both of his hands. He kissed her tenderly, running the tip of his tongue over her bottom lip and then nipping at the plump fullness. Pulling back, he untied the wet silk from around her neck and peeled the fabric from her skin, sucking in a breath at the sight of her breasts. Lush, so full and firm and yet so soft . . . he cupped them lovingly while rubbing his thumbs over her beaded nipples.

"Wrap your legs around me," he said and then pivoted so that the waterfall washed over her shoulders and down her breasts. She arched her back, letting the water sluice over her. Her skin seemed to glow in the muted light and Travis thought it was the most erotically moving sight he had ever seen.

Travis turned into the cascading water, kissing her as the water poured over both of them before stepping just inches away and into the mist.

Krista clung to him and pleaded, "Travis, I need you inside me. Make love to me." She kissed the tender inside of his neck, loving the slippery feel of skinny-dipping.

Travis chuckled. "Then we're good to go?"

"Yes . . . please!" She playfully pounded on his shoulders. "Oh!" she exclaimed when he entered her with a long, smooth stroke. She gripped his shoulders and wrapped her legs around him. He helped by cupping her ass and thrusting upward while kissing her. He backed up into the waterfall letting the water spray over his shoulders and down his chest. Krista clung to him, arching her back so he could go even deeper. Pleasure, warm and liquid, pooled and spread like heated honey.

He murmured words of love in her ear, whiskey-rough, intensely sexy words that mingled with the hiss and splash of the water. Threading her fingers through his wet hair, Krista arched her back, giving him full access to her breasts. He sucked and licked while riding her slow and easy as if savoring each stroke. The fringes of an orgasm began to build. She gasped when he nipped hard on her nipple causing a short burst of pain that exploded into rippling waves of pleasure and took him right along with her.

"Travis!" His name was a throaty gasp. Still tingling, she clung to him, nuzzling her face into his neck while he was still buried deep within her. Still feeling little aftershocks of pleasure, she kissed his stubbled cheek. "That was . . . amazing . . . *beautiful.*"

His answer was a sweet, lingering kiss.

Travis knew in that shining moment that he loved her. Yes, it was too fast, too soon, and it would scare the hell out of her if he voiced his feelings, so he kept it to himself, hoping that he could think of a way to make it all work out. He stood there for a few minutes letting the water lap around them while he held her, loving the feel of her wrapped around him . . . never wanting to let her go.

"We have to go back," he reluctantly murmured into her ear.

She nodded into his neck.

"We're going to have to find our clothes."

She nodded again, seeming to be half asleep.

"Worn out?" Travis asked with a chuckle.

"Mmmmm, yes."

"Okay, you swim out to the edge of the pool and I'll find our clothes, okay?"

" 'Kay."

"Can you do this?"

"Think so."

Travis laughed and kissed her on the tip of her nose before they both dove beneath the water. He swam around until he located all their clothing but put the wet mess into a pile and then located the thick towels provided by the resort. After wrapping a towel around his waist, Travis went over to the side of the pool where Krista dangled tired and naked. Reaching down, he offered two helping hands and lifted her easily out of the water. He wrapped a towel around her and asked, "Can you walk?"

"Of course," she scoffed, but wobbled a bit.

"Sure you can," Travis said with a chuckle. He picked up the sopping pile of clothes and then put his arm around her waist.

They walked through the woods with only the moonlight for guidance. Music and laughter mixed with the sound of waves crashing to the shore reminded Travis that he was far from Nashville, but surely they could find a way to make this work. He just had to.

Krista was rather quiet and he wondered if she was thinking the same thing. They paused at the steps to the back porch. "You're coming in, right?"

She hesitated just a second but it was long enough to make Travis worry. "Sure." She smiled but there was something about the way she held the beach towel tightly against her body that spoke volumes to Travis. She was nervous. Skittish.

And it scared the hell out of him.

"How about a cold beer out here on the porch?"

She nodded. "Sounds good."

Travis smiled. I'll be back in a minute." He headed into the house. The longer he kept her here the more likely she would spend the night, which was what he ultimately hoped for. After uncapping the longneck bottles, he headed back outside and handed her one before joining her on the swing. She took a sip and curled up against him with her legs tucked up under her towel.

She seemed to relax and they sipped their beer in a companionable silence broken by sounds of the night. Bullfrogs croaked in the distance and the buzz and screech of insects mingled with the sounds of the sea. The tall skinny cypress trees whined and creaked in the sultry breeze.

"See any beady eyes out there?" Krista asked with a little shiver.

Travis tightened his arm over her shoulders. "Scared?"

"Not with you here."

Travis smiled into the darkness, ridiculously delighted that she thought he could protect her from things that go bump in the night. He chuckled when the thought occurred to him that he would slay a dragon for her.

"What?" She swirled her fingertips over his bare chest.

"Nothing."

"Tell me."

"Promise you won't laugh?"

"No."

"I was just thinking that I would slay a dragon to protect you," he said in a rush. "Well, the dragon would probably slay *me* but I would die trying. You asked. Go ahead. Laugh."

Krista's fingers stilled and she looked away. Travis felt a little surge of what-the-hell-did-I-do panic. He gently cupped her chin and tilted her face so that she had to look at him.

"Aw, damn, Krista." His heart turned over at the sight of a fat tear rolling down her cheek.

She swiped at the tear. "If you're messing with me, cowboy, I'll kick your ass."

Travis chuckled and she gave him a glare and a shove at his chest. "I mean what I say."

His grin faded. "So do I," he said softly, running a finger down her cheek. "You don't know me well enough to trust me, but we're going to change that."

"I'll warn you that it won't be easy."

"Neither is staying on a bucking bull for eight seconds. You'll find that I'm damned determined when I go after something."

A very slight smile tugged at the corners of her mouth. "So, are you going after me?"

He grinned. "Well, I've got a bum shoulder and a bad leg, but yeah. I'm going after you with all I got, Krista Ross. I'm just giving *you* fair warning."

Krista frowned. "Travis, you've got me feeling like I've just stepped off of the Dolphin."

"You mean that roller coaster that takes you smack-dab into the lobby of the hotel?"

She nodded, her blue eyes big with emotion.

"So, are you going to toss your cookies or get back on for another ride?"

"Both."

"Explain."

She took a deep breath and let it out. "I'm scared, excited." She smiled shyly. "A little weak-kneed. But I'm willing to get back on for another ride, Travis."

Willing to and *wanting to* were two very different things in Travis's way of thinking. Krista looked torn between wanting to bolt and wanting to kiss him. "Krista, I know I'm moving way too fast for your comfort zone. The last thing I want to do is to scare you off. Let's go for a soak in the hot tub with a couple of cold beers and then watch a movie or something. Low-key. No pressure. How's that sound?"

"Wonderful." She smiled, but then giggled.

"What?"

"I was just picturing you slaying a dragon."

Travis chuckled. "You're never gonna let me forget that one, are you?"

⟋ chapter
nine

After a long soak in the hot tub, Travis announced that he was starving. Krista decided that there was nothing sexier than watching a man grill a burger in the moonlight. Of course, the fact that he was shirtless, wearing a beach towel slung low on his hips, helped in the very-sexy department. He hummed while he worked, pausing to take long pulls from his beer bottle. Krista was content to watch him from her lounge chair, sipping on her own frosty beer. God, she had forgotten how good a cold beer tasted. She wore one of Travis's T-shirts instead of her towel and the masculine smell of his cologne infused in the soft cotton was driving her nuts.

While Travis grilled, he gave her barbecuing tidbits, but she wasn't paying a bit of attention to what he was saying. All she could think about was how cute his butt looked, the way the breeze ruffled his hair, the ripple of muscle when he flipped a burger. But what really turned her inside out was his smile. Warm and engaging with a hint of mischief, his smile put Krista at ease. For a guy who had droves of female fans, he sure seemed unaffected by it all.

"How do you do it?" Krista asked softly.

Travis placed a thick slice of cheddar cheese on the burgers and then turned to face her. "Do what?"

"Stay grounded."

He shrugged. "I guess I just remember where I came from, which is a small ranch in Nowhere, Texas. My daddy struggled to stay afloat. It was tough goin' some-times, but the one thing that could bring a smile to his face was to see me rope a steer and ride a bull."

"Ah, so that's why you did it."

Fanning the charcoal-scented smoke with the spatula, Travis asked, "What do you mean?"

"You risked your neck on the rodeo circuit when you would have rather been making music but you didn't want to disappoint your daddy."

Travis shook his head. "That's not true."

Krista angled her head, giving him a level look.

"Okay, maybe a little true. There was some pretty good money involved, you know," he said, moving the burgers from the grill to a plate.

"Money that saved the ranch?"

"Making the same kind of money in this crazy music business was a long shot." He shrugged. "Besides, even though rodeo stars aren't famous like NASCAR drivers, I did have a loyal following that helped me sell records. So it all worked out in the end."

Krista grinned. "Yeah, right. You've just been outed again, *bad boy.*"

He pointed the spatula in her direction. "Don't you go

starting the you're-such-a-nice-guy stuff. God, you make me sound like such a dweeb."

"*Nice* is pretty doggone sexy in my book."

Travis arched a dark eyebrow. "Oh, well then, on the other hand . . ."

"Come here, cowboy." Krista crooked her finger at him and Travis was on her in three strides across the small patio. He straddled the lounge chair, cupped his hands around her waist and lifted her up like she was nothing. With a little moan, Krista wrapped her arms around his neck and her legs around his waist and then kissed him. He smelled like charcoal and tasted faintly of beer and Krista couldn't get enough.

"Are you going to feed me?" Krista asked, a bit breathlessly.

Travis chuckled and then replied, "Sure thing, because girl, you're gonna need all the energy you can get."

Krista laughed. "You're a big talker, Travis Mackey."

He joined her on the lounge chair, feeding her bites of cheeseburger grilled to perfection, but as it turned out, they wound up crashing on the couch after consuming the meal, falling asleep wrapped around one another.

Krista woke up briefly sometime in the middle of the night with her head on Travis's shoulder and her legs tangled with his. She braced herself for the feeling of panic, the urge to bolt, but it didn't happen. Instead, she nuzzled the crook of his neck and with a contented sigh placed her hand on his warm, bare chest and fell back asleep.

Over the next few days, Krista and Travis fell into a pattern. In the mornings while Travis and the band rehearsed, Krista worked in her office in between making runs to the amphitheater with bottled water, food, and anything else they needed. As celebrities went these guys were pretty laid back, making so few demands that Krista's job was easy for a change. This gave her the chance to watch them perform and she had to admit that they were amazing. Her eyes, however, were mostly for Travis even though Brody Baker the crazy bass player did all kinds of antics to grab her attention just to tick Travis off.

Krista would have lunch with the band and then hook up with Travis after he worked out with Victor, the evil trainer. The long afternoons were spent soaking up the sun, and then came leisurely dinners where Travis would try out new grill recipes for his cookbook. Afterward they would take slow walks on the beach as the sun dropped from the sky.

The nights were filled with making love.

A sense of peace and contentment seeped into Krista's bones, and for the first time in her life *she relaxed*. Her smiles came easily instead of being forced and when she ran in the morning she didn't feel the need to push, but found herself pausing to watch dolphins frolicking in the water or seagulls in flight.

On the morning of the concert Max caught up with Krista while she was walking back from her run on the beach. She paused when he waved at her.

"Hey there," Max said with a grin. "Are you excited about the concert?"

Krista nodded.

"Are you still ticked about not having the Beach Boys?"

Krista scraped her toe across the frothy surf and playfully splashed Max with droplets of water. "Rub it in all you want."

"Now, that's not very Krista-like. What's come over you?"

Krista put her hand up to shade her eyes from the bright sunshine and gazed up at Max. "As if you didn't know. Andi tells you everything."

"Are you in love with Travis Mackey, Krista?" Max asked quietly, without his usual teasing tone.

"How can you *know,* Max?"

"Do you think about him constantly?"

"Pretty much."

"Get hot the moment he walks into the room?"

"I prefer to say tingly, but yes. God yes."

"Let him pick what to watch on television?"

Krista chuckled and then wrinkled her nose "Guilty. Last night I pretended to enjoy a show about monster trucks."

"Sweetheart, you're a goner."

Krista took a deep breath and blew it out. "Now what?"

Max ran his fingers through his dark hair while looking out over the ocean for a long moment. Turning serious eyes to her, he said, "That part is up to you, but there are a couple of things I want you to know. Krista, you know you do an amazing job here at Wild Ride, but I want you to promise me that if you want to leave, that you will."

Krista had to talk around the lump forming in her throat. "I can't imagine leaving here . . . *you* or Andi."

Max shook his head. "That's not what I asked. Promise me that you won't put working for me ahead of your happiness."

Krista swallowed and then said, "I promise."

"Good. Now promise me that if this cowboy does anything to hurt you, you'll tell me. I'll kick his ass, famous singer or not."

With a gurgled laugh, Krista launched herself into Max's arms.

"I'll always be here for you," Max said and then kissed the top of her head. "Remember that." He gently pushed her back a step and looked down at her. "Krista . . ."

"I hear a *but*. You can shoot from the hip with me, Max. Say what you want to say."

Putting his hands on her shoulders, Max said, "This guy is a celebrity. You've dealt with a lot of them and they don't always play by the rules."

"Travis isn't like that. He's grounded. Down to earth."

Max nodded. "Yeah, but sweetie, what's going to happen when Travis leaves here? Goes on the road for months at a time? It's one of the things you hated about your mother. Do you think you want to get involved in a relationship like that?"

Max was one of the few people who knew about her childhood, about her mother's long absences. With a sigh Krista picked up a shell and tossed it into the water. "I keep telling myself that it's too early in the game to worry about that." Shaking her head she continued, "But Max, I don't want to end up like my dad. My God, Max, I'm falling for the wrong guy. Leave it to me to wait all this time to give my heart to the absolute wrong person."

Max shook his head. "I don't think it's always a choice. Krista, you can't change how you feel about someone." He put a finger underneath her chin, forcing her downcast eyes to look up at him. "Krista, did you ever think about the fact that it was as hard for your mother to leave you as it was for you to not have her around?"

"Don't go there, Max," she warned.

"You wouldn't expect Travis to give up his music for you, would you?"

"Of course not. It's in his blood . . . oh *God*." She closed her eyes. "Mama cried every time she left. Sobbed. Hugged me and Daddy." She looked up at Max and a tear slid down her cheek. "I didn't make it easy for her."

Max wrapped his arms around her. "You were a child, Krista. Now, maybe you understand? The carnival was in my father's blood. I hated moving all over the damned place, but my childhood made me who I am."

"Why does life have to be so complicated?"

Max shrugged. "Maybe it's not. Maybe we *make* it complicated. Love is really pretty damned simple."

"Then how come I'm so confused?"

"Give it time. After the concert tonight, Travis's band is leaving and you'll have him all to yourself." With a grin, he added, "Just remember to get your job done. This doggone wedding is taking up way too much of my time." He gave her a little shove. "Now, go check on the details for the concert and then take the rest of the afternoon off and get all dolled up for the big event."

"Thanks for talking to me, Max."

"I said that I'll always be here for you and I mean it."

"I know." She stood on tippy-toe and gave him a kiss on the cheek. "Andi is a lucky girl."

Max chuckled. "She's a piece of work, but I love her. Now go find your cowboy."

Krista headed into the woods and followed the sandy path paved with brown pine needles that led to her house.

She had some work to do but she had promised to have breakfast with Travis. She could smell the bacon frying as she mounted the steps to the back door and her stomach rumbled in response. She knew he'd have cheesy grits and fluffy scrambled eggs. Good lord, she was going to have to add another mile to her morning run. Krista grinned. It would be worth it. She hadn't realized how much she missed warm comfort foods, a cold beer on a hot day, and worn blue jeans.

Krista stood on the back porch for a moment, leaning on the railing. Her mind was still trying to process the conversation that she had had with Max. There were so many reasons why she should turn and leave, so many obstacles in the way of a serious relationship. She had childhood issues and then there was *her* job and *his* career. Closing her eyes, she inhaled a deep, shaky breath. So deep in thought, Krista was startled when Travis's strong arms wrapped around her from behind. She shivered at the touch of his warm lips against her shoulder bared by her racer-back sports bra. While he placed little kisses up the curve of her neck, she melted against him.

"Hey, I want to ask you something." His voice was a low rumble in Krista's ear.

She nodded, still wrapped in his arms. "Okay."

"You know that after tonight the band and crew will leave the island."

Krista nodded again.

"Well, I was wondering . . . make that *hoping,* that you would move in with me. I'll have more time to spend with you after tonight."

Krista's heart started thumping double-time. "I have to work, though, Travis," she stated cautiously.

"I know. And I'll be writing songs." He gently turned her around to face him. "But I want to wake up in the morning next to you."

Krista hesitated. Saying yes would be a huge step in their relationship. A step that scared the hell out of her.

"I don't mean to push," he said softly.

"You're not."

"Then why can't you look at me?"

Krista opened her eyes, which had been squeezed shut. "Because you're exactly the type of person that I shouldn't be falling for."

"Oh." He took a step back and folded his arms across his chest. "Okay." Angling his head, he said, "But at least you admit that you have fallen for me."

"Travis, I've fallen for you faster than the Dolphin on the first spiral turn." God, he looked so cute with his hands jammed into his jeans pockets. He wasn't making this easy.

"That would be flattering, except I hear a big 'but' in there somewhere." He tried to grin but didn't quite succeed. His brown eyes looked wary.

Krista took a deep breath and blew it out. "You don't just have a career. Music is your life. It was that way for my mother with her art. I don't want to get involved with someone who will up and leave me for weeks at a time. I know that drill and it isn't fun."

"So, are you saying that we should end things?"

Hot moisture gathered behind her eyes. Not trusting her voice, she gave him a sad nod.

"I could argue with you. Tell you that if it gets to that point between us we'd find a way to make it work. All of the guys in the band except for Brody, 'cause no one will have him, are married. But I won't push you into something that doesn't feel right."

Krista nodded again. "Thank you for understanding."

"So, you're leaving, then?"

"Yeah."

"Okay." He took a step back and while nodding, repeated, "Okay."

Krista frowned. "You're not mad at me?"

"Of course not. Your honesty is refreshing."

"Then, you're okay."

"I *said* I was okay."

"Good, it's for the best."

He remained silent with a slight frown on his face.

"Well then . . ." Krista turned to go; actually took a step away from him, but then made the mistake of glancing over her shoulder. He looked so damned unhappy that it clawed at her heart. "Travis . . ."

"I'm *okay*." He made a shooing motion with his hands. "Go."

Fighting back tears, Krista nodded, and this time she didn't look back.

~~ chapter

ten

With his hands fisted at his sides, Travis watched Krista walk down the sandy path until she rounded the bend and he could no longer see her. "I really don't need this," he grumbled under his breath. "I've got a concert to perform tonight." He paced back and forth on the porch. "If this is the way she wants it then . . . fine. Fine!" He plopped down on the first step and for a moment propped his elbow on his knee and rested his chin in his hand. "Who needs Krista Ross, anyway?

"Ahhh, dammit, I do," he growled, answering his own rhetorical question. Pushing up from the step, Travis jogged down the path, ignoring the pointy pine needles that poked into his bare feet. He rounded the bend where the path became narrow. "Whoa!" Travis skidded to a halt, almost barreling into Krista. "You . . . you were coming back?" His heart hammered in his chest while he waited for her answer.

"Yes." She looked away.

Travis took a step closer. "You've been crying."

"No, I haven't." She brushed at her eyes. "It's sweat."

"Liar."

"Yeah, well, I've become pretty good at lying to you and to myself."

Travis took another step closer. Krista looked ready to bolt, so he put his hands on her shoulders. "So, tell me the truth, Krista."

Closing her eyes, she hesitated with a deep breath, but then looked up at him. "I don't want it to be over between us, Travis."

"Since I was chasing after you like a lovesick puppy, it's pretty clear how I feel."

"But—"

Travis put a finger to her lips. "Let's talk about it over breakfast." He wagged his eyebrows and said, "Cheesy grits. Bacon, crisp, just the way you like it."

Krista groaned. "Do you know that I've had to add a mile to my morning run because of your cooking?"

"But it's worth it, right?" He took her hand and they began walking back to the house. "Better than all that sprouty stuff you were used to eating?"

Krista shook her head. "Tastes better, but not better for me."

"Aw, hogwash. My granny's ninety-two and she eats down-home cookin' every day of her life." Travis put his finger to his lips. "Shh, don't tell Victor, my evil trainer, what I've been eating."

Krista slanted him a look. "I guess you've got to keep that sexy six-pack for the ladies."

Travis shrugged. "I look at it as part of my job and

don't take the screaming ladies too seriously. There were buckle bunnies on the rodeo circuit, too."

Krista chuckled. "Buckle bunnies?"

"It's what they call rodeo groupies. Krista, I'm not attracted to women who want a piece of me and nothing more. Too easy, too quick and meaningless." He paused at the steps to the back porch. "I have fun with it but I don't take myself too seriously." He shrugged again. "But the whole sex-symbol thing sells records. I owe it to all the people who depend upon me to put food on their table to work hard and hey, if wearin' tight jeans and wiggling my ass does the trick, then I'm gonna do it."

Krista frowned up at him. "I was only kidding."

Travis pulled her into his arms. "I know. But it *is* something you'll have to deal with."

"Well, I'm going to get a crash course tonight."

"Enough about all that." Travis tugged her hand. "Let's go eat. I'm going to need all the energy I can get."

"For the concert?"

"No," he whispered in her ear. "For making love to you."

"You are a smooth talker, Travis Mackey," Krista said as they entered the house.

"Is it working?"

"Maybe."

"That's a start."

"I'll go shower while you finish fixing breakfast."

Travis gave her a quick kiss on the cheek. "Sounds like a plan." He watched her leave the room and then headed to the kitchen. He hadn't brought up her moving in with him again, not wanting to scare her off. "Take things slow, Mackey," he said under his breath while he whisked a bowlful of eggs. Asking her to move in had been a lame-brained idea, he thought. Too much too soon. Ah, but that was the problem. He didn't have forever; he only had a few weeks.

Checking on the bacon in the warmer, Travis decided to use a new method of attack. He would tease. Make her want him so badly that *she* would be the one making the moves. Pursing his lips, Travis nodded, thinking that for a beat-up cowboy, he was pretty damned smart. *Just play it cool, Mackey,* he thought to himself. He chuckled when he remembered Brody telling him to flex his muscles. Could he do that without falling onto the floor laughing? *Hmmm, she did say he had a sexy six-pack.* "Thank you Victor the evil trainer," he mumbled, trying to think of a reason to remove his shirt. God, was he desperate or what?

Feeling ridiculous, Travis splattered some bacon grease on his T-shirt. He waited until he heard Krista's footsteps coming into the kitchen and then reached for the edges of his shirt, turning towards the doorway while he tugged the shirt over his head. "Bacon grease," he explained at her curious look.

"Oh, make sure you treat that before you wash it."

"Treat it?"

Krista chuckled. "Never mind. Remind me to wash it for you, okay?"

Travis nodded, feeling more than a little silly. Krista was wearing one of his shirts, making his mouth go dry. He wondered if she was nude underneath the worn cotton T-shirt that hit her about mid-thigh.

"Sorry," Krista said. "I didn't have anything other than my sweaty work-out stuff to wear. I hope you don't mind?"

"Not at all." Travis realized that he was staring and turned back to the stove, glad to have something to occupy his brain other than her lack of underwear.

"It smells heavenly in here. I'm starved. Can I help?"

"You can pour the coffee," he said without looking at her, forgetting that the coffeemaker was right next to him. When she reached for the carafe, her breast brushed his arm, making him jump and flip scrambled eggs everywhere.

"You okay?" Krista gave him a curious look.

"Uh, I always get a bit edgy on the day of a concert." This was sort of true.

"Maybe you just need to relax. Unwind." She gave him a suggestive smile.

This wasn't going to be easy. "I'll soak in the hot tub later," he assured her. "That always does the trick."

"Oh, that sounds nice," she said with a sexy I'll-join-you smile.

A heartbeat of silence passed and Travis knew Krista was waiting for him to ask her to join him. "The eggs are ready," he said, hoping his smile didn't look as strained as it felt. He waved a hand toward the small table. "Have a seat."

"Okay."

Travis brought heaping plates of eggs, bacon, grits, and toast to the table and tucked into his food so he wouldn't say something stupid like *you look hot in my shirt, now let's go make love all day long, every which way we can.* That smoldering thought brought on a hot visual that made Travis choke on his eggs.

"You okay?"

He nodded, taking a big gulp of orange juice.

"Concert nerves?"

He nodded.

She nibbled on her toast. A little frown furrowed her brow.

They ate in silence and Travis noted sadly that so far his plan was a total flop. Everything she did, from sipping her coffee to licking strawberry jam from her lips, was turning him on, while *she* on the other hand seemed totally unaffected. Too bad there wasn't something heavy to lift . . . striking a muscle-flexing pose would be, well, too obvious.

"Travis?"

"Hmm?"

"I asked if you wanted me to clean up."

"Oh, no, I'll do it."

"I'll help," she insisted. "Boy, you really are distracted."

"I guess I am," he said, tightening his ab muscles as he stood up, feeling like an idiot. When she looked concerned, he added, "Don't worry, I'll put on a good show, Krista."

"You just look so tense."

And you just look so edible. "I'm fine. Really." He took the dishes over to the sink, turned around and leaned against the sink, trying to strike a seductive pose. His elbows slipped on the slick surface and he almost landed in a heap on the floor.

"Travis!"

"I'm okay!" He held up his hands, feeling heat creep up his neck. This was becoming a disaster.

Krista tilted her head to the side and gave him another curious gaze. "Travis, what's going on here?"

"I'm trying to . . ." His face felt even warmer.

Krista raised her eyebrows and waited.

"My plan was . . ."

"Plan?" Frowning, she drew out the word.

"Okay, I had this harebrained idea to try to make you, um, really, you know, hot for me and then, well, play hard, sort of, to get. You were as skittish as a newborn filly and I thought if you . . . well, thought that, *oh man,* never mind." He put the heel of his hand to his forehead. "I'm a dork."

"So, let me guess. Taking off your shirt just as I entered the room was *planned.*"

"Mmmm, guilty." He cringed.

Her lips twitched.

"Hey, you said that my six-pack was sexy," he said.

"It is."

"I suck at being . . . what's the word?"

"Coy?"

"Yeah, that."

"Cowboy, you are so damned cute."

Travis groaned. "Cute? That ranks right up there with *nice.* Chicks don't dig adorable. Nice is . . . nice is . . . boring."

"Oohh, so I can call Mary Hart on 'Entertainment Tonight' and give her the scoop that bad boy country star Travis Mackey is really nice and a cutie-pie and knows his way around a kitchen?"

"Cutie-pie? You're killing me."

"What if I told you that nice turns me on? That cute makes me melt?"

Travis shivered when Krista crowded his space, traced a fingertip down his chest and over his abs.

"Still want to be bad to the bone, Travis?"

"Nice is good. I can do nice."

Krista chuckled. "You were really going to play hard to get?"

"That was the plan."

She played with the snap on his jeans, popped it open, and then looked up at him expectantly. "So, just how hard are you to get?"

He swallowed. "Not . . . so very."

"Mmm, good," she said while running a finger over the zipper.

Travis sucked in a breath. "Krista . . . you don't have to do this."

She smiled, blinking away moisture burning behind her eyes. "You just confirmed your nice-guy, cutie-pie status with me. Most guys would be dragging me into the bedroom and you're giving me a choice."

"I just want you to be sure you want this to go forward."

She shook her head. "I know I've been blowing hot and cold."

"Uh, make that *running* in the opposite direction. It isn't exactly good for a guy's ego."

Krista put a hand lightly on his chest, loving the warm solid feel of his skin. "Travis, I wasn't running from you. I was running from myself. My past, my parents." She looked up at him, took a deep breath, and then said, "I'm tired of running and of pretending to be someone other than myself. You gave me back all of the things I've been missing. Wanting. *Craving.*"

Travis grinned. "Like cheesy grits?"

"Yes."

"Juicy burgers?"

"God, yes."

"Worn jeans and sloppy T-shirts?"

"No doubt!"

He cocked an eyebrow at her. "Country music?"

She caught her bottom lip between her teeth and then softly admitted, "Yes."

"What about cowboys?"

"*Especially* cowboys."

"Gotcha covered." Travis put his hands around her waist and pulled her against him with a grin. "After all, what else is there?"

"I can only think of one thing." With a slow smile, she moved ever so slightly against him.

"I'm all over it."

When he lowered his mouth to hers, Krista stood on tiptoe for better access. She wound her arms around his neck, molding her body to his. Her movements caused her T-shirt to creep up, allowing Travis to find her bare bottom. Still kissing, he groaned into her mouth and lifted her up. Krista circled her legs around his waist and he carried her to the bedroom. After lowering her to the unmade bed, he said, "God, you look good in my shirt."

"It smells like you."

"That's a good thing, right?"

"Quite a turn-on."

"Maybe you should move in and leave all your clothes at the hotel." Damn, he hadn't meant to say that. He held his breath.

By the look on his face, Krista knew that Travis wished he hadn't mentioned moving in. "I'm not going to bolt," she assured him. "And if any buckle bunnies or groupies or whatever throw themselves at you tonight, well, let's just say that they'll have to go through me." She jammed a thumb at her chest.

Travis laughed.

"Hey, I'm little, but tough as nails."

"I believe you."

"Nobody messes with my man." It was meant as a joke, but the thought of Travis being her man sent a little thrill up her spine. *Her man.*

"Chicks fighting. Sweet." Travis chuckled as he joined her on the bed. "Can there be mud involved?"

She punched him playfully in the arm. "Yeah, *that* would score me brownie points with Max."

"You don't even know how to throw a punch," Travis said while running a hand up her leg.

"Hmm, care to call my bluff?"

Leaning in, Travis nibbled on her neck. "Yeah, and I seem to recall that you couldn't stand the thought of hurting me."

Krista sucked in a breath when his warm, wet mouth found her breast. "Oh yeah? I think I'm gonna put the smackdown on you right now, cowboy."

Travis fell back onto the pillow laughing. Krista loved the deep rumble of his laughter. Playful was fun. Teasing was fun. She realized that at this very moment she was truly happy. Relaxed.

And totally turned on.

With a little whoop, she flipped over onto Travis and sat up. With another whoop, she tugged the big T-shirt over her head and tossed it to the floor. "There's not any rule about making love on the day of a concert, is there?"

"You think you're gonna wear me out?"

"Yep."

"I'm in pretty good shape."

"We'll see."

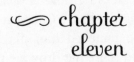 chapter
eleven

Travis lifted his hips so that Krista could peel his jeans off. "Wow, you were going commando," she observed with a laugh.

"Underwear is overrated," Travis said, sucking in a sharp breath when Krista lightly cupped his balls and then wrapped her hand around his shaft.

"Oh, I agree."

Travis scooted up to a half-sitting position and watched her small hand move up and down, making him pulse and swell. Just when he couldn't take it anymore, she stopped and traced a pretty, pink-tipped fingernail over the head of his dick, swirling the pearly drop of pre-come until he was wet and shiny. God, she looked so delicate and fine-boned next to his big body. And she was giving herself to him . . . uninhibited, trusting, and *good lord*, she wasn't holding back. This is what he wanted, but it scared him to think that he had the power to hurt her.

This will work out, he vowed. *No matter what it takes.*

Travis arched upward when he felt the tip of her tongue on his sacs, moving back and forth until he was wet and on fire for her. The sight of her blond head between his thighs bobbing and moving while she licked, nibbled, and kissed him was so damned erotic. Travis watched, clenching his stomach muscles, clenching his jaw in an effort to keep from coming. She looked up and then flipped her hair out of the way, leaning to the side so he could see her mouth on him. He watched her mouth move over him, the pink tip of her tongue darting out. He took a deep, shaky breath, inhaling floral perfume mixed with the heady scent of sex.

"You're gorgeous," she breathed, pulling her head back to look at him. "So hard, so powerful. I want you inside me."

Travis nodded, thinking she was reaching for a condom, but she looked at him with a smile and said, "But first, I want *this*."

He sucked in a breath and fisted his hands in her hair when she took him deep into her mouth and began loving him with a fierce intensity that not only stole his breath, but also went straight to his heart.

With his eyes closed, Travis was trying to recover from his white-hot climax when he realized that she had just slipped a condom on him. With a weak chuckle he pleaded, "Ah, Krista, give me a minute."

"I can't wait," was her breathless reply as she grabbed his shoulders and swung her leg over his waist to straddle him once more.

Travis opened his eyes when he felt the heat of Krista's body wrap around his penis. Her sigh of pure feminine pleasure made him smile. Cupping her breasts, he circled the pads of his thumbs over her stiff nipples until she made a little whimpering sound deep in her throat.

"Travis, I don't think I can move. My legs are like Jell-O."

"Then just hold on." With a chuckle that became a groan, Travis pushed his shoulders back against the pillows and thrust his hips upward while holding her around her waist.

"No, I need . . ." she panted. "Travis I want . . ."

Understanding, he gently turned her onto her back. "You need *this,*" he growled, pumping deep and hard.

"Yes. God, yes. More." Arching up, she met his thrusts and then wrapped her legs around his waist.

"Like this?" He slipped his hands beneath her, loving the smooth feel of her warm skin, while giving himself leverage to go deeper and faster.

"Yes! M-more."

Krista felt so delicate beneath his body that Travis was afraid that he should hold back, but she arched her hips, urging him on. Her shoulders pressed into the pillows and she threw her arms wide, fisting her fingers into the sheet. Her eyes were closed, her lips moist and parted. Travis watched, slowing his rhythm for a few strokes. Pulling his penis almost all the way out, he paused to glide one hand over her breasts and then downward until he reached where their bodies were intimately connected while savoring the sight of her body glistening with a fine sheen of sweat.

"Travis, don't *stop.*" She bit her bottom lip and arched upward.

Krista's throaty plea washed over him like warm summer rain and he slid back into her soft heat with one long stroke. When she gasped and then cried out, Travis pushed deeper, climaxing with a long, hot wave of pleasure that made him shudder, taking her right along with him. With a weak moan, he wrapped her in a full-body embrace and then rolled to his side. "You are incredible," he said gruffly and then kissed her softly. "Just *incredible*."

"So are you, cowboy."

Her trembling smile hit Travis right smack in the gut. He held her close and she nuzzled the crook of his neck while entwining one slim leg with his.

"I could stay like this forever," she said with a sigh.

Travis smiled and was about to ditto her feelings when he felt her body stiffen as if she wished she hadn't said that. He kissed her on top of the head and then paused for a long moment. His heart thudded harder than when he was on the back of a bull waiting for the chute to open at what he was about to say but dammit, he wasn't one to pussyfoot around. After clearing his throat, he began, "Krista, I know we haven't known each other long and this sounds like a cheesy line, but I have to tell you that I've never felt about a woman the way I feel about you."

There, I said it. He waited for her reply, holding her tightly so she couldn't scoot away from him. When she remained silent, his heart thudded even harder but he finished his statement. "I'm falling in love with you." He had this whole this-won't-be-easy-but-we'll-work-it-out speech ready for her arguments, but her silence was killing him. "I've already written a song about you," he said with a nervous edge that made him sound like a pansy-ass.

"You did?" Her voice was barely above a whisper.

Travis released the breath he had been holding. *Okay, this is a start.* "Yes, and I've got an idea for another one." Silence again. "We can do a sexy music video together," he tried with a weak chuckle. *Well, damn.* "You know, Krista, I feel like it's one step forward and then two steps back with you. Help me out here. Talk to me." He kissed her on top of the head once more. "Please."

Krista took a shaky breath. She *couldn't* talk. Her throat had gone all tight on her and her nose twitched something fierce. She was in real danger of blubbering like a ninny. *He wrote a song for me?* She opened her mouth but her throat was still malfunctioning. All she could manage was a strangled gurgle.

"Krista?"

Sniff. Gurgle.

"Are you okay?"

She nodded into his neck but he wasn't buying it.

"No, you're not," he accused and rolled her onto her back. Propping his head up on his hand, he looked at her and said, "Aw man, you're crying. Why are you crying?"

Krista took another deep shuddering breath, swallowed hard, and managed, "B-because you s-said." She paused and then finished in a whisper, "that you're falling in love with me."

Travis frowned down at her.

"And"—she poked him in the chest for emphasis—"you w-wrote a sssong for me." She poked him harder. "And you just gave me the best orgasm *ever.*"

"Really?" *Cool.*

She nodded.

"Then what may I ask is the doggone problem?" His voice was laced with confusion.

"I'm happy!" She pointed to her face. "These are *happy* tears!" She sighed and muttered, "Men!"

"So, then, just humor me. Are you falling in love with me, too?"

Krista shook her head.

"Oh."

"I'm past the falling stage, cowboy."

He gave her one of his bone-melting smiles. "We'll make this work somehow. You know that, right?"

"I *don't* know that. But the point is that I'm willing to try." Krista pulled him down for a long kiss, thinking that she finally *got* how her father had felt about her mother. "Music is your passion. I totally get it and I don't expect you to change. It won't be easy, but I want to give it a try." She smiled up at him. "Let's try, Travis."

"That's all I can ask for," he said, leaning in to mold his body to hers. "The best orgasm ever, huh?" he asked against her lips.

"Oh, boy, that Stetson is never gonna fit back on your big head." She pushed at his chest. "It was probably just a fluke. You could never do it again."

"Is that a challenge?"

"You betcha," Krista threw back at him, but she was already halfway there just being in his arms.

"Well, that's a challenge that I'm definitely *up* for." He kissed her softly and then said, "I'm nervous, you know."

"Oh, Travis, I was only kidding."

"Not about *that.*" He traced a finger down her cheek. "I'm nervous about the concert. About you being in the audience. What if you think I suck?"

"You're joking."

He shook his head, feeling rather stupid for confessing.

"Travis, I've been listening to you rehearse for the past two weeks. You and your band are amazing. Surely you know that."

Travis shrugged and looked away from her probing gaze. "The music has always been in me, that's for sure, but the success came so fast after my accident that I guess I wasn't prepared. God, Krista, sometimes I get up there on stage and I think all those people are going to suddenly start throwing tomatoes at me." Okay, now he really felt stupid. He had never told anyone this before.

Krista put her hand on his chin, forcing him to look at her. "First of all, you have a very distinctive, not to mention incredibly sexy voice. I can't even explain it. Sort of rough and smooth at the same time. God, and such *emotion*. You rock, cowboy."

Travis opened his mouth to thank her but she wasn't finished.

She poked him in the chest. "Plus if anyone even thinks of throwing anything at you, I'll kick their ass. And that includes bras and panties, I'll have you know."

Travis leaned back against the pillows and laughed. "You know you are a quite a piece of work?"

"You mean that in a good way, right?"

He chuckled. "In a very good way. And here I was worried about you riding on the back of my Harley."

Her eyes lit up. "You've got a Harley?"

"I've got all kinds of toys."

"Well then, let's play," she said with a wicked grin.

"Woman, you're gonna kill me."

"You'll die happy," she teased and leaned down to plant kisses on his chest. She was heading south when a loud voice startled them both.

"Travis!" A loud male voice boomed followed the sound of footsteps heading their way. "Where the hell are you?"

"What the . . ." Travis began.

Krista scooted beneath the covers just as the door to the bedroom swung open.

"There you are!" Brody boomed, strolling boldly into the room in nothing but a pair of board shorts that hung so low on his hips that they defied gravity. "Hey there, Krista," he said with a nod as if it were a natural thing to burst into the room where she and Travis had been on the verge of making love. "People are looking all over for you! We've got that damned video to shoot and they want footage on the beach." He ran his fingers through his choppy blond hair, messing it up even more than usual.

Travis frowned. "What time is it?"

Brody threw his hands up in the air. "Almost noon, bro! Get dressed and get your ass over to the shoot. Personally, I think it should be *me* being filmed barefoot and shirtless strolling down the beach, but *nooo,* they want you."

"Brody, you can leave now," Travis said, trying not to grin. Krista had the covers up to her chin.

"Hey, you should be thanking me. That fancy-schmancy director is having a hissy fit. I figured you two might be in bed and I didn't think you wanted everyone to know so I took it upon myself to come looking for you."

"Go, Brody." Travis pointed toward the door.

"God, I get no respect. Bass players are just taken for granted." With a shake of his shaggy head he turned to leave but said over his shoulder, "Krista, if Travis was a disappointment, well, you know where to find me."

"I can't believe he just waltzed right in here pretty as you please." Her Southern accent had reared its head, full-blown and, as far as Travis was concerned, sexy as hell.

Travis grinned. "Brody Baker is hell on wheels. There are three things he can't say no to: a dare, a bar fight, and a woman, not necessarily in that order.

"He's a talented musician."

"That he is, which reminds me, I have to get over there to the shoot before my manager comes banging on my door." He kissed her on the cheek. "Not that I wouldn't rather spend the day in bed with you."

"I'll be waiting right here after the show."

"Then there *won't* be an encore," he said with a grin.

"Give your fans what they want, Travis. Just remember that I'll be demanding my own personal command performance." Blushing a deep shade of pink, Krista pulled the covers up over her head. "I can't believe I just said that."

Travis chuckled and tugged the covers down so he could see her face. "You are so damned cute. This next CD is going to be filled with songs inspired by you." He gave her another kiss and then reluctantly rolled from the bed. "I really have to grab a shower and go."

"I should go, too. I've got some last-minute things to take care of before the concert." She scooted from the bed, but then asked, "Travis?"

"Yes?"

She shook her head. "Never mind."

"Go ahead. Ask me anything."

She paused and took a deep breath. "What's the title of the song that you wrote about me?"

Travis came over and sat next to her on the edge of the mattress. "Well, you know, you kept running from me, backing off, basically driving me nuts. I thought that if I could just hold on to you long enough, then I'd have a chance." He paused to pick up her hand and then kissed her palm. "I was about ready to give up when I realized something."

"Go on," she prompted when he hesitated.

"Well, I realized that for a very long time, I had been doing things for other people. Not that I didn't want to, but well, I rode bulls for my dad and paraded around posing for ads for my sponsor." He looked at Krista and said, "I'd do that all over again, mind you, but—"

Krista put her hand over his. "Travis, it's okay."

"I do the concerts to please the fans when all I really want to do is play my guitar and write songs. Not that I'm not grateful." He smiled at her and said, "But I realized after spending time with you . . . falling for you, that I *need* you. So, that's the name of the song. 'I Need You.' Pretty simple, really. I need you, Krista. I need you in my life. For the first time in a long time, it was all about what I wanted, what I needed." He frowned. "Aw, damn, please tell me that those are happy tears."

Krista nodded. "Yeah, happy tears." She sniffed and then threw herself into his arms so hard that he fell back onto the bed. She planted wet kisses all over his face until they both fell back against the pillows in a fit of laughter.

"I really have to shower," Travis said. He wiggled his eyebrows. "You could shower with me."

Krista groaned. "I can't. I need to get ready for

tonight." She gave him a quick kiss and then rolled from the bed. "See you tonight."

Krista found her sports bra and spandex shorts, tugged them on, and headed out the door, trying to focus on what she needed to do in preparation for the concert. *I need a run on the beach to clear my head,* she thought, and turned toward the sound of the waves crashing against the shore. But instead of running, she found herself jogging and then slowing to a walk. At one point she stopped completely, lifted her face to the warmth of the sun and, spinning in a circle, let out a whoop so loud that she startled some seagulls into flight.

Krista inhaled a deep breath of briny air and found that she couldn't stop smiling. She no longer needed to run as fast as she could from her past; instead, she turned from the beach and started walking straight toward her future.

Worth the Wait

⤳ chapter
one

"**Y**ou're not scared, are you, Jenna?"

"Of course not," she scoffed, giving Cole Forrester a roll of her eyes.

"Embarrassed then?"

"Now *why* would I be embarrassed?"

"I seem to remember that you're a screamer."

Jenna's mouth dropped open. He remembered? God, that had to have been fifteen years ago.

Cole arched one dark eyebrow at her. "Are you *still* a screamer?"

Jenna felt one corner of her mouth twitch. "Okay, yes, I admit it, but I'm not embarrassed, for goodness' sake. Lots of people scream."

"Then what's the problem? Come on," Cole pleaded and gave her a hard-to-resist smile.

Jenna sighed. "I'm just tired, that's all. I want lunch and a long hot shower."

"Well, that's a lame excuse." He slipped his big hand

over hers and tugged. "Come on. The brochure says it's the best way to start our vacation."

Jenna gave him a shake of her head and stood her ground.

"Oh, come on, Jenna, let's do it. Everyone else is."

The schoolteacher in her wanted to tell him that they didn't need to follow the crowd, but she was beginning to feel like a fuddy-duddy. Oh wait, she *was* a fuddy-duddy. Maybe she should just do it.

Cole must have seen her hesitation, because with another persuasive grin he pressed her further. "Oh, come on." He tugged on her hand a little harder, causing Jenna to stumble forward.

"Oh!" Jenna caught herself when her free hand landed on the solid wall of his chest. The tips of her fingers encountered warm, bare skin exposed by the three open buttons of Cole's yellow polo shirt. She blinked up at him, wanting to protest, if only she could find her voice, which had seemed to have left the building.

"You know you want to." Cole gave her a little nudge with his elbow.

Jenna tried not to smile. She really didn't know why she was being so stubborn, other than that she wanted to make it clear to Cole that he wasn't going to be calling the shots. They had an agreement and she was going to stick to it even if it killed her . . . and it probably would. "I'm just not in the mood," she protested and then cringed. *Oh, why did I just put it that way?*

Ignoring, *okay trying to ignore,* the tingle in her fingertips—God, his chest hair was silky—she groped for another reason to deny him other than the admittedly lame I'm-not-in-the-mood excuse. "It's small," she protested weakly. "The ride would last, like, maybe a minute."

Cole nodded his dark head in agreement. "Yeah, bigger and longer would be better, but it would still be a fun ride and a great way to get things going. Size doesn't always matter, you know," he added with a wicked grin.

Blushing furiously, Jenna managed to say, "Go on by yourself, Cole." She removed her hand from his chest and tugged her other hand from his firm grasp. Waving her hand in the direction of the sleek blue roller coaster shaped like a dolphin she said, "Just look at the line. Do you really want to wait?"

He shrugged his broad shoulders and gave her a level look. "Some things are worth the wait," he responded with his mouth close to her ear.

The low timbre of his voice oozed over Jenna like hot fudge on a scoop of vanilla ice cream. Her stomach did a little flippy-floppy thing and she barely resisted the urge to put her hand to her midsection. It was the same damned flippy-floppy feeling that Cole Forrester had been causing since his sister Halley's third-grade pajama party when he had run by in Batman underwear and a towel tied superhero-fashion around his neck. *God, why did I agree to this vacation?* Closing her eyes, Jenna inhaled a deep breath and then blew it out. "Okay," she reluctantly agreed. "I'll ride the Dolphin with you."

Cole gave her shoulder a nudge. "That's my girl."

His girl. Jenna gave him a tight smile and headed for the long line of tourists waiting to ride the flashy blue roller coaster into the lobby of the Wild Ride Resort hotel. Jenna knew it was only an expression, but it drove home the fact that she *wasn't* his girl nor was she ever likely to be. Cole Forrester was her best friend's brother, a great guy, but a real player. Most of the women in their hometown of Sander's City either had dated Cole or wanted to . . . her included, in the "wanted to" category. Past tense. At twenty-nine and heading for the big three-oh Jenna was looking for forever and she seriously doubted that the word *forever* was in Cole's vocabulary.

Trying not to sigh, Jenna looked up at the twisting, turning roller coaster and tried to ignore the rush of excitement when Cole's bare forearm brushed against hers. She remembered the feeling of slow dancing with him at Reese's and Halley's wedding where she had been the maid of honor and Cole had been the best man. It had been exquisite torture: a dream come true that was destined to go nowhere.

And now this.

"I must be crazy," she mumbled under her breath and pushed her sunglasses up on her nose.

"Pardon me?" Cole asked with a frown.

"Nothing." Jenna glanced up at him out of the corner of her eye and forced a smile, glad for the sunglasses that hid her eyes. With a lopsided grin Cole gazed upward, watching the Dolphin spiral into the first turn. Cole was tall, dark and George Clooneyish handsome, making Jenna question her sanity at insisting that the vacation be a strictly platonic, you-go-your-way-I'll-go-mine-once-we-get-there plan. *Oh, what was I thinking,* she wondered with a shake of her head.

When Reese Taylor had gotten called up to the major leagues to pitch, he and Halley were forced to put their honeymoon on hold. Getting their money back from Wild Ride Resort was impossible because it was so last-minute. So Jenna and Cole had come to the rescue and had bailed them out by offering to take the trip off of their hands. It had been Cole's suggestion and a good one . . . in theory. Jenna didn't start teaching school for another week and Cole had vacation time coming from his job as marketing director for the Sander's City Flyers, the minor-league baseball team for which Reese had played.

The reality of the situation was that Jenna had agreed to a weeklong honeymoon vacation at the popular adults-only resort with a man she had had a major crush on for most of her life. She swallowed a moan as she took a few steps forward in the slow-moving line. "Insane," she muttered.

"It will be worth it," Cole responded, shading his eyes against the glare of the Florida sunshine.

Jenna nodded, embarrassed that she had uttered her thoughts out loud, a really bad habit of hers. She let Cole think that she had been referring to the long line and not the impossible situation she found herself in. Not that this vacation wasn't in many ways a welcome change from her rather tame small-town school-teaching existence. But still, it royally sucked that she was here with the man of her dreams . . . and yet she wasn't. *God.*

The heat of the tropical sun beamed down on Jenna's strawberry-blond head, making her glad that she had applied sunscreen to her fair skin. She envied Cole's dark complexion and made a note to herself to be really careful not to get fried. She might have to slather on sunscreen, but she couldn't wait to sink her toes into the warm sand. Inhaling the scent of the sea, Jenna couldn't help but smile in spite of the ridiculous situation she found herself in.

They made small talk while the long line progressed. Cole, as always, had a way of making her feel at ease. As her best friend's big brother, Cole had known Jenna most of his life and they shared many of the same interests, especially baseball.

"I wonder if Reese will get the chance to pitch this weekend?" Cole asked with a sideways glance in her direction.

"I hope so. But I hate to miss his major-league debut."

Cole nodded. "Reese and I got off on the wrong foot but I realize now that he's one hellava guy."

"You mean when you punched him?" she asked drily.

"You know about that?"

"Halley is my best friend, Cole."

He shrugged and gave her a sheepish look. "I thought Reese was playing her. I'm a bit overprotective about the people I care about. But I know now that he's a great guy and he's worked his ass off to get to the big show. I hate to miss his debut, too, but I'm glad we could take this trip off of their hands. Besides, I've heard so much about this place and the waiting list to get a reservation is almost a year in advance."

"I've been told that it gets wild when the sun sets."

"Me too," Cole replied. He looked at her for a long moment and then said, "Jenna, I know we have an understanding about this trip, but I want you to be careful."

Jenna was a bit annoyed that he thought she couldn't handle herself. She raised her chin a notch. "You don't have to play the big-brother role, Cole. I can take care of myself," she replied a bit more sharply than she had intended.

An expression that Jenna couldn't quite read passed

over his features, but then he smiled. "I'm sure you can, but maybe we should stick together, just for tonight, okay? Just until we get acclimated."

Jenna hesitated and then finally nodded. "Just for tonight."

"Okay." He looked as if he was going to say something else, but then turned his attention back to the roller coaster.

"Next?" the attendant said and motioned Jenna and Cole to the Dolphin, but Cole shook his head.

"We'll wait for the front seat," Cole said and let the couple behind them go ahead. Turning to Jenna, he asked with a huge smile, "After waiting this long we might as well do it right, don't you agree?"

God, Cole's smile still had the power to make her melt. This week was going to be torture. Unless . . .

"I totally agree," Jenna replied and just that quickly she made a huge personal decision. Screw the whole platonic plan. She was sharing a honeymoon suite on a tropical island with Cole Forrester, and by God if she couldn't have forever, then at least she was going to make the most of this one week that she had with him in paradise. Of course, this would take some cooperation on Cole's end, but surely she could manage that, right? There, with that decision made, Jenna turned to Cole with a big smile of her own and said, "I couldn't agree with you more."

❧ chapter
two

Cole stepped back to let a young couple go ahead of them in line while thinking that something had just happened, but he couldn't quite put his finger on it. Jenna's smile looked a little . . . *danger-ous* and he wondered if she was going to let her hair down and get a bit wild at this resort. He glanced at her out of the corner of his eye and thought, *nah*. Of all of Halley's friends, Jenna had always been the most shy and reserved, but she suddenly had that feminine gleam in her eye that said that she was up to something. That thought made Cole frown because he had known for a while that he was in love with Jenna Wagner.

Cole glanced again in Jenna's direction, admiring her profile while wondering what the hell he was going to do if she decided to go man-hunting while on this vacation. *She won't do that, will she?* Cole was still pondering this when Jenna leaned forward, resting her arms on the metal railing, giving him a very nice view of her butt showcased in a pair of snug white shorts. Cole noticed that the guy in line behind them, some chump in a Hawaiian shirt and a backward baseball cap, was admiring the same view, making Cole want to smash his fist in the guys grinning face.

Cole must have involuntarily growled or something because Jenna suddenly turned to him and asked, "You okay?"

"Sure." *Yeah, right. I'm okay if you discount the fact that I'm staying at a sexy adults-only resort with the woman I love but whom I've promised to keep my hands off of while she cavorts with other single men. Yeah, I'm fine and dandy.*

Cole sighed, drawing another look from Jenna. She patted his hand, which had a white-knuckled grip on the metal railing, as if he were one of her high-school students. "You're probably just a bit tired, too," she assured him in a soothing voice that made him feel about ten years old. "We'll have to go back to the room and grab a quick nap. I want to be fresh for the Travis Mackey concert tonight, don't you?"

Cole nodded absently while his brain conjured up a picture of Jenna *in bed* in their lavish honeymoon suite. God help him, there was probably a heart-shaped hot tub and champagne on ice just waiting for their arrival.

And he had promised not to touch her . . . "God!" Oops, he said that out loud.

"Weren't you the one who said it would be worth the wait?" Jenna asked.

Cole nodded, glad that Jenna had mistaken the long line for the source of his frustration. "So, are you still a screamer?" he teased. "My eardrums haven't recovered from the last time I rode a roller coaster with you."

"Sorry." Jenna chuckled as they slipped into the front seat of a car shaped like the nose of a dolphin and let the attendant lower the metal bar across their laps. "I was scared to death."

"But you rode the rides with me all day long at that amusement park when I took Halley and you guys that one summer. You were the only one who rode the Beast with me." Cole gave her a questioning lift of his eyebrows.

Jenna lifted her sunglasses up and peered at him. "Well, *yeah!* I was *so* trying to impress you. You were Cole Forrester, big man on campus at Sander's City High. I was a lowly, freckle-faced freshman and you were what . . . team captain of both the football and baseball teams?"

"So you don't like roller coasters?" Cole asked as the Dolphin jerked forward and then began the slow ascent of the first hill.

Jenna grinned over at him. "I love them! I get scared to death but I like the danger and excitement." She raised her hands over her head and elbowed him to do the same. "I love the rush but also knowing deep down that you're actually safe. Better hold your ears, Cole. I'm about to start screaming," she warned as they crested the hill. "Wow, the view from up here is amazing! Just look at the ocean . . . whoaaaaa!"

She wasn't kidding. As soon as the Dolphin zoomed down the first hill, Jenna let out a horror-movie-worthy scream and didn't stop. In fact, she screamed even louder through the first spiral turn, but Cole noticed with amusement that she refused to hold on to the metal bar. Her shoulder kept slamming into his and her red-gold hair blew across his face. When they hit the next hairpin turn and the second hill Jenna came up in her seat, held down only by the metal bar. Three more jerky but smaller hills came in quick secession, followed by a flat stretch that whizzed them into the hotel. By the end of the ride Cole was laughing so hard that he had to wipe tears from the corners of his eyes. After the sleek roller coaster came to a smooth stop in the upper lobby of the hotel, Cole lifted the metal bar and then stepped from the car. Still chuckling, he held out his hand to assist Jenna out.

"Whoa!" she said in a shaky, slightly hoarse voice and basically fell against him when she stepped out of the nose-shaped compartment.

"You okay?"

"Define okay."

"Well, for starters, can you walk?"

"Uh," she said and then swallowed. "That's doubtful."

Cole slipped his arm around her waist and had to grin. Her hair was windblown in wild disarray around her face. Her sunglasses had slipped to the very tip of her nose and she was having a hard time standing. While the noisy crowd pushed past them, Cole led her over to a plush sofa and helped to ease her into a sitting position.

"You had better stay here and rest while I go and check us in."

"Okay." Jenna flashed a wobbly grin up at him. "*That* was a rush. Definitely worth the wait."

Kneeling down beside her, Cole gently removed her sunglasses. "Sorry, Jenna. I didn't realize that the ride would shake you up so much."

She shrugged her slim shoulders. "I think it's a combo of a long flight followed by a bumpy boat ride, ending with a roller coaster."

Cole nodded. "And you mentioned that you're hungry and tired."

"That, too." She blinked up at him.

Patting her knee, he said, "You sit tight. I'll get our room key. We can order some room service and then you can nap. Sound good?"

Jenna gave him a bit of a loopy grin and then leaned forward, bringing her mouth dangerously close to his. "Sounds perfect. Thank you."

Her voice, still husky from screaming, was such a damned turn-on that Cole unconsciously leaned even closer until his lips were almost brushing against hers. He could feel the warmth of her mouth, and the light, floral scent of her perfume filled his head. He was almost kissing her when a voice in the back of his brain growled, *Don't! Follow your plan.*

"I'll be back as soon as I can get our room." Cole quickly pushed up to a standing position, feeling a bit shaky himself. *Jet lag,* he told himself, knowing full well that it was Jenna Wagner that was throwing him off kilter, not one measly hour's change in time zone or a roller-coaster ride. "Stay put, okay?"

Jenna nodded, looking a bit confused and . . . disappointed? Had she wanted him to kiss her? Should he have kissed her? With a mental shake of his head, Cole kept walking toward the escalator that led to the front desk while reminding himself that he *had* a doggoned plan, and that he should stick to it.

Cole swiped a hand over his face while he got into the back of the long line of tourists waiting to check in to the hotel. His master plan for this week had seemed simple enough, especially considering that his previous love life had consisted of juggling women instead of trying to capture the heart of one. That, of course, was part of the problem.

Cole, since as long ago as he could remember, had been considered a player. Okay, he had *been* a player. A psychology major that he had dated briefly in college had explained to him (after he had given her the it's-not-you-it's-me speech) that his fear of commitment was a direct result of the early death of his mother. Of course, Cole had scoffed at the idea, but deep down he knew that there was some truth to the notion that he was afraid of feeling the same heartbreaking loss that his father had felt, and that the only way to prevent this was to avoid falling in love.

This whole not-falling-in-love thing had been working pretty darned well for him until on a dare at a bachlorette party sweet little Jenna Wagner had planted a kiss on him that had knocked his socks off. Cole still shook his head when he thought about it. A simple kiss. His sister Halley had seen his reaction and had warned him to stay away from Jenna. She had told him that her best friend didn't need to have her heart broken by a playboy like him.

Cole chuckled, drawing a glance from the couple ahead of him in the slow-moving line. He had tried! But in the small town of Sander's City, avoiding someone was next to impossible. He would bump into Jenna at the grocery store, at Flyers games, at the local diner, and at parties of mutual friends. And God help him, he would notice it, no *feel* it, as soon as she entered a room or the ballpark or wherever, and then he would slowly gravitate toward her, quite unable to resist. But like the good brother and that he was, Cole had refrained from asking Jenna out on a date.

Then, there had been Reese's and Halley's wedding. Nearly a year of planning, parties, fittings . . . *God,* and *still* Cole had been the perfect gentleman . . . quite a feat, actually, considering his track record . . . a track record that during this time had come to a screeching halt. To put it quite simply, other women ceased to attract him. Instead, he had found himself quietly falling deeply in love with Jenna.

The actual wedding had blown him away. Jenna had looked radiant in emerald green with her red-gold hair swept up from her neck and curling in little tendrils around her face. Slow-dancing with her had been amazing, but then watching her dance with other men had been sheer torture. Jealousy had been a foreign feeling for Cole, but where Jenna was concerned he was definitely a goner.

Someone nudged him from behind and Cole stepped forward, realizing that he been lost in thought. Having Jenna on the brain had been happening to him a lot lately. He glanced up to where Jenna was waiting, wondering if she was feeling better, and then shook his head. *Here I am waiting to check into a honeymoon suite with a woman I'm crazy about. I've been celibate for months and my great plan is to remain that way even though just being near her drives me insane with wanting her.* Cole sighed. Jenna was fully aware of his playboy reputation. The last thing he wanted was for her to think he was simply trying to get into her pants. Everyone, including his own sister, thought that sex was all he was about, and he was determined to prove otherwise.

So, even though it was going to be damned difficult, Cole was going to take it slow with Jenna. He desperately wanted to make love to her, but he also wanted her to be in love with him. The only way to make that happen was to prove to Jenna that he wasn't the shallow playboy that she and the entire town of Sander's City thought him to be . . . well, not anymore, anyway.

Cole finally stepped up to the front desk and gave the perky clerk a weak smile. He scrawled his signature on some papers and absently listened to information about a buffet supper and the Travis Mackey concert that evening.

"You're all set," she finally announced and handed Cole the key cards. "You're on the seventh floor, down the hallway to the left. The honeymoon suites have private balconies overlooking the ocean. I hope you enjoy your stay at Wild Ride Resort. If there is anything at all that you need, don't hesitate to call."

"Thanks." Cole pocketed the key cards and headed back up the escalator. With a glance at his watch, he noted that he had been gone for nearly thirty minutes. He half expected to find Jenna curled up on the sofa asleep, but she spotted him as soon as he stepped off of the escalator and waved.

chapter three

"Ohhh . . ." Jenna tried to stand up but felt a bit woozy so she plopped back down onto the sofa. She drained the last sip of the cold, fruity punch from her hurricane glass, nearly poking herself in the eye with the tiny paper umbrella, and then smiled as Cole walked toward her down the wide hallway. People were laughing and chattering while calypso music from a live band drifted up from the lobby below. Waiters dressed in multicolored tropical shirts handed out welcome drinks right and left to eager takers.

Jenna had already consumed two but had declined another from a smiling waiter. Although the concoction tasted like Hawaiian Punch, she now suspected that there was a liberal amount of rum in the drinks. In hindsight, two potent cocktails on an empty stomach probably wasn't such a good idea. She straightened her spine, folded her hands in her lap, and attempted to look sober.

Jenna's heart thumped harder as Cole approached her. She

felt heat steal into her cheeks at the mere thought of making love to him, wishing she could control her blushing. Redheads didn't just blush, they flamed. She placed her hands on her cheeks while her internal schoolteacher voice reminded her that she was already hopelessly in love with Cole. Adding sex (that she was sure would be amazing) to the mix would more than likely raise the bar for any other man she happened to make love to, therefore basically ruining her for life. *Stay away from him* her schoolteacher voice persisted. *Find some other schmuck to ring your bell for a week.*

Jenna looked around. The place was crawling with single guys looking for action. She had heard that when the sun set this place went wild, so why did she need Cole Forrester, anyway?

Because I'm in love with him!

Don't let him know, she thought when he stopped in front of the sofa. *Letting him know how you feel will send Cole Forrester, the eternal bachelor, running into the arms of someone else.* Jenna also realized with a sinking heart that this place was crawling with gorgeous women. While she knew that she was attractive in a girl-next-door kind of way, she feared that she was no match for thong bikinis and boob jobs. She thought of her conservative tankini and sighed.

"Ready?" Cole asked, holding out his hand for her to grasp.

Jenna nodded while doubt bounced around in her brain. His hand felt warm and firm and sent a little shiver down her spine. She stood up and was horrified when she swayed . . . just slightly, but of course he had to notice.

"Hey, you okay?" he asked, and slipped his arm around her waist. "Still woozy from the roller-coaster ride?"

Jenna leaned heavily against him. "Actually I think it's more a reaction from two of those giant hurricanes on an empty tummy." Wrinkling her nose, she looked up at him. "Not so smart."

Cole chuckled. "I've always appreciated your honesty," he remarked as they began walking down the hallway.

Jenna smiled when his comment prompted a sudden thought. She did have one up in the competition. After a lifelong crush on her best friend's brother Jenna knew him pretty darned well. She knew guy things like his best-loved sport (baseball), his beer of choice (Bud light) and his favorite food (hot wings). He listened to classic rock, never missed a Will Smith movie, and read Stephen King novels. Jenna knew too, through Halley, that Cole had had offers for bigger, better jobs than that of marketing director for the Sander's City Flyers, but that he had turned them all down in order to stay near his dad.

When they paused at the door to their room while Cole fished into his pocket for the key card, Jenna realized that there were so many things that she liked about Cole, but she also remembered that Halley had warned her that her brother went through women like Jenna went through pantyhose. Okay, maybe having a fling with a guy that you're already in love with but who is certain to dump you isn't so smart. Jenna sighed and murmured, "Now, what do I do?"

Cole chuckled as he slipped the key card into the slot and then opened the door. "Lunch and a nap will make you right as rain. Don't worry; I won't let you miss the concert. Hopefully, our luggage has already arrived."

Thank God he misunderstood her remark, Jenna

thought as she stepped into the room. "Wow, this is beautiful," she observed and Cole gave a low whistle of approval. Tropic-themed but tastefully decorated, the room was big and airy. A huge paddle fan moved in a lazy circle while sunlight streamed through the open curtains, revealing a sliding glass door that led to a big balcony overlooking the ocean. Sturdy white wicker furniture stood in stark contrast to the sea-foam green walls. A wet bar, a mini-refrigerator and a small table with four chairs took up the far end of the room. But it was the king-sized bed . . . the only bed, that captured Jenna's attention. She tried to look away, but the bed was just so . . . *there,* taking up most of the space and all of her imagination.

The bed seemed to give Cole pause as well, because he stared at it with a frown. "I was hoping for a sleep-sofa." Still staring at the bed, he continued, "I can make do with the floor."

Jenna tried not to let his remark sting. After all, they did have an agreement, but gee, wasn't he going to try at all to . . . to get into her pants? Then, a horrible string of maybes whizzed through her brain. Maybe Cole wasn't attracted to her at all. Maybe she was more like a sister to him? Maybe the thought of sharing a bed with her turned him off! *Maybe* he couldn't wait to hit the tiki bar and troll for long-legged beauties because she just wasn't good enough! Well! Jenna let out a long sigh, thinking that unrequited love was *so* not fun.

Jenna realized with a sinking heart that this situation was going to be a lot more awkward than she had envisioned, and judging by the stricken look on Cole's face, and his wish to sleep on the floor for goodness' sake, he wasn't even remotely interested in a fling. So rather than have her self-esteem lowered even further, Jenna decided to nix the whole seducing-Cole idea.

So lost was she in her thoughts, Jenna hadn't realized that Cole had wandered over to the wide sliding glass doors at the opposite end of the room. He stood there with his back to her while gazing out over the water. As always, her heart skipped a beat just looking at him. Throw in a bed big enough to do undercover Olympics, an ice bucket with a bottle of champagne, and a silver tray laden with strawberries and chocolate for dipping, and it was enough to make a girl, well, get *really* turned on.

Jenna allowed her gaze to linger a moment longer. God, what she wouldn't give to have him slowly turn around with a sexy smile just for her. What would he do, she wondered, if she wiggled out of her clothes, plopped down on the bed and then offered him one of those fat strawberries while casting a come-hither look in his direction?

Oh, but of course she wouldn't, not even with two hurricanes under her belt. She might be in a honeymoon suite with Cole Forrester, but she was still quiet Jenna Wagner, high-school art teacher whose life was in pretty much of a rut. Jenna sighed, wishing that she had the nerve to seduce Cole, to make this week one to remember . . .

But then again, *maybe not*. Deep down, she knew that she wanted the whole package, not just sex. But since that wasn't likely to happen, she had better just keep her distance because boy oh boy, the sex part was looking pretty darned appealing right about now. Yes, she thought sadly, the you-go-your-way-I'll-go-mine plan needed to be back in place . . . pronto.

But she wasn't about to let Cole sleep on the floor!

"Cole?"

He turned to face her with an odd expression. "Yes?"

"You're not going to sleep on the floor. I won't allow it."

"Is that right?" Cole couldn't help but smile when Jenna raised her chin a notch and nodded firmly. Didn't she realize that she was tying him in knots? Even her prim and proper schoolteacher voice was a major turn-on. Perhaps it was because he had fought his attraction to her for so damned long, but every little thing Jenna did made him want to throw her onto the big-ass bed and make wild and crazy love to her.

Jenna visibly swallowed, and then with a sweeping gesture toward the bed announced, "The bed is huge. We can sleep there without even touching, no problem."

Ah, easy for you to say, Cole thought, and suddenly wondered if Jenna was over the crush that Halley had insisted that she had had on him.

"And I want to make it clear that I appreciate your concern for me, but I really don't expect you to babysit me all week long." She gave him a small smile. "I don't want to cramp your style."

Cole remained silent for a long moment, trying not to feel hurt that Jenna thought that he just couldn't wait to go swaggering around the resort in search of a willing woman. Unfortunately, his reputation for being something of a ladies man had grown to almost legendary proportions in Sander's City. Small towns had a way of taking little things like the fact that he had dated an actress or two while attending college at UCLA and giving them much bigger meaning than they really had. Being a high-school football and baseball star in a small town where local sports were the only real entertainment had added to his sex appeal. He was treated almost like a celebrity, which made him feel that many of the local women who came on to him were more interested in being seen on his arm than being in an actual relationship. Not that it bothered Cole too much, since the thought of settling down with one woman had never sounded appealing.

Until now.

"You won't cramp my style," he said stiffly.

"I will if I'm always with you. People will really think that we're . . . you know, *together*." She blushed to the roots of her hair.

"That will be perfect," Cole said when an idea popped into his head.

Jenna frowned and then her eyebrows shot up. "It will?"

"Yeah. I'm here for a little rest and relaxation. If people think that we're really honeymooners, then I won't have to worry about . . ."

"Fending off women?"

Cole nodded. "Right." He took a couple of steps toward her. "Uh, unless, I'll be cramping *your* style?" He waited, not realizing he was holding his breath until she answered.

"Oh . . . oh no. I'm here for some rest and to, you know, do other things like . . . uh, snorkel." She waved one hand in a dismissive gesture. "Not that I would have to fend off men." She chuckled and then looked away from him.

"Are you kidding? You'd be beating them off with a stick, Jenna."

She looked back at him with wide green eyes . . . eyes

that he could get lost in. "You always did tease me, Cole Forrester."

She thought he was teasing? Didn't she know just how appealing she was? Sure, she was more cute than beautiful, but so sweet, so damned feminine that she brought out every protective male instinct that he possessed. She was sexy in a down-to-earth, honest way that flat-out bowled him over. Taking another step closer, he said, "I'm dead serious."

"Y-you are?"

Cole nodded and lifted one eyebrow in question. "Think we can pull it off?"

"Being honeymooners?"

"It would take a little showmanship."

Her eyebrows shot up again. "Like what?"

Cole shrugged and tried to sound nonchalant. "Oh, I don't know . . . holding hands, maybe."

"Okay."

"A kiss here and there."

"Oh . . . right. Sure." She licked her lips as if thinking about kissing him, and Cole almost groaned. Jenna definitely had a mouth made for kissing. "Anything else?"

God yes. Cole shrugged, trying to look calm, cool and collected when he was anything but. "I'm sure we can ad lip . . . *lib* along the way."

Jenna nodded. She seemed nervous, but agreeable to his ridiculous (couldn't she see through him?) scheme. With a shy look in his general direction, she said, "I'm going to lie down for a little nap and sleep off my hurricanes."

Cole grinned. "Okay."

"You're welcome to join me . . . uh . . . you know, to

sleep." She bit her bottom lip and put her hands to her cheeks. "I'm blushing, aren't I?"

"Yeah," he said softly.

"I can't control it."

"I think it's cute."

She was silent at that comment, but then said, "This is more awkward than I thought it would be."

"We'll have fun, Jenna."

She smiled. "I know. You have a way of putting me at ease, making me laugh. I've known you almost all of my life, Cole. I trust you."

"Sleep tight. I'll wake you in time for a bite to eat before the concert." Cole smiled but cringed inwardly as he headed for the mini-bar for a cold beer and then headed out onto the balcony to drink it. Trust? What Jenna didn't know was that Halley and Reese could actually have gotten most of their money back because of an insurance policy on the trip. Cole had found this out when he approached the travel agent after offering to take the trip off their hands, but had kept the information to himself, selfishly wanting to take Jenna along. The other thing that Jenna didn't know was the true cost of the trip. The vacation had been a gift from Reese's parents to the young couple so that they could have a honeymoon to remember . . . and it had cost a small fortune for the honeymoon suite. Cole didn't mind. His job with the minor-league Flyers didn't pay a huge salary, but he had a knack for the stock market and had more money than he knew what to do with, especially with the low cost of living in Sander's City.

Cole tipped back the brown bottle and took a long swig of the cold, tangy beer. Jenna had paid only a small fraction of the cost of the trip and would have had a fit if she had known the true cost. On her teacher's salary, she would never have been able to afford to come, so Cole had fudged big time, quoting her a ridiculous figure, claiming it had been a special offer. Trust? Yeah, right. Jenna thought she was doing Halley a big favor or she never would have agreed to come with him. Not with big, bad playboy Cole Forrester.

Cole leaned on the railing, looking out over the ocean without really appreciating the magnificent view. He wished he could just be honest with Jenna and tell her that over the course of the past year, beginning with the bachelorette-party kiss and ending with Halley's wedding, he had fallen hopelessly in love with her. But Cole knew that she would think that he was just coming on to her. Damn, he had already almost blown it by coming very close to kissing her in the hallway. This taking-it-slow plan that he had concocted was going to be difficult. The most challenging thing, though, was going to be convincing Jenna that his feelings for her were sincere. His small-town reputation for being a big-time lover was going to be hard to overcome.

With a sigh, Cole drained the last of his beer and then sat down in a lounge chair. Wanting to feel the warmth of the sun on his bare skin, he removed his shirt and leaned back while inhaling the briny scent of the ocean. Cole relaxed, loving the feel of the sun caressing his skin. Somewhere in the distance he heard laughter, music, the screech of a seagull, and the crash of the waves hitting the shore. His eyes felt heavy and although he hated to move, he didn't want to fall asleep and wake up as red as one of Jenna's blushes.

With a groan, Cole pushed to his feet and entered the suite, silently sliding the door shut so as not to wake Jenna. The blast of cool air hit his heated skin, making him shiver . . .

And then his gaze drifted to Jenna. She was asleep, lying on her side facing him, looking so small in the great big bed. She had neatly folded down the dark green bedspread but was snuggled beneath a soft-looking green blanket. Her hair spilled over the white pillowcase. Cole could hear her breathing softly, drawing him closer to the bed.

Unable to help himself, he gazed down at her for a long moment. Her long eyelashes cast a slight shadow across her cheekbones. He smiled at the smattering of cinnamon-colored freckles dusting her perky nose . . . but it was her mouth that made his heart beat faster. Her lips were slightly parted, looking moist and oh so soft. Cole remembered how she kissed; she was tentative, a bit shy, but with an underlying heat that promised so much more.

Rather embarrassed that he was becoming aroused, Cole quickly turned away, almost knocking over the champagne on ice. Closing his eyes, he threaded his fingers through his hair and tried to find the humor in the situation but came up blank. With a sigh he toed off his Nikes and eased his weight onto the bed, realizing that he was exhausted. The long trip coupled with lack of sleep in anticipation of being with Jenna suddenly caught up with him. Cole slipped beneath the covers, carefully staying near the edge of the bed on his side. He rolled over, facing away from Jenna and closed his eyes, trying to will his tense body to relax so that he could catch some sleep.

chapter four

Jenna woke up by small degrees, scratching her nose, yawning, and then opening her droopy eyes. *Oh my.* Her sleepy gaze fell upon golden, tanned skin that looked smooth and touchable. She leisurely looked over at Cole's wide shoulders and then down his back, pausing to admire firm muscles that tapered to a trim waist. Her fingers itched to reach across the less-than-arm's-length space that separated her from her goal.

Jenna closed her eyes, hoping for the out-of-sight-out-of-mind thing to work, but then her senses became more in tune to everything else. She could hear the soft sound of his even breathing, smell the spicy scent of his after-shave, and feel the heat of his body so close to hers. Her body became aware and then aroused, making her want to wrap her arms around him and melt.

The urge . . . no, make that the *need*, to reach over and touch him became almost unbearable. Jenna wondered if Cole would wake up if she just barely grazed her fingertips over his back. With her heart pounding wildly, she eased her hand across the covers, but then snatched it back just before coming in contact with his skin.

Maybe she could snuggle closer, pretending that she had wound up that way by accident. Biting her bottom lip at her boldness, Jenna scooted a few inches closer. *God he smells good*, she thought, and then wondered with a hot little shiver what that golden skin would taste like.

Jenna let out a long audible sigh of complete and utter longing and almost levitated off the bed when without warning Cole rolled to his back, closing the small gap between them. Jenna held her breath when his shoulder almost brushed against her mouth. Jenna pressed her lips together to suppress another long sigh while gazing her fill. She had seen Cole shirtless many times over the years and had always thought he had a great physique . . . nicely defined with lean muscle without being too bulky. In her mind he had just the right amount of chest hair . . . dark and silky-looking, not too thick, and tapering nicely to . . . *oh God*, what did he look like *there?*

Stop! Jenna took a deep, shaky breath. Had she really been wondering what his . . . *oh no*, he stirred again, moving even closer, and then rolled onto his side, causing her to be up close and personal with dark chest hair and one flat nipple. For a moment Jenna went perfectly still . . . and then silently tried to scramble away, but her feet got tangled in the covers. She brushed up against his hard thigh and then ceased all movement, including breathing, when Cole sighed, mumbled something, and then flung a warm, heavy arm over her.

She was trapped.

Granted, Jenna could simply have nudged Cole awake, but she couldn't quite bring herself to do so . . . at least not yet. No, she wanted to savor the feeling of being curled up against his chest. Plus, from the many sleep-overs at Halley's she knew that Cole slept like the dead. No amount of adolescents screaming or pop music blaring could jar Cole awake.

Jenna smiled, remembering Halley's thirteenth birthday party when a truth-or-dare game had her sneaking into Cole's bedroom to squirt toothpaste on his forehead and stick a tampon in his ear. Well, she had managed the toothpaste part but chickened out of the tampon end of the dare. The next morning sixteen-year-old Cole had come roaring out of his bedroom in flannel pajama bottoms and his too-long hair spiked up with minty-fresh Colgate, hell-bent on wringing Halley's neck. Not wanting to see the demise of her best friend, Jenna had fearfully confessed, but Cole had simply grinned, rolled his blue eyes at Jenna, and then given her strawberry-blond pigtail a yank.

Jenna smiled softly. Cole had been so cute back then with rebellious long hair, a brooding bad-boy pout, and intense blue eyes. Thinking back, though, Jenna remembered that he had always seemed to have a quick grin and a teasing remark for her, and had even come to her rescue once when Danny Parker had tried to take her lunch money.

Taking a deep, Cole-scented breath, Jenna realized that her feelings for him were well beyond her teenage crush stage. Yep, she was in love up to her eyeballs . . . eyeballs that were at this very moment staring at his very fine chest. *Oh yeah,* the cute teenager had grown into a hard-bodied man.

Yikes! Jenna's eyes widened when Cole stirred, mumbled something, and pulled her even closer. His big hand slipped in a sleepy fashion to her hip, causing Jenna to roll closer and *ohmigod* . . . Cole was aroused.

Jenna's heart thudded and her whole body reacted, making her feel heavy-limbed, as if the blood trying to pump through her veins were made of warm honey. *This is insane,* Jenna thought, but at the same time wanted to rub her hand over the rock-hard erection that was right now pressed against her hip.

She had to wake him.

Swallowing, Jenna opened her mouth just as Cole shifted his weight forward and suddenly her lips were against warm, soft skin . . . God, make that *his nipple.*

She had Cole Forrester's nipple pressed against her mouth.

"Cole?" she tried but ended up sort of accidentally licking him since her mouth was still plastered against his chest. She couldn't get her hand between their bodies, so she tried tapping on his back. "Cole?" She said again, her voice muffled, encountering his nipple once more and a bit of chest hair.

"Hmmm?" Cole felt something warm and wet on his . . . *nipple?* He blinked, reluctantly trying to wake up from a delicious dream involving making love to Jenna on a roller coaster. He encountered flashes of red-gold and realized that Jenna's head rested just beneath his chin . . . and *God help him,* it was *her* mouth on his nipple. What was happening? Was he still dreaming? "J-Jenna?"

She tilted her head up, bringing her mouth so damned close to his that without really thinking, only feeling,

Cole closed the small space between their lips. *Ahh,* her mouth felt so soft, so pliant, and so very warm. Her lips parted and their tongues met, sending a jolt of white-hot desire coursing through him.

Threading his fingers through her hair, Cole tilted Jenna's head back against the pillow and deepened the kiss, loving it when she wrapped her arms around him and kissed him back. Slightly shy at first, she was suddenly on the same page, kissing him with gusto. When she slid her hands down his back, pressing him closer, Cole's desire shifted into overdrive. He moved his mouth from her lips to her neck, kissing and nibbling all the way to the swell of her breast above the V-neck of her shirt. Cole slid his hand beneath the hem of the soft cotton, moaning when he encountered satiny smooth, warm skin.

Somewhere in the back of his head a voice warned him to stop, but Cole ignored it. He wanted her too much and had waited for this moment for way too long. "God, Jenna." Cole kissed her again and she wasn't at all shy this time, opening her mouth to meet his, kissing him back with wild abandon, arching her body against him as if she couldn't get close enough.

Encouraged by her enthusiasm, Cole reached around and deftly unhooked her bra. Slipping his hand beneath the satin and lace, Cole cupped her breast, gently kneading the fullness. Pulling his mouth from hers, he said, "I want you in my mouth."

Her big green eyes, luminous, dilated with passion, gazed back at him. Her mouth was pink, swollen from his kisses. She nodded and whispered, "Yes . . . oh yes."

"Take off your shirt for me, Jenna," Cole pleaded and leaned back to give her room to do so.

She nodded, sat up, and then tugged her shirt and bra over her head, tossing them to the floor.

Cole sucked in a breath. "You have beautiful breasts."

"Freckled," she said shyly.

"Come here and let me kiss each and every freckle."

She blushed, reminding Cole that this was Jenna Wagner, and this was probably a big step for her. The annoying voice in his head also sternly reminded him that this was not the game plan. Far from it. "Jenna . . ."

"It's okay, Cole. I want this."

"But—"

Leaning forward, she put a finger to his lips. "Cole, we're both adults here." She nibbled on her bottom lip and then said, "There is obvious attraction between us, right?"

Cole didn't like where this was heading, but nodded his agreement.

"Then why don't we . . . um, that is, if you want to . . ." She lowered her eyes and swallowed.

Cole felt his heart sink. "Have a vacation fling?"

Lifting her gaze to his, she answered softly, "Yes."

"No strings attached?"

She shook her head firmly. "Oh, absolutely not."

Cole sighed, thinking that this was payback or poetic justice for all the times he had made the same speech. "What about after we get back home, Jenna?"

"Well, no one will ever have to know. There's no small-town tongues to wag here." Taking a big breath, she said, "I'm almost thirty years old, Cole. It's time I loved . . . I mean, *lived* a little."

Cole remained silent for a moment while his heart thudded and his mind raced. This was everything he wanted and yet nothing he wanted. Saying yes to her meant letting her think he was the no-strings-attached player that she thought him to be. But if he refused her, she would be humiliated. There was really no middle ground. He wished that he could just tell her his feelings for her but at this particular moment Cole doubted that Jenna would think his declaration of love would sound sincere. He could tell by the pink color in her cheeks that this wasn't easy. She seemed a bit troubled . . . confused.

"Why are you scowling? Oh God, you don't want me." She turned her face away from him. "I'm sorry, I—"

"Of course I want you." Placing his finger beneath her chin, he turned her face toward him and silenced her with a long, hot kiss. Pulling slowly away from her mouth, he licked her bottom lip and then asked, "Convinced?"

"Yeah." Her smile trembled a bit at the corners, reminding Cole just how sweet, how vulnerable she was, and yet the irony of the situation was that he was the one putting his heart on the line. *A vacation fling my sweet ass,* Cole thought grimly. Well, if sex was his weapon, he was just going to have to rock Jenna Wagner's world.

"Jenna?"

"Yeah?"

Cole leaned in and whispered in her ear, "I like to do things right. We'll start with the strawberries and champagne."

~~ chapter
five

J enna would have added her agreement, but her
voice had once again left the building. A moment later she had a fat, chocolate-dipped, strawberry in
her mouth. She took a big juicy bite and chewed while
watching Cole pop the cork on the bottle of champagne,
all the while wondering if it were possible for her heart to
pound right out of her chest.

He turned back to her and handed her a flute of bub-
bly with a smile that dissolved any last shred of resistance
or doubt. She wanted this man, always had. Resisting the
urge to tug the sheet up over her naked, freckled breasts,
she lifted her flute and tapped it to his with a delicate
clink. Jenna took a long swallow of the cold, fizzy champagne that warmed as it traveled down her throat to her
belly. She smiled at him over the rim while hoping desperately that she could make up for her lack of sexual experience with enthusiasm.

"I'll be right back," Cole said and then dipped another

strawberry in the dark chocolate sauce. He fed her a bite and then turned away, leaving Jenna sitting in the middle of the big bed. She licked chocolate from the corner of her mouth and then drained the glass of champagne, while wondering if it was too forward to remove the rest of her clothing. Cole walked over to the sliding glass doors and closed the drapes, leaving the room in semi darkness, and then disappeared into the bathroom.

Deciding that she should get naked, Jenna shimmied from the bed and removed her shorts and panties. She thought about striking a sexy pose on top of the bed, but doubted that she could pull it off and ended up slipping beneath the covers. This whole thing was sort of surreal but so exciting that she trembled.

Closing her eyes, she tried to squelch the guilt over telling Cole that she only wanted a vacation fling. What a bunch of hooey. She wanted the whole enchilada . . . but sternly reminded herself that Cole didn't. "Live in the moment," she whispered to herself. "If I can't have forever, this will have to do."

Jenna's heart kicked it up another notch when Cole came out of the bathroom clad in blue boxers. He gave her a soft smile and if Jenna hadn't known better, she would have thought that he looked a bit nervous.

"Music?" he asked.

Jenna nodded, since her voice was still MIA. She watched him pick up a remote and point it at the television until he found some sultry jazz on a music station.

"More champagne?"

"No," she managed to say in a voice just above a whisper.

"Me neither," Cole said and took her empty glass.

Jenna watched him slide the boxers past his hips. His

penis sprang forward, sleek and proud, making Jenna long to wrap her fingers around him and stroke him. Instead, she curled her fingers into the sheet and waited.

He dipped his finger into the chocolate sauce before joining her on the bed. "Open your mouth," he requested with a smile and touched the chocolate to her lips.

Jenna sucked the semisweet chocolate from his finger. Her heart thudded with the knowledge that he was going to take this slow and easy even though it was obvious that he was more than ready. Jenna was so excited that she wondered if she could take slow and easy, but didn't quite know how to voice her problem. *Forget the chocolate I want you inside me* might be a mood-breaker so she kept the need to ravish him to herself. When he turned back to the chocolate, Jenna wondered if saying *forget the chocolate* in a really sexy tone would work.

"Lean back against the pillows, Jenna."

She silently obeyed, easing her shoulders against the fluffy down pillows until she reclined in a half-sitting position. The sheet pooled to her waist and for a moment Cole just gazed at her. The gleam in his blue eyes made her feel sexy and beautiful. She sucked in a breath when he leaned over and swirled the chocolate over her nipple and then licked it off. *Ohhh, maybe slow wasn't so bad after all.* The only part of his body touching her was his hot tongue and she arched up, wanting more contact with his golden skin. "More," Jenna managed in a mangled whisper.

"Gladly," Cole said, mistaking her need. He twisted toward the nightstand and came back with more chocolate dipped fingers, repeating the sensual torture on her other nipple, licking with the very tip of his tongue.

"Cole . . ." God, this was sweet torture. "Please . . ."

He turned away again, coming back with two fingers covered in the thick sauce, and preceded to paint her pale skin with chocolate streaks. Jenna pressed her shoulders into the pillows, arching up while he licked lower and lower until her belly quivered, her breasts swelled, and her breath came in short gasps. If he didn't make love to her right *now* she was going to die.

The sultry wail of a tenor saxophone accompanied Cole's sensual assault. His tongue ticked, titillated and left her craving so much more. "Cole . . ." She needed the weight of his body, the heat of his skin. "Please . . ."

"Relax. Close your eyes."

Jenna obeyed, expecting more body painting, but gasped when with a cold drizzle of champagne hit her heated skin. Cole's low sexy laugh had Jenna opening her eyes in time to see his dark head dip to her body and lap away the liquid. Oh God, he continued south, tugging the sheet from the lower half of her body. He parted her thighs, nuzzled his hot mouth against her mound and then gave her swollen clitoris a light flick of his tongue.

With a surprised cry of pleasure, Jenna came instantly. Her orgasm was sharp, intense . . . and *embarrassing.* God, that had to be like a world record! What had it taken, three seconds? She was about to apologize, but Cole seemed impressed and said, "I always knew that you were a passionate woman."

He did? That thought filtered through her orgasmic afterglow, but before she could contemplate the meaning, he leaned in and kissed her. He tasted of chocolate and champagne and *sex,* a heady combination that had Jenna getting revved up all over again.

Cole turned and reached toward the nightstand for protection. A little shot of *I'm not ready for this* seeped into her brain, but then Cole turned back to her with a bone-melting smile that chased all her doubts away. She welcomed the weight of his body, and *finally* the feel of his skin sliding against hers.

"God, you feel so good," Cole whispered in her ear.

"And . . . mmmm, so do you." Jenna slipped her hands up and down his back, loving the ripple of muscle when he moved. She shivered when his warm lips nuzzled the tender inside of her neck, instinctively arching up while rocking her body against his. Her legs parted for him and Jenna cried out softly when he entered her with one smooth delicious stroke.

They moved in rhythm with the soft sultry music without even knowing it . . . Jenna wrapped herself around him until there wasn't one inch of her skin that wasn't touching his. She rocked slowly with him, surprised that he was so tender, so giving. Her pleasure began to swell, to build. She arched up, needing more of him . . . *all of him.*

Cole reached up and entwined his fingers with hers. He was familiar with sex, good at it really, but this was the next level of being with a woman. Knowing it would be special with Jenna, Cole still wasn't prepared for the emotion. He made love to her slow and deliciously sinking into her slick heat while savoring the feel of her skin, the taste of her mouth, the sound of her soft sighs that blended with the music.

When she cried out his name, Cole climaxed with a hot rush of pure pleasure. With his heart pounding in his ears, he leaned his forehead against hers, knowing that if she saw his expression, she would surely guess the intensity of his feelings. So much for taking it slow, Cole thought, wanting to kick his own ass. He had probably just driven home every playboy notion Jenna had about him.

This was not good.

"You were amazing," Jenna said softly.

Cole raised his head and smiled down at her. "And so were you."

She returned his smile with a shy one of her own. "I don't think we'll have any trouble convincing people that we're honeymooners."

"Not at all," Cole responded, forcing a light tone to his voice. He kissed her on the forehead and rolled to the side of the bed all the while wondering how his simple plan had gotten so screwed up so quickly. He wished he had the balls to grab her by the shoulders, look her in the eyes, and say, "Jenna, I've always adored you and over the past year I've fallen completely in love with you. I brought you to this island to show how much I care and a no-strings-attached fling is out of the question."

"Cole? Are you okay?"

When Cole realized that he had been staring at the wall he hesitated and then with a deep breath decided that he should just come clean and tell her how he felt. Screw it. With his heart pounding, he turned back to face her and said, "Jenna, I've always adored you and—"

"Cole, stop." She put a hand on his shoulder. "I don't want you to feel guilty about what just happened. I told you, I'm an adult and I can handle this . . . this agreement that we have. And I promise not to go all needy on you when we get home."

"So what goes down on the island stays on the island?" Cole asked, carefully keeping the disappointment from his voice. Well, he thought, so much for his little speech.

With a lift of her chin she smiled and said, "Yes, exactly."

Cole would have almost believed her but her smile trembled a bit at the corners and he wondered if Jenna wanted this no-strings bull as much as she pretended. But then again, maybe that was wishful thinking on his part. "Hungry?" he asked, wanting to change the subject.

"Starving!"

"I read in one of the brochures that you can get picnic baskets for the concert. How's that sound?"

Jenna smiled. "Perfect. I'll go get dressed."

When she leaned over and kissed him on the cheek, Cole's heart ached. If she dumped him after this week he was going to be one hellava mess.

⤳ chapter
six

"Oh no, every single spot is taken," Jenna observed as they approached the outdoor concert area of the resort. The large semicircle of lawn that surrounded an amphitheater looked like a continuous patchwork quilt made up of beach towels and blankets where people lounged while waiting for Travis Mackey to appear. Like Jenna and Cole, many had opted for a picnic-basket supper offered by the resort.

Cole tugged on Jenna's hand, leading her to the edge of the grass a bit away from the crowd. "Come on over here. It's not the best spot to see the stage, but at least we can eat our dinner." He grinned. "From the looks of those speakers we'll be able to hear the concert just fine."

Jenna stuck her bottom lip out in a fake pout. "Yeah, but getting to see Travis Mackey in those tight Wranglers is half the fun."

"Hey, we're honeymooners, remember? You're only supposed to have eyes for me," Cole teased.

Oh, if only you knew, Jenna thought, but tossed a smile his way as she spread out a big beach towel. The truth was that she had a hard time taking her gaze off of Cole. He wore a casual, button-down blue shirt made of some soft-looking material that was loose-fitting and yet kept molding against his body when he moved. Three open buttons revealed tanned skin and dark chest hair. She really, *really* wanted to run her hands over the silky shirt and then slowly undo each button until she could feel his warm skin beneath her fingers.

Jenna felt a little daring in a flirty floral skirt and yellow halter top that bared her shoulders and showed more cleavage than she was used to showing. She had bought several new outfits for the trip, but had wondered if she would have the nerve to wear them. Even more daring was the lacy black thong that made her feel just a little bit naughty. Kicking off her sandals, she sat down on the blanket next to Cole, who was already opening the picnic basket that doubled as a cooler.

"We've got cold beer, but I thought you might like some raspberry tea," Cole said.

"Oh, raspberry tea is my favorite."

Cole gave her a smile as he twisted off the lid and then handed her the cold bottle. "I know. And I have chicken-salad sandwiches."

"My favorite, too," she said softly.

"Brownies for dessert," he whispered in her ear. "I've known you for a long time, Jenna. I know more than you can imagine."

"Well, you sure know me a lot better now," Jenna said and then put a hand over her mouth. "Oh, *why* do I always say what I'm thinking?"

Cole tilted his head back and laughed. "See, I know that about you, too."

Jenna nudged his shoulder, enjoying the playful banter. She had been worried that after having sex things would be awkward, but she felt even more relaxed with him. The sexual tension that had crackled between them for the past year had melted into something that suddenly felt very warm and very real.

Cole handed her a sandwich and she bit into the crusty French roll. "Mmmm, this chicken salad is the kind with grapes and pecans. I'm in heaven!"

Cole angled his head at her and said, "That's another thing that I like about you, Jenna. You enjoy simple things that others overlook or take for granted."

Jenna shrugged. "I guess that's the artist in me. I tend to see the beauty in the smallest of things, even chicken salad." Jenna wondered if her admission screamed "small-town schoolteacher" when she was trying to come out of her shell. Her answer, though, seemed to please him, because he gave her a warm smile that made her want to tackle him right then and there.

They ate their sandwiches in companionable silence, but Jenna was keenly aware each time Cole's arm brushed hers. Every little thing he did somehow seemed sexy and made her awareness of him skyrocket. When he twisted off the cap of his beer bottle Jenna admired his long, tapered fingers, remembering how they had felt caressing her skin. When he leaned back on his elbows, his shirt molded against the contours of his chest. God, and the man even had sexy feet. Jenna chuckled at the thought.

"What?" Cole glanced her way.

"Nothing."

"Tell me."

"You have sexy feet," she said, and then felt the heat of a blush in her cheeks.

He looked down at his feet. "Really? Now how can my *feet* possibly be sexy?"

Jenna took a drink of her tea and then scooted down to the edge of the beach towel. After removing his flip-flop, she put his foot in her lap. "Well," she began, "for starters, your toes are cute."

He arched an eyebrow. "Cute?"

Jenna nodded. "See, your big toe is nicely shaped and your other toes," she continued while touching each toe, "are in perfect alignment. None of that middle toe being taller than the others or bunions or anything." She ran her fingertip over his arch. "Nice curve here," she said, trying to remain serious. Lifting his foot up by the heel, rubbed her hand over the bottom of his foot. "Ahh, very smooth."

"So, that's why my feet are sexy?"

"Your feet are sexy because they are attached to the rest of you."

Cole laughed. "You said that out loud, you know."

"I know."

Cole came up to a sitting position. "Are you flirting with me?"

"I do believe I am." She surprised herself by kissing his big toe. "Or at least with your feet."

"Well come up here and flirt with the rest of me." He patted the space beside him on the towel.

"Okay." She scooted back up to his side and he put his arm around her but instead of flirting, she leaned her head against his shoulder. The sun looked like a giant orange ball as it dipped lower on the horizon, streaking the sky with purple and red. When the band started warming up, the crowd buzzed with excitement.

Cole leaned next to her ear and said, "Hey, why don't you sit between my legs and you can lean back against me."

The low timbre of his voice next to her ear gave Jenna goosebumps even though the night air remained warm and sultry. "Okay," she readily agreed and scooted between his legs. She leaned back against his chest, loving the silky feel of his shirt against her bare back and the solid warmth of his body. The spicy scent of his cologne filled her head and, of course, she spoke her thoughts. "You smell so good."

He chuckled and nuzzled his nose next to her neck. "And so do you."

Cole's warm kisses on her neck made Jenna tingle all the way to her toes. "The concert is about to begin," she said, trying to keep her voice steady.

The crowd roared and lights flashed when Travis Mackey bounded onto the stage and began singing his latest hit song but Jenna and Cole were all but oblivious to anything but each other.

Cole tried to concentrate on the concert but Jenna's bare shoulder caught his attention and he felt compelled to kiss her smooth skin. He brushed her hair to the side and kissed the tender inside of her neck. When she sighed and relaxed against him, Cole whispered in her ear, "You smell good but taste even better." Unable to resist, he slid his hand beneath her skirt and onto her thigh. "Your skin is so smooth, so warm," he murmured against her neck. When he nibbled lightly on her tiny earlobe, she shivered.

As if on cue, the lights on the stage dimmed and Travis Mackey said, "I learned from my bull-riding days that if you want something bad enough, you had better hold on tight and never let go. Krista Ross, this song is for you." A hush fell over the crowd while Travis Mackey seemed to sing directly from his heart while alone on the stage with a stool and his guitar. His whisky-smooth voice drifted into the night, washing over the crowd like the gentle waves lapping against the shore.

Cole's hand caressed Jenna's thigh in small circles, keeping in rhythm with the slow beat of the song. The heat between her thighs drew his caresses closer until his fingers made contact with the hot silk of her panties. Her quick intake of breath made him bolder and he slipped his middle finger beneath the lacy edge until he felt wet heat drench the very tip of his finger.

"Cole, you can't . . ."

"Oh, but I can. No one can see my hand. Relax and just enjoy." Cole nibbled on her neck while he slipped his finger between her slick folds. She arched her back when he circled his finger over her clitoris and continued to lightly caress her until she bit her bottom lip and shuddered in his arms.

"My God," she breathed and then put her hand over her mouth while leaning heavily against his chest.

"Don't be embarrassed. You are so beautiful when you come." Cole whispered. "Hey, would you mind listening to the concert from our balcony? Some of the other things I have in mind can't be done even in secret."

"Okay." Her reply was husky, breathless.

"I'll grab the basket, you get the beach towel."

"Sure."

"Oh, and Jenna?"

"Yes?"

"Let's hurry."

She giggled and they both scrambled to their feet. Cole had to hold the picnic basket in front of him to hide the very big tent in his pants. He could not for the life of him remember wanting a woman more than he wanted Jenna right this very minute.

They half ran, half stumbled all the way back to the hotel, almost falling into the elevator when the doors opened. Jenna, breathless and giggling, surprised Cole by pushing him up against the elevator wall and proceeded to frantically unbutton his shirt.

Splaying her hands on his bare skin, she said, "You've got the most magnificent chest in the entire world."

Cole chuckled. "That might be stretching it a bit."

"Nuh-uh." She placed warm kisses in the middle of his chest and then looked up at him with a shy smile that turned him inside out. "It's perfect. You're perfect."

Yeah, physically, thought Cole with an inner sigh. He wanted her to see so much more than his damned six-pack. Jenna was a cute but sheltered little schoolteacher looking to sow some wild oats with the town stud. End of story. He was a fool to think otherwise. He was surprised at how much it hurt, but forced a smile. "Like my sexy feet, huh?"

"Cole Forrester, there isn't one inch of you that isn't sexy but . . ." Her eyes widened a bit and she abruptly stopped talking.

"But what?"

chapter
seven

Jenna was saved from answering when the doors of the elevator opened with a whoosh. She quickly stepped out and headed down the hallway carrying the big beach towel. *God,* she had almost blurted out that even though she found him incredibly sexy from head to toe, it was how she *felt* about him that made her melt. She would love him even if he had a doggone beer belly. Jenna had to giggle at the thought of Cole sporting a jiggling beer gut.

"What?"

Jenna jumped. She hadn't realized that he was standing right behind her holding the key card in his hand. She was trying to think of an alternative answer to her beer-belly visual, but suddenly realized that Cole had a frown on his face. "N-nothing really."

Still frowning, Cole slid the key card in the slot and held the door open for her and then closed it with a quiet click. "Jenna, we need to talk."

"Okay." *Oh, those are never good words,* she thought with her heart banging against her chest.

Cole sat the picnic basket down and flicked on a light. He seemed nervous, but somehow determined. "About this whole fling scenario that we've cooked up." He paused and ran a hand through his hair. "I don't want a fling, Jenna, I—"

"Don't." Jenna's thumping heart suddenly felt like a lump of lead sinking to her toes.

"Jenna, hear me out. I—"

"I know. I don't know what we were thinking." Her hands took on a life of their own, fluttering in the air like drunken sparrows. "It was a stupid idea." Her pride bubbled to the surface, making her ramble on. "Let's call the whole thing off and go back to our original plan of going our separate ways. We can chalk up our . . . *my* earlier behavior to temporary insanity." Oh, God, she could feel heat in her cheeks but raised her chin a notch. "I'm going to head on over to that Moonlight Madness thing that they talked about in the brochure."

"Jenna, let me finish . . . *explain.* You've got this all wrong."

"So you do want a fling?"

"No . . . I want—"

"I'm leaving."

"No! Wait! You're not going to Moonlight Madness alone!"

"Watch me." Jenna ignored Cole and hurried to the door before he could see her tears. He followed but tripped over the picnic basket and came down on his hands and knees with a thump and a curse, giving Jenna the opportunity to slip out the door ahead of him. As luck would have it, the elevator doors were open and she rushed over and jammed her finger on the lobby button, looking up in time to see Cole hurrying toward her. The fact that he was limping slightly caused a twinge of concern but the doors closed before he could make it to the elevator.

With a loud sniff, Jenna angrily swiped at a tear. "How damned stupid could I possibly be?" she said through clenched teeth. Putting her cool hands to her warm cheeks, Jenna shook her head and moaned. "God, I basically threw myself at him, offering him everything, asking nothing in return. He must think that I'm pathetic." The doors opened and Jenna walked out into the lobby while wondering how in the world she was going to last a week under these conditions. *Maybe I should just go home*, she thought, and swiped at another tear. But then she squared her shoulders, sniffed one last time and decided to go on over to the Moonlight Madness carnival and have the time of her life . . . or at least pretend.

The empty lobby felt eerily quiet. Her footsteps squeaking on the marble floor was the only sound, making her feel very alone and vulnerable. "Suck it up, Wagner," she muttered and stepped out into the sultry night. She walked past the shimmering pool while glancing over her shoulder, half hoping to see Cole hurrying after her. He wasn't, causing a lump of disappointment in her throat.

She could hear Travis Mackey singing, but knew that the concert had to be almost over, so she headed in the opposite direction—toward the big gates that were only opened at night for Max's Moonlight Madness. Having heard that the carnival was a bit wild, like Mardi Gras, Jenna was admittedly nervous; she suddenly wished she were wearing more than the tiny floral skirt and halter top with nothing underneath but a thong. Going back to the room to change, though, wasn't an option, and would be an admission of some sort of odd defeat on her part, so Jenna walked through the big gates with her head held high and her heart pounding like a big bass drum.

She didn't have to worry about her attire since very little clothing seemed to be the norm. Because people were just starting to trickle in from the concert, Jenna was able to admire the cobblestone streets and quaint storefronts that sort of reminded her of Main Street in Disney World.

Despite the pretty exterior, there was a hint of anything-can-happen-here in the air. Jenna tried not to feel uneasy, but as the crowd swelled and rum punch flowed, she felt a bit out of her element . . . "Don't be such a wimp," she muttered and accepted a plastic glass full of a red rum punch.

Sipping the cold, fruity concoction, she paused at the street corner and looked around, and then moved on when she realized that she was searching the crowd for Cole. The scent of buttered popcorn popping in an old-fashioned cart mingled with the aroma of cotton candy and fried elephant ears. Jamaican music had people dancing in the street. Laughter flowed as easily as the punch and although part of her wanted to join in, Jenna stood off to the side. She wanted to lift her arms in the air and sway her hips to the beat of the drums, but couldn't quite gather the nerve. She downed the rest of her drink, hoping for some Dutch courage.

"Would you like to dance?" asked a husky masculine voice near her ear.

Jenna turned around to face a handsome shaggy-haired

blond that she recognized as the bass player in Travis Mackey's band. "No, thank you."

He gave her an exaggerated pout.

Jenna had to smile. "I loved the concert, though."

"Thanks, pretty lady."

A moment later Jenna spotted him dancing with someone else and wondered if she shouldn't have taken him up on his offer to try to get her mind off Cole. Try as she might, she kept looking for him, becoming increasingly aggravated with herself for doing so.

And then she spotted him standing directly across the street.

After noting the dark scowl on his face, she noticed that his blue shirt was buttoned up unevenly and he was barefoot, reminding her that he had hurried out of the room in quick pursuit. His persistence in finding her would have cheered her up except that she knew he had come for her simply out of concern. She reminded herself that Cole had just crushed her ego by squelching a fling after they had already done the deed *thank you very much*. Oh, now she really wished she had taken the cute bass player's offer to dance. She thought about grabbing the next available guy and dirty dancing with him right under Cole's nose, but instead she ducked into the first open doorway.

Jenna pushed her way though strings of purple beads into a small room that smelled of incense. Candles flickered, sending shadows dancing on lavender walls. An Oriental carpet covered the floor and the muffled sound of tinkling music could be heard coming from behind a closed door. Wondering what she had wandered into, Jenna turned to leave when the door opened.

A dark-haired exotic-looking young woman entered with a flourish. "Welcome," she announced with a dramatic wave of her arm. Thin gold bracelets jangled, mingling with the music. "Come with me and we will explore what your future holds."

"Oh, I don't—"

"Follow me!" The bracelets jangled again as she waved her hand over her head and swished through the doorway.

Jenna hesitated, but then, mumbling about curiosity and the cat, followed the woman into a tiny room not much bigger than a closet. A small table and two chairs took up almost all of the space. Jenna jumped when the woman firmly closed the door.

"Sit!" The woman ordered, whirling around so fast that her long skirt billowed and her very long, dark hair almost hit Jenna in the face.

Jenna sat but said, "I really don't want my fortune told."

"Yes, you do," the woman scoffed in a thick accent that Jenna wasn't sure was fake or real. She was leaning toward fake.

Jenna clasped her hands in her lap and politely inclined her head. "I beg your pardon, but I really don't—"

The fortune-teller's hand waved across the table making Jenna scoot back her chair. "You most certainly do. You want to know about the sexy man looking for you."

Jenna's heart skipped a beat. Sexy man? Okay, that was a was pretty broad statement, but she couldn't help but ask, "What sexy man?"

"The one that you are in love with."

"I'm not—" she began but was cut off with a pointed

look from the Gypsy lady. "Okay," Jenna said slowly. "Why is he looking for me?"

After a dramatic flip of her dark hair over her shoulder the woman splayed her hands on the small table and then closed her eyes. "I feel . . . anger. You pissed him off."

Jenna almost laughed at her unexpected candor.

"Why did you run from him? Are you crazy?"

Okay, this was getting creepy.

"He loves you so very much."

"Loves me?" Jenna blurted out and snorted. This woman was obviously a hack, a fake. "I really should go."

A red-tipped finger wagged in her face. "You must listen to Lola."

"Your name is Lola?"

Lola rolled her eyes. "No," she said, dropping the accent. "My name is Mary Jane Barone and I'm from Brooklyn, but I know what the hell I'm talking about so listen up. Sheesh. This poor guy has it bad for you."

"Okay," Jenna said to be polite, but wasn't convinced.

"This sexy man," she began with the exotic accent back in place, "is frantic to find you."

"What's his name?" Jenna asked, narrowing her eyes at Lola . . . Mary Jane, *whatever.*

Lola waved a hand impatiently. "I always have to prove myself to nonbelievers. Ahhh, something with a C, ahhh, Colin . . . no, Chris . . ." she paused and snapped her fingers. "Cole."

Jenna swallowed and then sat up straight in the chair. "Cole is in love with me?" she squeaked.

Lola arched one winged eyebrow. "Ah, so now you want to cut through the crap."

"How did you know his name? Is this a game? Did he put you up to this? You don't even have any cards to read or a crystal ball or whatever?"

"Stop!" Lola morphed into Mary Jane. With her palms up in the air and her Brooklyn accent back in full force, she continued, "It's a damned curse if you have to know, *Jenny.*"

"Jenna."

"Whatever."

"So you can like read minds?"

Mary Jane a.k.a. Lola snorted. "Honey, I wish. It would be great if I could solve crimes or win the lottery, but the only thing I can predict with accuracy for some ungodly reason is emotion, especially love." She leaned forward. "You know, the real deal. Unwavering and all that." She snorted again. "That's why I've never been married. I know when a guy is full of bull. This guy Cole loves you, Jenny." She angled her head and said, "And you are crazy in love with him. It's like rolling off of you in waves."

Realizing that she was losing all sense of reality, Jenna was starting to believe that Mary Jane knew what she was talking about, but still . . .

"I can sense your doubt." Mary Jane shook her head so hard that the big hoops dangling from her earlobes smacked her on her cheeks. "Think of it this way. What guy would spend the fortune that it costs to stay at Wild Ride if he wasn't serious about you?"

Jenna lifted her chin a notch. "My situation with Cole is a bit different. We're going Dutch on this trip and I paid my thousand dollars up front."

Mary Jane's eyes went wide and she snorted. "A thousand bucks? You gotta be kidding. That won't pay for one night. Honey, this ain't a Holiday Inn."

Something flipped over in Jenna's stomach. "He lied to me," she whispered.

"Oh come on, surely you had to know a resort like this would be expensive."

Jenna shook her head. "I'm just a small-town girl way out of my league."

"He knew you wouldn't come if you couldn't pay your way."

"I thought you could only predict emotion."

Mary Jane smiled softly and reached across the small table to grasp Jenna's hand. "I understand pride."

"You're right, I wouldn't have come, but it was wrong for Cole to lie to me."

"And yet you have lied to him about how you feel about him."

Jenna took a deep breath of incense-scented air and then shrugged. "Yes, I did. I let him think that I wanted a vacation fling. I figured if I couldn't have forever with him, I might as well have one week. God, I was so stupid."

"He doesn't want a fling."

"I know."

"Cole wants forever, Jenna."

With a frown, Jenna snatched her hand away. "How can you possibly know this? He's not even in the room for you to feel his vibes."

Mary Jane cocked a dark eyebrow. "Close enough. Your sexy man is right outside the door."

chapter eight

Cole impatiently untangled himself from the plastic beads and was about to exit the weird little room when he thought he heard Jenna's voice. "Okay, I'm losing it," he muttered. Cocking his head to the side, he strained to hear the voices over the noise coming from outside. He inched closer to the closed door. The voices were feminine, becoming increasingly agitated.

"If you don't believe me then open the door!"

"Okay I will! And if you expect me to pay for this nonsense—"

The door swung open and Cole was suddenly face to face with Jenna and a tall, exotic woman who he guessed was the fortune-teller.

Jenna's green eyes opened wide when she saw him. "Cole!"

"See!" The exotic-looking woman tapped Jenna on the back. "Now, do you believe me?" Her Brooklyn accent was at odds with her appearance. She gave her big hair an arrogant flip over her shoulder and then placed her hands on her hips. "Well?"

"No, I don't!" Jenna answered.

"But he is standing right there!" She pointed at Cole.

"I mean the *other* part," Jenna urgently hissed.

Cole took a step toward Jenna. "What's going on?"

The Brooklyn Gypsy said, "Jenna, I told you, I can feel these things!"

"That's a bunch of . . . of hogwash!"

"Listen here you little small-town teacher, I know my stuff."

Cole looked at Jenna. "Feel what? Know what?"

They ignored him as if he wasn't squeezed next to them in the tiny room. Cole was surprised when sweet little Jenna turned and with her hands fisted on her hips, glared at the fortune-telling chick, and said, "Mary Jane, *zip* it!"

"I will not *zip it*." Turning her fury on Cole she demanded, "Tell her!"

"Tell her what?" Cole all but bellowed.

"That you love her, you dolt!"

The room was suddenly silent except for the noise trickling in from the carnival and the soft tinkling of the mood music. Cole was about to throw caution to the damned wind and admit that he was in love with Jenna but she turned on him accusing green eyes that were swimming with tears.

"You brought me here under false pretenses. A week at this resort costs more than my car."

Cole's declaration died in his throat. "You wouldn't have come otherwise."

"I *shouldn't* have come." She avoided looking at him.

Cole felt as if she had just sucker-punched him. "Why not?"

"Because . . ." She swallowed and a lone tear slipped out and ran down her cheek.

Seeing her cry felt like another blow to his gut. He took a step toward her but his attention was diverted by a snort from behind him.

"Oh pul-ease," Mary Jane muttered in a nasal tone. "Can the soap-opera theatrics and just be honest with each other, okay?"

Cole blinked at her for a moment and then smiled broadly when it all became clear to him. "I hear ya." With the smile in place, he turned around to explain himself to Jenna.

But she was gone.

Cole felt panic well up in his throat. "Where'd she go?"

"Damned if I know. She musta slipped out." Mary Jane gave him a shove that sent the bangles on her wrists jangling. "Go on! Go after her and for God's sake tell her that you love her!"

"But what if—"

"No buts . . . hurry before she gets lost in the crowd." She gave him another hard shove.

Cole stepped outside into the humid air, letting his gaze flick over the crowded street, hoping to catch a glimpse of Jenna's red-gold hair. He pushed past people swaying to the calypso music, tipping back cups of rum-laced punch. Laughter, becoming increasingly raucous, shot alarm down Cole's spine. Jenna shouldn't be wandering around in the wild crowd alone. Cole knew that she couldn't have gotten far, but had no idea which direction to turn. With a silent prayer he weaved through the sea of people while cold sweat rolled down his chest.

Jenna ran through the rowdy carnival with tears blinding her eyes. When she nearly knocked over a clown on stilts, she forced herself to slow to a swift walk. Taking a shaky breath, she realized that she had wandered over to an area dotted with carnival-style rides. With a guilty little shiver, she knew that Cole would be worried and probably combing the crowd in search of her. Running had been the cowardly way out, but Jenna was too scared to put her heart on the line. Being turned down for having a fling was one thing, but if Cole tossed her love back in her face, she feared she would have a total meltdown.

Someone pushed Jenna from behind and she stumbled. The crowd seemed to have swelled, gotten louder, rowdier . . . a bit wild. The humid air felt thick, making it hard for Jenna to draw a deep breath. She yelped when she felt her butt being pinched and swung around with her best schoolteacher glare.

"Hey baby." The tall stranger gave her a leering grin.

"Back off."

He lifted his hands in the air. "Okay. Chill baby, I was just playing."

"Play with someone else," she answered with more bravado than she felt. The truth was that she felt a bit, okay a *lot* out of her element and more than a little frightened, suddenly hoping that Cole would find her. Running had been more than cowardly; it had been stupid.

Deep down Jenna knew there were undercover workers keeping a close eye on things, but this sexy, sultry, anything-goes atmosphere was just a bit too much for her to handle all alone. She decided that she should make her way back to the hotel room, but had no idea which was the way out.

Nibbling on the inside of her lip, Jenna moved forward with the crowd, not realizing that she was actually in line for a ride until she was near an arched entrance that read TUNNEL OF LOVE. *Oh great.*

"Would you like to ride with me?" asked a rather good-looking guy in line behind her.

"Uh . . ." He seemed nice enough, but still . . .

Jenna was saved from answering when she saw Cole swing his long legs over the metal fence and then jump into the line next to her.

"Hey!" the guy protested, giving Cole a challenging glare. "What the hell do you think you're doing?"

"She's with me, buddy." The steel in his voice warned that he meant business and the guy backed off.

"I'm not going on this ride with you, Cole."

"Please?"

Okay, she had expected this big alpha male to bully her into going. His simple plea was hard to resist. "I . . ." When she hesitated he brought out more ammunition and flashed her his sexy smile. Jenna returned it with a frown. "Okay, but don't you dare try anything!"

"I'll keep my hands to myself."

"When we get off of this stupid boat ride, we need to talk."

"Agreed." He nodded, but his smile faded. "Jenna, don't ever run off like that again."

"I'm not a child and you're not my keeper." Okay *that* sounded grown-up. Jenna suppressed a groan, thinking she sounded like one of her students.

"You're right about the child thing. I don't see you as a child at all." He gave her a smoldering look that made her insides quiver.

"I was perfectly fine by myself." *Liar.* She glanced at him. She knew *he* knew she was fibbing, but Cole scored points for not saying so. Jenna would have assured him further but the ride attendant ushered them into the first in a line of small boats that were bobbing in the narrow lane of water leading into the tunnel of love. *God,* she thought. *Of all the rides, why did I have to choose this one?*

The boat was so narrow that the sides of their bodies were firmly touching from shoulder to knee. Jenna felt the familiar jolt of awareness and really wished she could scoot away from him. The boat began lazily floating through the water toward a dark tunnel. Cheesy elevator-style music floated toward them. If Jenna hadn't been so nervous, she would have giggled. Instead, she said the first thing that came to her mind. "That Lola the fortune-teller was a hack."

"I thought her name was Mary Jane."

Jenna snorted. "Yeah, her *real* name. She admitted that she was from Brooklyn."

"So you didn't believe what she told you?" Cole asked softly.

Jenna shrugged, inadvertently making her bare arm caress his. The small boat swayed slightly in the silent water. "Who believes in that sort of hogwash?"

"You."

He knew her all too well. She was a Pisces, an artist, a dreamer . . . *a believer.* She believed in all kinds of hogwash. "Do you?" She threw the ball right back at him.

This time he shrugged. "I don't know. What exactly did Lola tell you?"

"None of your business." She tried for her crisp schoolteacher voice, but it came out all husky. In a moment they were going to be plunged into the dark tunnel of love. *God!*

Cole turned to look at her. His eyes glittered in the moonlight. "Tell me."

The little boat entered the tunnel just as Jenna began to answer. *Might as well give him a laugh,* she thought with a grim smile. "Mary Jane said that . . ." she paused when they were in complete darkness.

"Go on."

"No." She could feel the heat of her blush.

"Please." His voice was soft, pleading.

Damn him!

"She . . . she said . . . she said that . . . we were . . ."

Silence. Lapping water. Even the cheesy music ceased or maybe she just couldn't hear it over the loud banging of her heart. Jenna took a deep breath and then finally blurted out, "She said that we were in love." Her voice seemed to echo off the walls. She held her breath and waited for laughter.

"Do you believe her?" Cole asked softly.

"Do you?" She tossed that hot potato right back at him.

"On my end."

Jenna's heart bounced like a pinball in her chest. "What does that mean, exactly?" She tried to sound off-hand, but her voice quivered.

He chuckled, but not a snarky chuckle . . . oh, no, a low, sexy rumble. "It means that Lola was right. I love you, Jenna. I've known this for a while now. I would have been straight up with you, but, well, I didn't think you'd take me seriously. That damned playboy rep I've got was getting in the way. I didn't think you'd believe me. When Halley and Reese couldn't use this honeymoon, well, I thought this was the perfect opportunity to show you how I feel about you. Of course, you blew my plans all to hell."

"I did?" Her heart was pounding so hard she thought she would surely rock the small boat. She squinted in the dark wishing that she could see him better. How doggone long was this tunnel?

"I planned to take things super-slow so you wouldn't think I was . . . you know."

"Trying to . . ."

"Yeah."

"Sorry I messed that up." God, she hoped her blush didn't glow in the dark.

"Jenna, was Mary Jane right?"

She smiled in the darkness. "On my end?"

"Or do you just want a fling?" His voice shook just a tiny bit.

"She was spot-on."

"Come on, Jenna. Say it."

"I love you. I've loved you for as long as I can remember and I have a pretty darned good memory."

"Woohoo! She loves me!" His voice bounced off of the walls and the little boat bobbed back and forth.

Jenna laughed softly. This type of behavior was so out of character for Cole that it touched her heart. She twisted in the vinyl seat and threw her arms around his neck, almost capsizing the boat. "Kiss me, you fool!"

He did. The boat bobbed and rocked, causing water to splash all over the place but they didn't care. They were still kissing when the boat emerged from the tunnel, but they didn't notice until the roar of applause from onlookers pulled them apart.

"Why is there such a crowd?" Jenna asked, blinking up at Cole. God, he was so . . . *hot*. She giggled, thinking that *hot* was a term that her ninth graders would use, but it fit. Cole was off the charts in hotness. She opened her mouth to tell him her astute observation and that she really wanted to do a charcoal sketch of him—preferably nude—but the roar of falling water caught her attention. "What's going on?"

Cole grinned and then leaned over and said in her ear, "We're about to take the plunge."

Jenna didn't grasp his meaning for a moment, but then gasped. "A waterfall? We're going over a waterfall?"

Cole nodded. "You're gonna scream, aren't you?"

"Oh my God, yes."

"It's too late to back out now, so just hold on tight."

"I'm not backing out. I'm so ready. How about you?" she challenged.

"More than ready. Believe me."

Their gazes locked. "I do," she answered.

"Jenna," Cole shouted over the increasing roar of the water, "you can close your eyes."

"Oh no!" She looked up at him. "My eyes are staying wide open. I don't want to miss a thing."

He grinned down at her and then kissed her on the tip of her nose. "Me neither."

Jenna leaned into his shoulder and wrapped both of her arms around his bicep. Her heart beat faster as the little boat neared the edge of the waterfall. The crowd cheered them on and Jenna bravely loosened her grip on Cole's arm to give them a very brief wave . . .

And then they were plunging over the edge! Jenna screamed, but as promised, kept her eyes open as the little boat careened nose-down, causing a misty spray of water and wind to whip at her face. Jenna had never felt so alive as they hit the bottom pool with a huge splash that washed over the boat, drenching them both. Her screams turned to laughter as she pushed her wet hair out of her face.

Cole, who was laughing as well, helped her out of the boat. Jenna fell into his arms, laughing, kissing, and bursting with happiness. *He loved her.* "I love you, Cole Forrester," she said against his lips. He picked her up and swung her around, sending water droplets flying from her hair.

"So you don't just want me for my body?" Cole asked.

Jenna looked up at him, still plastered against him. While his tone was teasing, his blue eyes were serious. "There is so much more to you than that, Cole. You're smart, loyal, and funny . . . I could go on forever."

"I wasn't fishing."

"Well, you caught me, hook, line, and sinker."

He chuckled. "That was pretty corny."

"We're in love. We're allowed."

"Ahh, Jenna." He bent his wet head and kissed her again, oblivious to the crowd, the noise, the surroundings. Jenna filled his arms and his head, and, by God, his heart. "Let's go back to the room," he whispered in her ear.

"You don't have to ask twice."

"Jenna, let's hurry."

"You know the way out of here?"

Grabbing her hand, he nodded. "Come with me."

Cole wound his way through the crowd with Jenna in tow. She held tightly to his hand and it occurred to him that she must have been frightened in the Moonlight Madness all by herself. He realized that he had always felt protective of her, but this was a whole new level of possessiveness and he was going to put a big-ass diamond ring on her finger for the world to know it.

"Cole!" Jenna tugged on his hand. "Your legs are too long," she panted. "I can't . . . I can't keep up."

"I can fix that." He bent at the knees. "Hop on my back. I'll give you a piggyback ride."

"You've got to be kidding."

"I've never been more serious. Hop on."

"I'll feel ridiculous."

He gave her a glance over his shoulder. "Do you want to get back to the room quickly or not?"

"You convinced me." Jenna wrapped her arms around his neck and her legs around his waist. He hoisted her up and off he went. She giggled, feeling like a teenager, while Cole wove his way through the crowded carnival, carrying her on his back as if she weighed nothing. She bounced up and down as he jogged, which made her acutely aware that her legs were spread with nothing on but her tiny skirt and her thong rubbing her in just the right places. Her breasts rubbed against his back as well, and by the time they reached the entrance to the hotel she was . . . well, really aroused. "Hurry," she whispered in his ear.

Cole jogged into the hotel. His bare feet slapped against the marble floor as he crossed the lobby to the elevator.

"You can put me down now. I'm heavy."

"You're a feather."

"Good answer. I'm loving you more and more." She

nibbled on his earlobe while they waited for the elevator to arrive.

"Mmmm, stop. You're driving me crazy."

"Payback for the ride," she purred in his ear. "You know, a piggyback ride in a thong is quite interesting."

"You mean . . . ?"

"That I'm hotter than a firecracker? Oh, *yeah.*"

"Good god." Cole punched the up button with his thumb. "Ten seconds and we take the stairs."

The doors whooshed open and they all but fell into the small space. Cole jammed his thumb on the button for the seventh floor and then let Jenna slide from his back. "God, your wet clothes are like a second skin. Turn around and look."

Jenna pivoted to the mirror on the back wall and gasped. Her yellow halter was sucked against her skin like plastic wrap. Her cotton skirt was almost transparent, showing the outline of her black thong. She sucked in her breath when Cole came up behind her and untied the knot at her neck.

"Cole! What if someone . . . oh!" Her eyes widened when he peeled the wet fabric from her breasts. The sight of his big tanned hands cupping her white flesh was . . . *God,* almost too much. Jenna was already on sexual overload. If he touched her nipples she would probably come right then and there. "Cole, you have to stop." His thumbs circled closer to her pointed nipples. Her knees were turning to water. "No, I'm going to . . ."

"Come?"

She nodded, blushing furiously.

With a low chuckle he removed his hands and Jenna let out a held breath that morphed into a moan. They turned and looked at the red digital numbers that weren't changing nearly fast enough.

"Come on," Cole growled. He glanced at Jenna, who was fumbling with her wet top. "Hang in there."

What seemed like eternity but was only a minute or two went by until finally the bell dinged and the doors slid open. Cole grabbed her hand and they rushed down the hallway. He put the key-card in backwards and cursed. He put it in upside down and cursed again. After dropping it, he finally inserted it correctly and pushed the door open and flicked on one light. They tumbled into the room peeling off wet clothing, laughing.

Jenna fell backwards onto the big bed while Cole fumbled for a condom and rolled it on with lightning speed. She gasped when he pushed her legs wide and entered her with one hard, swift stroke. She wrapped her legs around his waist, arching her back, taking him deeper, matching him thrust for wild thrust until mere seconds later Jenna cried out his name.

"Wow," Cole said leaning his forehead against hers.

"Ditto," Jenna answered with a breathless laugh. "That was amazing but too fast."

"Once more with feeling?"

"Just once?" She raised her eyebrows and gave him a teasing grin.

Cole chuckled. "You know I can't back down from a challenge."

"Never could."

"You know me pretty well."

"I'd like to know you better."

He gave her quick kiss. "Give me a minute."

"I'm counting."

Angling her head, Jenna watched Cole retreat to the bathroom, admiring his very fine naked buns. Reaching for the remote, she found some classic rock, turned it on low for mood music, and then fluffed the pillows, waiting for his return. She could not keep from smiling.

Cole Forrester loved her.

He walked back into the room and their eyes met. Everything was the same and yet completely different. He gave her a warm smile that was almost shy and her heart melted. Jenna shook her head.

"What?" He lifted one dark eyebrow and stood there completely nude with his shoulder against the door frame, making her mouth water.

"You're gorgeous, you know that?"

Color rose in his high cheekbones.

Jenna frowned. "Oh Cole, there I go saying what I'm thinking. You've heard that so often—"

"It's different coming from you."

"You're blushing. I thought you might be angry."

Still holding her gaze, he walked over to the bed and sat down. "The only thing that would make me angry is if you run from me again." He traced a fingertip down her cheek and gave her a smile. "You know, I've never said the L-word before."

"I believe you. You know Halley said pigs would fly when she fell in love."

Cole nodded. "It was tough seeing our mom die and Dad mourn for her. As kids we sure missed her, but it was as if Dad had lost a huge piece of himself. I didn't want to open myself up to that kind of pain. But after seeing how happy Reese made Halley, I had a lightbulb moment and realized that having that kind of love for only a while would be better than never having it at all. And I know that even knowing that Dad would only have mom for a few years wouldn't have changed a thing. He still would have married her . . . oh damn, Jenna, I didn't mean to make you cry." He wiped tears away with his thumb. "Please don't—"

Jenna cut him off with a tender kiss. With her hands on either side of his cheeks she deepened the kiss, loving him more with each minute. Without breaking the contact, she swung her leg over his lap and pushed his shoulders back against the fluffed-up pillows. She moved her mouth from his soft lips and licked the rough stubble on his chin, nibbled a bit and then nuzzled his neck while letting her breasts barely graze his chest. His hard penis, already sheathed in a condom, brushed teasingly against her mound. She was wet and oh so ready, but wanted this to be slow and easy.

"Jenna . . ."

"Not yet." She leaned in and licked one flat brown nipple and he sucked in his breath. Not nearly finished, she swirled her tongue in the silky springy hair on his chest, going lower and lower, leaving a trail of moist kisses over the hard ridges of his abdomen. He smelled of soap and warm skin, tasted of salt and man. Her nipples tightened, grazing his skin, sending hot tingles to her groin. She licked his thigh, cupped his sac in her hand, and then let the very tip of her tongue lick him there.

"God, *Jenna*." His voice was strained. "Ride me, now!"

Jenna scooted up. "Give me your hands." Her eyes locked with his as she laced her fingers through his. She scooted up over his body until she straddled his waist. Stretched wide, she enveloped him with her slick heat, taking all of him deep inside until he filled her completely . . . so big, *so hard,* sweet pain, and yet not quite. Using his hands for support, Jenna raised herself up to her knees, pressing into the mattress, and then with a little cry sank all the way back down. Squeezing his hands tighter, Jenna moved quicker. Closing her eyes she bit her bottom lip while riding him harder, faster, until her thigh muscles protested. The hard-rock music blared in the background, urging her on.

"Jenna, let me—"

"No!" Her voice was a croak. "I want this . . . *you* . . . filling me . . . *Cole.*" Sweat trickled between her breasts. Her thigh muscles burned, but she couldn't stop now, not when she was so close. Cole angled his palms upward, making his arms stiff to give her the leverage she needed. He thrust his hips upward, matching her rhythm. She could feel his penis thicken, pulse, while she hovered on the brink of an orgasm . . .

And then she shattered. Pressing her palms against his, squeezing his fingers, she arched her back and neck while wave after wave of pleasure ripped through her body. She felt Cole lift his hips to push into her as far as possible while he hoarsely cried out her name.

"Oh my." With a weak chuckle, Jenna fell against him like a limp rag doll. He gathered her in a full-body embrace and they kissed, long and deeply. Jenna shivered with tiny aftershock ripples of pleasure, wanting the kiss to go on forever.

Finally she pulled her mouth from his, but couldn't resist one last lick across his full bottom lip. Her thighs quivered, but she couldn't bring herself to break their intimate connection. She loved the feel of him buried deep.

"I'm going to have a hard time walking tomorrow," she said with a little giggle. "I'm going to look like I've been on a week-long cattle drive."

Cole chuckled while cupping her breasts. Her nipples were super-sensitive and she gasped when he tugged and licked. "You've been riding a cowboy, not a horse."

Jenna chuckled and then tweaked his nose. "You're not a cowboy."

"I can be." He nibbled sharply on one nipple and then soothed the pointed peak with a soft lick. "I can be anything you want me to be."

Jenna tucked a finger underneath his chin, forcing him to look up at her. "All I want is you."

"Ahhh, Jenna." He threaded his fingers through her hair and then kissed her. "You've had me ever since that kiss on the dance floor at Shakey's."

"The bachelorette party? Cole, that was over a year ago. Why did you wait so long?"

He shrugged his broad shoulders. "God only knows, but Jenna, you were worth waiting for."

She angled her head at him. "You said that some things were worth the wait to me this morning while we were in line for the Dolphin, but you weren't talking about the roller-coaster ride, were you?"

"Nope." He brushed a lock of hair behind her ear. "I was referring to you."

Jenna swallowed the hot moisture gathering in her throat but her voice was still husky when she spoke. "I can't believe that was just this morning. So much has happened in one day." She lowered her eyes and asked softly, "Have I convinced you not to sleep on the floor?"

"Have *I* convinced you that I'm in love with you?"

Jenna's throat closed up again, but she managed a throaty "Yes."

"Good, then we're on the same page."

"Yeah, of a romance novel," she said with a watery giggle.

"Ooh, those have lots of sex."

"And you know this *how?*"

"Halley gobbled them up like potato chips."

"Halley? Your sister claimed not to have a romantic bone in her body," she said and then gave Cole's shoulder a playful nudge. "You still haven't answered my question. How do *you* know romance novels are full of sex?"

"I . . . uh, might have peeked in her books once in a while."

"Peeked?"

"Okay, searched for the good parts."

"In other words, the love scenes."

"Guilty. I dog-eared every one of them. I'm thinking we need another one right about now." He cocked an eyebrow at her. "Are we still on the same page?"

Jenna tapped the side of her cheek with her fingertip. "Hmmm, being an avid romance reader myself, I have to tell you that there is a lot of conflict leading up to the amazing sex."

"Conflict?" he asked weakly.

She nodded. "Yeah, something like two people who were already crazy in love with each other but neither one of them knew how the other one felt."

Cole grinned. "We've got that one covered. Okay, are we good to go?"

She tapped her cheek again. "Well, then you have to have some sort of misunderstanding . . ."

"Like when the girl thinks the boy wants a fling when he really wants forever?"

Her finger stopped tapping. "Yeah, like that," she answered softly.

"We cleared that up, though, right, Jenna?"

She nodded.

"Then we're ready for the amazing-sex part."

"More than ready."

"I'm going to give you a dog-ear-, underline-, and highlighter-worthy love scene."

Jenna laughed. This playful side of Cole was endearing. He flipped her over to her back and began kissing her neck. "Do you know what *I* love best about romance novels?" she asked. She gasped when he took a nipple between his teeth and tugged.

"The hot sex?"

"You are such a guy. No, the happy ending."

He paused in his trail of kisses down her abdomen and looked up at her. "Yeah," he said softly, "happy endings are a good thing."

Arching one eyebrow, Jenna said with a smile, "But my second favorite thing is the hot sex."

"That's my girl," he responded with a low chuckle.

Jenna smiled. "You called me *your girl* this morning and I was so wishing it was true." She put a hand over her eyes. "I shouldn't have admitted that."

Cole gently peeled her fingers away from her face. "I meant it this morning and I mean it now. Jenna Wagner, you *are* my girl. Are we still on the same page?"

Jenna nodded.

"Good." He resumed his hot trail of kisses. "Now about that love scene . . ."

about
the author

LuAnn McLane lives in Florence, Kentucky. When she isn't writing, she enjoys long walks with her husband, chick flicks with her daughter, and tries to keep up with her three active sons. She loves hearing from her readers. You can reach her at luann@excessstreet.com or visit her Web site, www.luannmclane.com.